To Marc,

Moneymaking Music

Enjoy!!

Your Complete Guide to Making, Keeping, Protecting, and Growing Your Music-Success Fortune

by Jeffrey P. Fisher

Jeff Fisher
2/'03

ProMusic press

236 Georgia Street, Suite 100
Vallejo, CA 94590

Library of Congress Catalog Card Number: 2001095834

Production Staff: Mike Lawson, Publisher; Patrick Runkle, Editorial Director;
Stephen Ramirez, Art Director

ProMusic Press is an imprint of artistpro.com, LLC
236 Georgia Street, Suite 100
Vallejo, CA 94590
707-554-1935

Also from ProMusic Press
Music Copyright for the New Millennium
The Mellotron Book
Electronic Music Pioneers

Also from EMBooks
The Independent Working Musician
Making the Ultimate Demo, 2nd Ed.
Remix: The Electronic Music Explosion
Making Music with Your Computer, 2nd Ed.
Anatomy of a Home Studio
The EM Guide to the Roland VS-880

Also from MixBooks
The AudioPro Home Recording Course, Volumes I, II, and III
I Hate the Man Who Runs This Bar!
How to Make Money Scoring Soundtracks and Jingles
The Art of Mixing: A Visual Guide to Recording, Engineering, and Production
The Mixing Engineer's Handbook
The Mastering Engineer's Handbook
Music Publishing: The Real Road to Music Business Success, Rev. and Exp. 5th Ed.
How to Run a Recording Session
The Professional Musician's Internet Guide
The Songwriters Guide to Collaboration, Rev. and Exp. 2nd Ed.
Critical Listening and Auditory Perception
Modular Digital Multitracks: The Power User's Guide, Rev. Ed.
The Dictionary of Music Business Terms
Professional Microphone Techniques
Sound for Picture, 2nd Ed.
Music Producers, 2nd Ed.
Live Sound Reinforcement
Professional Sound Reinforcement Techniques
Creative Music Production: Joe Meek's Bold Techniques

Printed in Auburn Hills, MI
ISBN 1-931140-12-X

Dedication

For my family ...

Thanks for enriching my life, inspiring my muses, indulging my whims, and making me laugh.

Introduction

"The beginning is the most important part of the work."—Plato

Forget about breaking into the music business.

Start your own music business and succeed with it instead. You no longer need to be stuck in the machinations of record labels and other old ways of thinking about music success. In today's music industry, you alone are fully responsible for your own career. And you must take charge of all aspects of that career. Your success depends on how well you promote and sell yourself and on how well you manage all your professional activities. Now, more than ever, it is possible to have a successful music career free from traditional constraints. It is the Age of the Independent. Welcome!

This book shows you how to make money selling your music products and services. And there is a new paradigm in the way money is made in today's music industry. The shift away from record labels is creating a modern breed of independent music professional. And that transformation is what makes this such an exciting time.

It used to be that acts could build a local following by playing live and building on that notoriety. While that model still works, the Internet makes it possible to build an international fan base. One band confessed that their MP3 had over 20,000 downloads. Through this outlet they have been able to play their music for more people than they ever could staying local.

There are virtually limitless opportunities for you to make some bank with your music beyond performing, too. You can compose songs, write jingles, do TV and film scores, get into music production, help others manage their careers, and more. The new qualifications for success are versatility and diversity. You need learn a wide-range of skills and take a specific, proven approach. You must establish goals and figure out how to accomplish them.

Use this resource to successfully create your own personal music career. When you diligently follow the advice in this book, you can move past a mediocre music career into a thriving, exciting, and moneymaking music business. The answers you need are here in *Moneymaking Music.*

What's Inside

Moneymaking Music is your personal guide to making, keeping, protecting, and growing your music-success fortune. Money is its primary focus and we'll be spending a lot of time together discussing the finer points of cash: how to get it and what to do with it. You discover how to make a living both inside, outside, and on the fringes of the today's music industry. You learn the particular business-building techniques that help you map your musical journey, get what you need to know, understand the industry (and how you make money from it), diversify your music products and services, promote effectively, increase sales, make more money, save more money, invest your resources, and work your way toward your very own music success fortune.

This book has five parts:

Part One: *Get Ready for Your Success.* Here you discover the secrets to success and how to model your personal music career.

Part Two: *Find the Music Money.* Study the many moneymaking music activities and then choose those that let you earn the most money from your particular skills.

Part Three: *Master Ruthless Self-Promotion.* Effectively promoting your music career allows you to meet your success goals. Use the techniques presented here to do it right.

Part Four: *Manage Your Music Career.* Follow this step-by-step plan to start, protect, and keep your musical activities on track.

Part Five: *Grow Your Music Success Fortune.* Don't just survive; make your life better.

For several years now, I've focused on music industry issues. What I've seen is a lack of meaningful or practical resources that tell you how to really make money with your music by following definitive, tested, and basic business principles. This book provides all the specific techniques and advice that can help you avoid the pitfalls and manage your successful professional music career. It is my sincere hope that you find in these pages everything you need to make your musical endeavors—and your life—more productive, successful, satisfying, and profitable.

Special note. While I believe this book provides definitive advice for making it in the music industry, you should know that it was conceived and written with another resource in mind. This book provides the *business* knowledge you need to succeed with only a smattering of promotional help. Another book I have written, *Ruthless Self-Promotion in the Music Industry,* provides extensive information about how to successfully promote and sell your music business career. It doesn't have the business focus this book contains. In essence, these two books work together to provide a complete education for the aspiring music professional.

A Little about Me ...

I work from my Bolingbrook, IL, project studio on a variety of music, writing, and multimedia productions. I have operated my company, Fisher Creative Group (FCG), since 1991. Through FCG, I provide digital content creation including words, music, sound, and visuals.

I composed, recorded, and released a two-volume buy-out music library called *Melomania* and a CD, *Atmospherics*, of my original instrumental music. I've also written and published four music and sound industry books: *Profiting From Your Music and Sound Project Studio, Ruthless Self-Promotion in the Music Industry, How to Make Money Scoring Soundtracks and Jingles,* and this book you now hold.

There is also an ever-growing wealth of information on my website at ***www.jeffreypfisher.com***, and in my free *Moneymaking Music Tip of the Week* e-mail newsletter. Send me an e-mail with "subscribe" in the subject to start your subscription. Few authors would give you their phone number (630/378-4109) and e-mail address (jpf@jeffreypfisher.com) so readily. I want you to know that should you need additional help or just want to share your stories, I urge you to contact me.

Pro/Files

Throughout this book you'll meet several people working in different parts of the music industry who are realizing their personal vision. The Pro/Files included in this book came from an on-line survey of real people facing and overcoming the real challenges of today's music industry. Some are just getting started while others are seasoned veterans. They all have something useful to say, and you can benefit from their advice. Also, you can get more answers by either visiting their Web sites or contacting them directly.

Now Commit!

Take a moment now to read the paragraph below, fill in your name, and complete it by adding your signature. Your agreeing to this pledge is a crucial first step. Every time you open this book, it will remind you of your commitment to taking the necessary action to realize your life's ambition.

I, ______________________________________, do hereby commit myself to the endless pursuit of knowledge necessary to helping me achieve my goals of musical success. Signing below signifies that I will do everything necessary to reach my goals. I also understand that certain skills and actions are required to succeed and that I now pledge myself to improve my professional skills, cultivate the proper attitudes, and take the appropriate actions. I also recognize that I am solely responsible for my ultimate objective. Some may help; some may hinder, but I am fully accountable. There is no easy road to success. Thus I, here and now, promise to persist in my efforts to get what I want, need, and deserve. By signing below, this I vow as my personal obligation and commitment.

Signed,

Are you ready to begin your journey toward doing, being, and having what you really want? Let's get started ...

Contents

PART ONE:
GET READY FOR YOUR SUCCESS

"Progress is impossible without change; and those who cannot change their minds cannot change anything."— George Bernard Shaw

Successfully making your way in music requires both a map and your commitment to follow it. Your career can't be haphazard and serendipitous. You need to prepare for your journey by carefully reviewing some fundamental concepts and completing several exercises. These steps assure a solid foundation on which to build your moneymaking music career.

CHAPTER 1

Moneymaking Music Philosophy

"I believe that most artists write and create motivated by the goal of sharing their music with as many people as possible and view the financial reward as a natural and welcome outcome as opposed to it being their singular motivation."—Alanis Morissette

If you've read my other books, dropped by ***www.jeffreypfisher.com***, or subscribed to my *Moneymaking Music Tip of the Week* by e-mail, you already know I concentrate on making money in the music and sound industry. If you are new to my work, let me share my philosophy with you. It's simple, really: Create your own personal moneymaking music wealth machine by increasing your income substantially doing the work you love and most enjoy, reduce both your business and personal expenses by spending less, invest your savings, and use the income generated by those investments to support your current and future lifestyle.

Though the title of this book hints at the more mercenary aspects of earning your living in the music industry, money should not be the major focus of your work. Never lose sight of the real reasons you choose to pursue your music career. The money you earn from your music affords certain life choices that stay out of reach of those people struggling to survive. Money enables you to lift your quality of life, but it is not your whole life. If some musical thing makes you happy, but doesn't pay, keep it in your life anyway. Getting joy and fulfillment doesn't have to come with greenbacks.

And please don't just work for work's sake or just to make money. Get the most out of everything you do by looking beyond the immediate gains. You can inspire people, help them realize *their* dreams, serve as a role model for kids, foster changes in attitudes, and, yes, simply entertain. All this can happen as you realize your own dreams, achieve success, make money, and participate in new enriching and satisfying experiences for your own life.

According to Aaron Ahuvia, University of Michigan-Dearborn School of Management professor and co-author of the study *Income, Consumption, and Happiness*, "The connection between people's income and happiness tends to level off at remarkably low levels, somewhere in the $20,000 range. It never hurts to have more, but it doesn't help very much either." He further claims that people who earn substantial incomes are no happier than people of more moderate means.

Most people are happiest when they do something beyond its financial gain. Creating, relating, and just being true to ourselves are infinitely more satisfying than cold, hard cash alone. According to Ahuvia: "People who are chronically dissatisfied with how much they earn (which has little to do with actual income) tend to be unhappy with their lives in general."

Some people who have a job that they hate prefer to leave the work behind and go home to more satisfying activities. They work for money and get their satisfaction elsewhere. When you do the work you love, the lines between work and play blur. Don't worry about that. You may find that merging both your professional and personal lives can both make you more successful and provide more satisfaction. Now, this is not to say that you become some workaholic spending every waking moment on your career. What you should do is arrange your life in ways that let you pursue the activities you most enjoy while earning the income you need to support your lifestyle.

THE DAY JOB DILEMMA

Making the move from working a job you either hate or don't find fulfilling to doing the music work you love and crave is an important step on the way to your music success fortune. You need to reduce your dependence on being an employee and instead run your own career as a self-employed small business. While you may still hold down a day job to help you through the lean times or to pay the bills while you hone your craft, make the major thrust of your musical pursuits satisfy the aching thirst of your creative spirit.

Work for money. *You can get a menial job just about anywhere that lets you earn money without taxing your time or creative resources. Food service,* *retail, and factory work spring to mind. You put in your time, collect your pay, and go home to do your real life's work.*

Work in the music world. *There are two ways you approach this. You can work in the periphery of the industry, such as a record or music store, or you can land a steady gig inside the industry, such as in a studio or at a label. The peripheral side keeps you surrounded by music, but its greatest drawback is it probably won't further your career in any real sense. Working inside the industry, however, does allow you to both gain invaluable experience and build a contact network of people who could help you with your career. One caveat: if you get involved in the music industry this way, you may find yourself working on other people's music projects and sacrificing your own. You are in the music industry, but not necessarily in the way you planned.*

Work outside the music world. *Here you immerse yourself in activities that have nothing to do with your music ideas. For some, it may swallow up any hopes of ever making your way in music (this was the dilemma I faced years ago). For others, the contrast afforded by doing something different from music actually works in their favor to support their creative endeavors.*

Here's one additional suggestion. Consider doing your music activities ***before*** *your day job, if possible. This helps your mind focus on what is really important to your life—your music—before you go off to earn your necessary pay.*

Your musical endeavors can both feed your body and nourish your soul. Your work also enables you to *build a life,* not just put cash in your pocket and bread on your table. I've always felt the real key to success is to discover your innate abilities and then pursue the work that lets you use those skills to their fullest. Do what makes you happy. Express your creativity. Build meaningful relationships with other people. Make enough money to cover your basic expenses. Stay out of debt (a mortgage is fine; credit card debt isn't). And put aside a little money for your golden years. Follow your bliss, as Joseph Campbell put it, and make your professional and personal life so much more rewarding and satisfying.

MUSIC SUCCESS FORTUNE

Because you are reading this book, I assume you want music to be a significant part of your life. You want to compose, play, record, teach, eat, sleep, and breathe music. You also want your involvement in music to pay the freight. Whether you want your music to supplement a day job or be your only source of income, this resource can help. How do you define a music success fortune? There are three parts.

Music. You plan to make music central to your life, whether that's playing, recording, managing, or any number of music-related activities. Music brings great satisfaction to your life; you wouldn't be reading this book if you didn't feel compelled to pursue a career in this creative field. Confucius said that "music produces a kind of pleasure which human nature cannot do without." This enjoyment comes to those who listen, and to those of us who make music. We drown in the melody, our hearts beat to the rhythm, and our souls relish the joy that only music can bring.

Success. You want to achieve some level of success with your musical pursuits. The prudent way to define success is: living the life you want to live in the way that you choose to live it. Success is a personal thing; it's a lifestyle choice. For some, having a gold record is success. For other people, supporting a family through musical activities is success. Your vision of success is as distinct and unique as you. Never measure your success against another person's. You must first define what success means to *you*. Then, proceed to arrange your life in ways that let you achieve the success you want on your own terms. You can let music fund your entire lifestyle, be self-supporting, or just put some extra bucks in your pocket. While there is nothing wrong with doing your music because you want to, there's also nothing offensive about wanting your music to help you earn some money either. Getting paid for your music work—even if only a small amount—can make the work just that much more enjoyable.

Fortune. You need to amass some wealth to support the successful lifestyle you want. Wealth comes in four forms: money, skill, relationships, and experiences. Like success, your money fortune differs from that of another person's. Many people won't settle for less than a million dollars, while others are content making a few thousand here and there. The skills you acquire add up to a highly personal wealth. Your ability to accomplish certain tasks, musical or otherwise, is certainly as valuable as the money you're able to earn. Whether you choose to also convert your skills into monetary wealth is a choice left up to you. Your relationships with people—family, friends, and music business associates—reward you in ways that are difficult to measure. Finally, it's no good to hermit yourself away either. You need to experience other people, places, and things and have people experience what you have to offer, too. These experiences enrich our lives in ways that help us grow as human beings. Seeing more of the world and participating in all its splendor adds a different, yet crucial wealth to your personal fortune.

RECIPE FOR SUCCESS

There are only five essential ingredients to being a success in today's music industry:

- Depend on yourself and your talent
- Go into business for yourself
- Create notable music products and services that people want to buy
- Promote those products and services so people do buy them
- Manage the business effectively, especially its financial aspects

Depend on yourself and your talent. You are the one most responsible for your own career path. And your talent must be as good or better than other people already doing the same work. While you'll rely on other people to make your success real, it's your personal ambition and individual effort that usually means the difference between success and failure.

How do you keep your life focused on growing and maintaining your music career? One word: desire. You must desire to make your life bigger and better. At the same time, you must also desire to make *other* people's lives bigger and better through your musical work. Without these two intrinsic and explicit desires, you will severely impede your progress. You must really want to be successful, but you can't indulge your whims at the expense of alienating people either. You have an obligation to share your music gifts in ways that other people appreciate and need, too.

Every person's journey is different and unique. The best this book can do is to provide the basic skills you need to make your journey effectively. Your talent will serve you, your tenacity will drive you, and what you learn here can save you from making horrible mistakes. However, I can't make you follow this advice. I can't make you pick up the phone and call prospects. I can give you the marching orders, but I can't make you follow them. It is you who must take the initiative and work hard on building your career.

Take charge of your own life. Don't live someone else's idea of what your life should be. Concentrate on what matters most to you. Figure out what you want to do and be. And then use your talent, initiative, and all the resources available to you to go out and live your dream. Also, start today. There is no reason to put off your journey. Even if your chosen career path may at first seem an insurmountable task, you need to get going now. If you never begin, you'll never get there. Resolve to start taking steps right now.

You won't regret it. Ever. You'll only regret the shoulda, coulda, wouldas.

Go into business for yourself. This central concept is how the music industry works today. And it is vital that you recognize, understand, and exploit this issue. According to the Bureau of Labor Statistics, 26 percent of the U.S. work force are self-employed with another 17 percent claiming they'd like to go independent. However, the creative industries have traditionally been more independent than the rest of the U.S. population. I suspect that over 90 percent of the music industry is self-employed. The vast majority of those earning money in music do so on their own, taking charge and running their music career as a small business. Even a band signed to a major label is considered independent; they don't work for the label.

If you sell something—music products such as a CDs and/or services such as performing—you are in business, whether you like it or not. There are specific advantages to running your own business that include legal, financial, and promotional benefits. Being in business for yourself forces you to become more accountable, too. You make plans, study what is happening with your business, and then revise your plans accordingly. This combination of careful planning coupled to good informational feedback reminds you of where you are and where you are heading. You begin to make better decisions and the right choices, and you learn to trust your instincts in ways that make your business stronger.

Do you have to sell out to make money with your music? Selling out implies compromising your art. Promoting what you do to people who like what you have is *not* selling out in any way. However, the commercial aspects of today's music industry do have a way of interfering with your artistic vision and your personal pet projects. Balancing art and commerce is no easy task. They are often diametrically opposed forces. Your art is often *not* a commercial success.

What to do? The best strategy is to let your more commercial ventures fund your artistic side. Work for the money you need to support your lifestyle doing what must be done. Save a portion of the money you earn and then use your free time and some of those funds to do your want-tos. In other words, take on projects that pay enough to support your personal, more artistic pursuits. First earn the money you need to survive and then go make your art!

SELF-EMPLOYED MONEY ADVANTAGES

The term self-employment is a bit misleading. It implies that you work for yourself. On a base level that is somewhat true. You are responsible for your own endeavors. Also note that the self-employed really work for others—their clients! So although certain freedom and flexibility comes with self-employment, there is still an underlying sense of service to others that you cannot neglect. The ultimate irony is that many creative people end up spending more time on other people's projects than they spend on their own.

One distinct advantage of running your own business is the expenses that you pay out of your personal pocket can now be covered by the business. It is this conversion of certain, specific personal expenses into business expenses that often makes running your business so attractive. It is also the reason that many self-employed business owners get audited by the IRS each year; it is open to abuse.

Also, some people may feel they can pull a fast one on the IRS by not really being in business. It's simple: only accept cash for the work you do and never report the income. You may get by with this, but you'll probably never land any real, well-paying gigs as those business clients would require transactional records. Plus, if you never report the income you make, you can't report the expenses either. In brief, you miss out on all the distinct advantages you get by running a legal business. My advice? Stay out of the underground economy. If you're truly serious about your career, set it up as a real business. If you are currently working below IRS radar, I'd strongly urge you to consider transforming your current situation into a viable and legal small business.

Create notable music products and services that people want to buy. If you genuinely want to make money with your music, you can't be self-indulgent and only do what you want. No matter what you sell, you must reconcile your music art with the vagaries of commerce. You must reasonably consider the market—what other people want and, most importantly, what they are willing to buy. There are essentially five ways to make money in the music industry:

• Create something musical such as writing songs or composing soundtracks and jingles.

• Perform something musical such as playing solo or in a band.

• Package something musical such as recording and producing music in your project studio.

• Sell something musical such as wholesaling and/or retailing music-related content.

• Support something musical such as teaching lessons or managing an act.

Versatility and diversity really come into play here. You need to be able to create different products and perform different services. Your act can't just produce studio CDs; you must also tour and play live. You can't just produce music in your project studio, you must be able to mix live sound one day, a commercial tomorrow, post a video after that, and then do sound and music for a Web site. You need to offer a little of everything related to your central music career.

This strategy works for two reasons: First, it makes earning money easier and steadier. Your entire product and service line ties together and brings the maximum value to each buyer. This approach helps you create clients that keep buying from you over and over. Second, it can help you better satisfy your creative spirit. You take on new and exciting challenges that can help you eliminate boredom and burn out.

Coca-Cola thoroughly market-tested their notorious New Coke before releasing it. They found that people actually preferred the new taste over the original. What they failed to test was whether people would actually *buy* the new version. People didn't, and new Coke failed. Learn from this infamous example and make sure you don't repeat its mistakes. Are the music products and services that you sell what people really want to buy?

Promote those products and services so people do buy them. Many succumb to the miserable trap unleashed on the misinformed. These hapless souls believe their work is the most important thing and that promotion is beneath them or it's something that other people do. Let me reassure you that promoting your music products and services is the most important part of the moneymaking music philosophy. People are assaulted with messages every single day that entice, titillate, and distract. As a whole we've become rather adept at filtering out the noise. This phenomenon makes it difficult for promoters to get the attention of those who would buy their wares.

As you craft your saleable music products and services, you must always know how you will promote and sell them. You must put in as much—if not more—toward promoting your music as you put into making it. The world does not beat a path to your door to see what you have to offer. You must take a proactive approach and persist in your efforts to bring your message to the right people. Just as you can't rely on a single product or service to support you indefinitely, you can't rely on a single promotion to bring you a flood of new customers either. What I can guarantee is this: people *will not* seek you out without targeted promotions on your part.

Understand this basic tenet of promotion: success breeds more success. Once you achieve some level of success, it is often easier to maintain it. This tenet is why top rated songs on MP3.com stay on top, because people see them first, click on them first, and therefore keep these artist's numbers up. Promoting your successes increases your overall impact exponentially. This fact is why promotion is such a critical component to your success.

YOUR MANY HATS

When you manage your music career as a business, you take on many jobs and the demands that go with both music and business. Obviously, you are the primary content supplier behind whatever music products and services you provide. Also, you are the one person in charge of all aspects of your burgeoning business, which means that you are the general manager, the marketing manager, the promotion manager, the production department, the order fulfillment and shipping and receiving department, customer relations manager, office clerk, bookkeeper, web master, graphic designer, copywriter, gopher, janitor, and often more! Of all these hats, the two most crucial are those of the artist and the promoter.

When you put on your artist's hat, you are infinitely creative and capable with your music and the technology to produce it. You see all the possibilities inherent in your art. When you put on your promoter hat, you ask the pertinent questions, listen carefully to what people tell you, study their behaviors, and discover what people really desire. By focusing on what people want, you see the real market for your creative music products and services.

Author and former U.S. Labor Secretary Robert Reich said that there are two creative personalities that are vital to the new economy: the geeks and the shrinks. In his book The Future of Success, *Reich wrote: "The geek (artist) draws on his endless fascination with the medium—a technology, a science, a visual art. The shrink (promoter), by contrast, draws on her fascination with people. The geek understands it— the possibilities within a given medium. The shrink understands them—what [people] could possibly want or need."*

Manage the business effectively, especially its financial aspects. Don't stick your head in the sand while your career spins uncontrollably around you. Formulate a reasonable plan and work it hard. Have a sound financial strategy that lets you manage your money effectively: income, expenses, taxes, debt, investments, and more. Also, take charge of all the business aspects that directly effect you including the legalities of your career, protecting your creative properties, and insuring yourself and your assets.

SHORTCUT TO SUCCESS

There is no great mystery to success in any venture. You just need to do whatever it takes to get whatever it is you want. And you can accomplish all this in just three steps. One, decide the course. Two, figure out what you need to do to get there. Three, take action. I have and continue to use this simple strategy throughout my professional life. It has served me well, and I've no doubt that you can benefit from this, too.

MUSIC SUCCESS FORMULAS

Everybody wants to know some magic formula for fame and fortune in the music industry. I could be flippant and just say hard work, talent, and dumb luck. While those three notions often do result in success, they do not tell the whole story. You must develop and leverage three concepts to help you achieve the goals you've set for yourself: reputation, relationships, and knowledge. So, how do you build a reputation, cultivate meaningful relationships, and use knowledge to your best advantage? These three formulas can help.

Image + Credentials = Reputation. You must establish an image for your music industry career. An image wraps up everything you are about into a tight, neat package that's easy to promote and sell. You manufacture this image to appeal to the people who buy your music. You become the image, and all that it represents, while your promotions serve to enhance and support it. Put simply: your image, and all that you prepare and use to represent it, makes it easier for people to remember you.

Part of developing your image is discovering your unique artistic voice. Your voice represents your core values, what you are about, and what you are trying to say. This voice manifests itself both in the work you produce and the image with which you associate. You should have a vision of your music career that complements and supports your image and voice. Ask yourself these two questions. What is your personal vision of today's music industry? How do you see yourself and your career as part of that vision?

You earn credentials in two ways: what you sell and what other people say about what you sell. Your music products and services are a record of your abilities and serve to prove your talent. For example, a band must have a live act. This goes beyond just playing;

they need to be entertaining. No band is legitimate without a CD either; it's a testament to their skills and professionalism. You can't sell your services as a soundtrack and jingle composer without a demo of your past work. You can't be a music success *at all* without something tangible to prove your ability to deliver what you claim. Comments and reviews from the media and testimonials from satisfied clients are other critical credentials you must secure. These third-party, mostly impartial endorsements also make you more legitimate and help reassure suspicious buyers. The last credentials are awards such as winning a battle of the bands or, ultimately, a Grammy.

With a carefully crafted image and supporting credentials, your career earns a deserved reputation. That reputation instills confidence and trust in people who would buy your music products and services. Reputation is why Sting goes platinum fast. Your reputation will bring you the success you desire, too. People will say "this band rocks" when they mean the band has a reputation for good music and being entertaining. Or "this composer delivers" when they mean she does her work on time, on budget, and meets the client's needs. Everything you do must serve to enhance, augment, and further disseminate your reputation.

People are skeptical. Chances are they've never heard of you and they are afraid to make a mistake. When you earn and have their trust, people will listen to what you have to say and take your recommendations seriously. Having a believable track record helps to reduce new prospect and client fears. Because of your reputation, these buyers are less skeptical and therefore more likely to open their wallets. Reputation and trust form your "brand" where you lend your name and goodwill to your (or other's) products and services. People trust your brand and therefore trust what's offered. They will know, based upon your past reputation, that what you sell will be of a certain kind, quality, and value.

You help other people = Other people help you. Your success doesn't happen in a vacuum. You need to organize, nurture, and maintain a network comprising people who can help you with your music business career. You must work hard to connect and reconnect with people and build relationships carefully. The crucial point of this relationship building is both give and take. You need to give of yourself and provide value that other people can use, first and foremost. When you take this approach, most people will respond in kind out of a sense of obligation. In a healthy relationship, everybody benefits and gets what they need. You also need to maintain relationships with your clients and keep them coming back and buying more of your music products and services. Ultimately, you'll build a pool of fans or anchor clients who always support your endeavors.

Knowledge + Action = Success. The more you know, the better your chances of making your music career better. Learn all you can about how this business works: read, take classes, and get real-world, hands-on experience. Use all that information effectively and take appropriate actions that move you closer to your goals. You must be ready and willing to drop everything and pursue an opportunity. Get up, get out, and get going. Knowledge and experience help you to make better decisions. You're better able to concentrate on what is really happening and focus your resources accordingly. Your gut will help you balance the risks with the possible reward. You'll be more agile and able to embrace change. You'll quickly spot trends, and move fast to capitalize on them. The music industry changes so rapidly that only the smart, results-oriented survive and thrive. That must be you.

CHAPTER 2

Money Making Music 101, or What You Need to Know Now

"Experience is what you get when you didn't get what you wanted."— Proverb

When you know and understand critical information about the music industry, you can better map your journey through it.

KNOW YOURSELF

To grasp fully what you *really* want, you must know what you are about. What are your dreams and aspirations? What skills do you possess? What are your strengths and weaknesses? Where did you come from and what have you already accomplished?

Who are you and who do you want to become? If I asked you these questions, what would you say? Typically, you'd probably say: "I write songs" or "I play guitar in a band." Rarely would you say: "I am a songwriter" or "I am a guitarist." We all need food, shelter, water, security, and safety. Once we meet these survival basics, we move on to the next level: our wants. Through our wants we build our self-esteem through learning, experimenting, playing, working, and achieving. Ultimately, we move from simply doing something ("I write songs") to *being* someone ("I *am* a songwriter"). Part of realizing your dream is to make that personal journey, to cease doing and start being.

These three exercises can help you find the answers you need. They should reveal where you came from, where you are at, and where you need to go with your life. The knowledge you've gained and the experiences that shaped your life help you trust your gut instinct, your intuition. Combine knowledge, experience, and intuition with your compassion and your ability to seize opportunities fast, and you emerge as a potent force ready for success.

Rewind and write the story of your life so far. I believe that certain events in your life often prepare you, unknowingly, for the future direction you take. Don't overlook your past; it is often an accurate predictor of your future. What has been your defining moment? What does the story of your life reveal about *you*? A simple biography that includes key moments from your past can be a cathartic and enlightening experience.

Describe the weird, wonderful, strange, and delightful things that have happened to you. Make sure you include your most vivid memories, both the worst and best events, your reactions, and how they shaped your current situation. Include your celebrations and problems. Salute your fortitude. Forgive your shame. Express your gratitude for all you've achieved. Describe your family, immediate and extended, and your friends, how you met them, what you do together, etc. Describe your home and neighborhood, why you live there and what you like and dislike. Indicate your favorite movies, radio and TV shows, music, books, bands, etc. and the impact your choices have made on your life. Detail your favorite foods, hobbies, clothes, and so forth. When you complete this exercise, review it carefully for insight into your life and yourself.

Fast forward and write what you'd like your life to be like, now and in the future. After looking at the past, start spinning some dreams for your future. Where are you today? Where have you been and where do you wish to go? Describe yourself literally, physically, emotionally, spiritually, and career-wise. Describe your vision of the future and your place in it. Also, describe your ideal place to live and work and why. Record your have-tos, like-tos, and want-tos.

Your have-tos. Take the time to determine all that you must do to survive. This includes your basic survival needs of food and shelter along with the fundamental events and issues that must occur to make your success happen. For instance, you *have to* create your music products and services. You *have to* find ways to promote them. You *have to* find people to buy them. And so on. Your list of have-tos can become rather long and cumbersome, but that doesn't diminish its relevance. This exercise helps you clearly think through all the steps that get you where you want to go.

Your like-tos. Next, record those things you would like to do sometime. This should include your wild fantasies along with whatever you think might bring meaning to your life. For example, you might *like to* travel the world someday. These like-tos tend to be two extremes: simple pleasures and wild, outlandish fantasies. You may get to these items someday, but they neither add nor subtract from the quality of your life.

Your want-tos. Finally, clearly define all those things you *really* want to do during your life and career such as you *want to* start a band, tour, and release an independent CD. These want-tos help you develop your overall strategy. They also provide the milestones for your career. Once you determine these milestones, you need to go back to step one and fill in all the have-tos that move you closer to these goals.

You might want to save these documents and review them again in a few years to see how well you stayed true to your dreams.

Press play and do something new. Is there something you always wanted to try, but never did? Now is your chance to both fulfill that dream and learn from the experience. To make the exercise worthwhile, record the event including what it is you will do, why you never did it before, and what you expect to get by doing it. After you do the new thing, write down what you did, when, where, why, with whom, and any other comments including your feelings. Compare the before and after for wisdom into your current state of mind.

FOUR SEPARATE PATHS

Many creative people try to do too many things at one time. It's part of the creative spirit that is so helpful when you need the muse and so destructive when either you never finish anything or you burn out by having too much going. One suggestion is to divide your life into four distinct parts. Pursue these four paths with conviction and enthusiasm. Set specific goals within these paths and update your choices as you accomplish goals and/or decide to take new directions.

• *One, choose a main or core goal for your creative music career and devote the lion's share of your time, money, and other resources to achieving that goal. This goal should be the one main activity that brings the most satisfaction to your life.*

• Two, choose a secondary goal that is more long-term in nature and doesn't require immediate attention to complete. Set aside a smaller percentage of your time to explore this goal.

• Three, devote some time to whatever you do that funds your lifestyle, be that a day job or other more commercial, moneymaking activities that you must have in place to meet your financial obligations. Though the core goal may provide some or all of your income, you may still need this other activity occasionally or when first starting out.

• Four, have another passion that balances your work. While this passion can be another creative outlet—painting, for instance—it should be wholly unrelated to your other three paths. Physical exercise is a good choice for this passion: working out, hiking, bicycling, or Tai Chi (my particular choice). Travel and going to school to study new areas are also good choices.

KNOW YOUR CLIENTS

Who is going to buy what you sell? What do these people want? You need to take the time to research these two questions carefully. You can't create something and then go hunting for somebody to buy it. You must take the opposite approach: research what people want and need and then transform your music products and services to satisfy those wants and meet those needs. Through this research, you will find your niche in the music industry. The days of mass marketing are long gone. If you must move 50,000 units of your CD to break even, you'd better re-evaluate. Today you must concentrate your resources on smaller pockets of people with similar interests and desires. Be more relationship centered and make contact and sales one person at a time.

Once you know who your market is, you can turn your attention to what they want and where you can find them. Say you want to score independent films and videos. You need first to find the people who produce such work and discover where they gather. Perhaps there is an association to join? A magazine? A trade show? Going to independent film festivals might be a good start.

Once you find prospects, you should start collecting information about what they need. What you discover by getting involved with these people will help you promote and sell better.

QUICK AND DIRTY MARKET RESEARCH

• *Looking to promote your band? Start with the local music scene. What venues and which bands are successful and why?*

• *Want to score soundtracks and jingles? Listen to radio, watch TV, and go to the movies and then ask yourself who buys this music and why?*

• *Considering an indie CD release? Visit a good record store and go online to do your research.*

• *Don't forget to ask current and past buyers of your music products and services about their interaction with you. You can conduct a survey or simply ask them the questions you need answered.*

• *Gathering intelligence about your competition is ridiculously easy, too. Visit their Web sites to see what they are up to. Get their promotional material. Read about them in the media. Ask other people their opinions, too. You may also discover additional data about your competition's buyers—the same people you want to buy from you.*

• *Pay attention to what's going on around you. People will tell you what they need. Are you listening? For example, inspiration for my books comes from two sources: things that happen to me personally and things that happen to other people with whom I have contact. I get a lot of e-mail, and people tend to ask the same questions repeatedly. This lets me quickly spot information deficits that I try to remedy through my written work.*

• *You can also join various trade associations, clubs, groups, and unions to gather information through their publications, at meetings, and during trade shows.*

• *Thanks to the web you can find information on just about any topic and any group. But don't neglect the traditional media. Scour the local and national newspapers, newsmagazines, and music industry magazines for insight and trends. A trip to the library can yield a wealth of information.*

Don't think of your clients as just a wallet, checkbook, or credit card. Help them in ways where their success is related to yours. Always center on your client and what she wants to achieve, not on what you sell. People usually want only two things: to gain something or to remove some pain. They want to make more money, be happier, improve their looks, feel better, or any number of possible gains. Further, they want to reduce or eliminate any pain in their lives by getting rid of some annoyance such as debt, bad memories, fat, depression, or any number of ills. You can also look at this gain/pain in the context of hope and fear. The gain is the hope of what we want to accomplish while the pain is our fears that we want to abolish. Knowing what specific gains and pains the people who would buy from you have, lets you frame your specific solutions to their issues in ways that increase your sales.

Sell benefits, not features. A feature is an attribute of something such as a color, style, or description. Benefits are what you get *from* something. Generally, people don't care about features. They are mostly interested in their benefits and their results. In short, people buy the specific benefits your music products and services offer to them, not the product or services itself. People don't buy your CD, they buy what the music does for them: entertains, stimulates, inspires, etc. You need to make sure your promotions transform every bland feature into an enticing benefit. These benefits motivate people to take action, to buy. Benefits, along with offers, testimonials, guarantees, and calls to action make promotions effective and are fundamental to making money with your music.

PEOPLE POWER

This book uses the terms lead, prospect, client, and buyer. How are they defined?

• ***Leads*** *fall into two distinct groups. People whom you think might be interested in what you do, and people who have already identified themselves to you as interested. Your job is to take those leads and see if they indeed are good prospects.*

• ***Prospects*** *are those people who turn out to be really good candidates for buying what you sell. Hot prospects either are ready to buy or have an immediate need. Warm prospects need a little more prodding before they are willing to part with their cash. Cold prospects are people who never become clients.*

• ***Clients*** *are buyers of your music products and services.*

KNOW YOUR COMPETITION

Though many musicians like to think they are the newest thing, chances are somebody has already or is currently selling something similar to what you do. You need to study your competition meticulously. Ask yourself what they are doing right and doing wrong? Why are they successful? Are there any gaps in what they provide that you can fill? Can you improve on what they are already doing substantially? If you are only marginally better, you will face a tough battle. One thing to keep in mind as you study your competition is this: Americans, as a whole, love to root for the underdog. If there are major players where you'd like to be, you might want to capitalize on your underdog status as you approach the market initially.

Right now it is oh-so-easy to make and distribute music that just about anybody can and unfortunately, just about anybody does! Competition is fierce today. There is great emphasis on making things better, faster, and cheaper. The music industry is not immune to this trend. There are two competitive situations that you must understand.

It takes less time and money to create, edit, master, and duplicate music content. Sophisticated digital tools make music production a snap. Sonic Foundry's Acid software is a prime example of this phenomenon. This means more people can make music than ever before. This is both good and bad. Some talented people can reach more ears, but there is so much garbage to sort through first that they may never be heard at all. This competitive fervor is not limited to music acts either. Soundtracks and jingle composers and project studio owners, to name two music industry fields, face increasing competition as technology improves both in features and market penetration. More people have the tools making it a buyer's market for those who need musical content.

It is far cheaper to make and distribute most music products today than ever before. Songs can be posted and downloaded immediately without the need for the physical media (the CD itself and its packaging). It used to take a substantial financial investment to bring a CD to market. Now those costs are minuscule. Again, the result is a flood of music content without an associated rise in listeners. According to SoundScan in 2000 only 88 albums sold over a million copies and only 200 sold over 500,000. That means fewer and fewer albums make up the greater percentage of sales. What should happen is the money that went into physically creating the music product should now be freed up for promotion that helps you stand out among the crowded music marketplace.

KNOW THE INDUSTRY

Do you know how the music industry works? Do you know how a songwriter makes money? A band? A film composer? Unless you know the specifics, you'll never know how to make any money. Along with your general industry knowledge you also need to know what's going on right now. What's trendy? What major issues are affecting the industry right now? Unless you've been living under a rock for the last couple of years, you know the tumult and turmoil in the music industry today. It's a business in transition, and nobody knows precisely where it's headed. Therefore, you need to keep abreast of it all to make sure you keep pace with the shifts. Read the industry trade press, a few e-zines, and visit a few Web sites to keep your knowledge current.

- Artistpro.com ***(www.artistpro.com)***
- Billboard ***(www.billboard.com)***
- EQ ***(www.eqmag.com)***
- Electronic Musician ***(www.emusician.com)***
- Getsigned.com ***(www.getsigned.com)***
- Gig ***(www.gigmag.com)***
- Guitar Player ***(www.guitarplayer.com)***
- Home Recording ***(www.homerecordingmag.com)***
- Keyboard ***(www.keyboardmag.com)***
- Mix ***(www.mixonline.com)***
- MusicDish e-zine and affiliate e-zines B2N and I2N ***(www.musicdish.com)***
- Musician on-line ***(www.musician.com)***
- Performing Songwriter ***(www.performingsongwriter.com)***

KNOW HOW YOU MAKE MUSIC MONEY

To be the success you envision for your music career, you need to establish, follow, and review a specific system. Your best strategy for making money in today's music industry is to go into business for yourself and take the independent route. Whether selling indie CDs, composing soundtracks and jingles, running a project studio, or any number of music-related occupations, going independent, and keeping your full rights to what you create, is the position you want to be in. You must expand the way you think about your music career and look for additional ways to make money, too. In short, you need a series of music products and services that fit together and complement each other. These complementary items give people choices, encourage them to buy from you repeatedly, and allow you to increase your per sale dollars by providing add-ons and add-ins or other package deals. Your success depends on two factors.

Your ability to create and sell your own music products and services. If you sell services, you must also sell products. If you sell products, you must sell services, too. You'll never make it with a single product or service. One product costs way too much to create and promote. So, create more products as soon as possible. You should also regularly repackage, update, and expand on what you create and sell and increase your income simultaneously. For example, if you've produced an indie CD, you need another one fast. One CD could be your studio opus while the other could be your live act.

Service sellers must be able to deliver multiple services to meet client demands, too. For instance, should you primarily produce album music, you severely limit your chances of landing good paying corporate gigs (radio commercials, multimedia soundtracks, etc.). Instead, you want to become a much sought-after person—a free agent—who sells your talent and experience to the highest bidder, just as the free agent in professional sports.

Your ability to find and create agreements that let you profit from other people's products and services. This approach lets you easily expand your business by simply adding new or additional suppliers. While you probably won't sell your music with lawn furniture, you can uncover other opportunities. Look for items that either come before, complement, and/or follow what you sell. You can partner, joint venture, affiliate, and/or set up cooperative deals and strategic relationships with these other sellers that let you earn money on your extra sales. Selling many of these extras can be low risk. You typically don't pay for them out of your own pocket until your client pays you first.

Outsourcing specific tasks and whole or portions of projects that you can't or won't do yourself lets you expand your music business and increase your revenues without placing additional constraints on your time. You could have multiple projects going on simultaneously, many outsourced, than you could handle on your own. You can also bring additional musical products and services to your clients that they would usually go elsewhere to get. For instance, if you produce music in your project studio, you should offer duplication services. This service can be outsourced or subcontracted to another firm that pays you a commission on the sales you generate. Additionally, a booking agent could sell a book about music promotion to an ingénue act. Selling the book lets you increase your sales dollars while simultaneously showing your real regard for the band's success. You want to help them succeed for two reasons: it's the right thing to do and when they succeed they'll bring you more business.

Running your own business, especially full-time, comes with a certain unpredictability. Your income can be rather erratic while your expenses come steadily. You know that whether you work or not, there will be bills to pay tomorrow. This situation forces you to work extra hard and even take on more projects than you can comfortably handle for the sole reason that there may not be any work the next day. This is a vicious cycle that is hard to overcome. One remedy is to work hard at building more revenue generating products and services that continually bring in regular amounts with minimal effort. Outsourcing is one example. Selling other people's products is another example. Still another tactic is to play a steady lounge piano gig at a local hotel every week while you pursue other musical ventures outside of that gig. The point is to bring in a steady cash stream and reduce your income fluctuations, therefore getting some much-needed peace of mind. You won't be forced to work overly hard just to make ends meet.

PRODUCT VS. SERVICE

It's easy to distinguish between products and services in most industries. Unfortunately, this distinction is somewhat fuzzy when it comes to music. Obviously, a CD is a product and playing live to an audience is a service. But what about a song? Is it a product? You can most certainly "sell" it. Or is it a service? You can write a song for somebody and that's service-like. Don't get mired in semantics. This book's techniques apply to selling all forms of music products and services, no matter how you define them.

Making or finding suitable products and selling them is one-half of the moneymaking music philosophy. You don't need to start your own factory to sell products. There are several approaches to consider.

Product produced on demand. Technology makes it a snap to create many products in-house and deliver them directly to the people who buy them. For example, you get an order for your independent CD, you grab a blank disk, burn the CD on your computer, print the graphics on your color printer, put the pieces together, and ship it to your client. This strategy is fine if the volume you sell is small. It's how I create and deliver my music CDs.

Downloadable products. Of course, you don't need to create a physical CD in many cases. You can upload your products and clients pay to download them. While a lot of music is given away as free MP3s, there are many other products that people pay for and download such as software, samples, MIDI files, books, and more. The nice thing about downloadable products is they are cheaper to manufacture. You don't have to spend money on their packaging and can either pass those savings on to the buyers or use the money you save to fund additional promotions.

Product manufactured in bulk. This is the method most people think of first when planning a new product. For example, you send your music master off to the duplication house that in turn creates the thousands of copies you need. The problem with this approach is you need an infusion of cash to pay for the duplication and packaging costs. While pressing a thousand CDs is not particularly costly, several thousand can run up a bill nicely. You have to be realistic with your projections and not make too many, lest you have boxes of unsold CDs in your garage for years. You also don't want to underestimate either or you might have orders for CDs that you can't deliver on time.

Products manufactured short-run. A viable alternative to the do-it-yourself approach and large-scale production is to find sources for smaller orders. While your per unit charges may be slightly higher than making thousands of a product at a time, your financial risk is appreciably smaller. You don't have to commit a lot of money to make 100 CDs to test the waters at gigs. Short-runs are especially attractive for swag (T-shirts, caps, cups, stickers, and such).

Products bought wholesale. You do not need to make your own products to make money, either. You can buy other products and sell them. You want to buy these products at wholesale prices (at least 50% of retail), so you can sell them at 100% retail. Look for CDs produced by other bands, swag, merchandise, even supplies. For example, a project studio can sell blank CDs, guitar/bass strings, music gear, and other merchandise to the people who record there.

Product bought at retail. If you buy products on behalf of your clients at full prices, it is a good idea to markup the cost slightly (10-15%) and earn a little extra money on the sale.

Product sold through affiliate programs. You can sell any number of products through deals you make on- or off-line. These programs have you doing the selling, but not the transactions. You promote a product, people order direct from the source or store, and you earn a commission, usually 5-15%, from the sales you generate. The Amazon.com affiliate program is just one example of this concept.

Product licensing. You do not have to either make or sell a product to make money. You can license *other* manufacturers to create and sell merchandise for you. When a band's logo or picture appears on a shirt, cap, or other doo-dad, you can bet that a percentage of the sale is going to the band. These licensing agreements typically return a royalty on sales to the copyright or trademark owner.

IS IT A MONEYMAKER?

As you consider the music products and services that you will sell, ask yourself this question: Will this activity move more products and services out the door and make more money or is it just a pipe dream? Your answer to this question, based on the research you do, should go a long way toward preventing you from making errors.

DEVELOPING SERVICES

Selling services is the other half of the moneymaking music pie. As with products, you can take several approaches.

Deliver services yourself. If you are a solo act, soundtrack and jingle composer, music producer, project studio owner, etc., you can develop and deliver your services to one client at a time. You will be paid according to whatever arrangements you agree upon. This is usually a daily or hourly rate multiplied by the time you work (Rate x Time = $) or a single project fee.

Add partners. Forming a band is just one example of adding partners to your service mix. Here you will split your income and expenses according to mutually agreed upon percentages, such as 50-50.

Hire employees. As a small business owner, you can hire people to work for you and pay them a salary for the work they perform. Their wages are a deductible business expense for you.

Outsource. Much of the work you do can be delegated to independent contractors whom you hire. These suppliers can be individuals or other companies. For instance, I hire voice talent to provide narration for audio-visual projects. This person is not an employee. She is an independent and free to pursue other work. Additionally, I hire a duplication company to copy and package CD projects that I complete for my clients. There are two ways to handle the money when outsourcing services. One, your supplier can bill you a fee directly. You can then mark up that fee, from 15-20 percent or more, and bill your client the higher amount. When your client pays, you pay your vendor. Two, your supplier can bill your client direct and kick back a commission to you (again, 15-20 percent is good).

Agent/dealer. One particular subset of outsourcing is using agents and dealers who sell for you in return for a commission on these sales. These people do not provide a service per se. Their function is to act on your behalf as your sales force. They earn their money by taking 10-15 percent of the money they generate for you. Having independent sales reps can be a good tactic because they free you from promoting. That lets you concentrate on delivering the music products and services you do best.

CO-OP DEALS

Which would you rather have, one person doing all the promotions and sales or dozens of people promoting your music products and services? Increasing your sales force can be a simple proposition. You need to set up cooperative agreements that are mutually beneficial between you and other people or companies. In short, you want as many people as possible selling your stuff in exchange for earning a commission on the sales they make. For example, a band could kick back a commission to anyone who gets them a gig. Personally, I set up an informal dealer program for my Melomania *music library CDs. By offering incentive (cash!) to people who sign up, I increase my sales force exponentially. This is the letter used to explain the program:*

Earn yourself some easy cash by selling my new Melomania music library

Here's how it works: You promote the Melomania CDs using the promotional materials we'll provide in your catalog, newsletter, or Web site. You take orders from your clients, deduct your commission, and send us the remaining amount with fulfillment information. We ship the CDs direct to your client. In other words, a standard drop ship arrangement.

Here's how you make money: You collect Melomania's full $99 price. You get over 50% off. That's right. You keep $50 and send the remaining $49 to us. You pay as you go—only when you sell CDs—keeping your $50 commission from every sale. You can even supply a customer label so the CDs look as if they came directly from you. Or you can stock CDs and ship them yourself if you prefer. Either way, this is by far the easiest way for you to make more money. Sell ten CDs, make $500. Sell 100, earn $5000! It's that simple. Sound interesting?

Here's how you get started: Anybody can join this program. Just buy one copy of Melomania at its full $99 price. After that you can sell Melomania, keeping your $50 commission on every sale as described above. We plan to release a new CD each year ... so you have the potential to keep earning money selling the expanding Melomania music library!

MAKING SALES

Once you have the music products and services established, you must understand the ways that you can sell them.

Sell direct. Make your sales direct to people and companies in person, over the phone, through your Web site, and back of the room at gigs. Selling direct means making the sale and delivering the product and service immediately or soon after. It also means you get 100 percent of the price. Direct product sales will put far more money in your pocket than any other kind of sale. And unless you use a manager, booking agent, or sales rep, selling your services direct will also keep your income high.

Sell to wholesalers. Exclusively the domain of product sellers, you deliver your wares at significantly reduced prices. The wholesalers or distributors then sell your products to retail outlets. Make sure you understand that distributors get your records to places where people can buy them. You still have to convince these people to actually buy your CD. Distributors don't promote; they are suppliers. The burden to promote and make sales is yours.

SELL SHEETS

Prepare a basic fact sheet to help distributors, wholesalers, retailers, and catalogs understand your music product(s). On your letterhead, print the details of this information:

- *Title*
- *Act name*
- *Label name*
- *Release date*
- *Format (CD/Tape)*
- *Retail price*
- *Discount terms (6-100-50% net 30; 101+- 60% net 60)*
- *Shipping fees*
- *UPC*
- *Contents*
- *Audience description / genre*
- *Brief act bio*
- *Tour dates*
- *Radio and music store appearances*
- *List stores that stock product currently*
- *Promotion plans (ads, web, publicity, etc.)*

Sell to retailers. You can bypass the wholesalers and go direct to retail outlets with your products. These retailers can include brick and mortar stores, catalogs, Web sites, and so forth. While some stores may buy your music products outright (at wholesale prices), many will prefer a consignment agreement. This basically means leaving a few copies of your product and the store pays you when (and if) they sell.

CONSIGNMENT AGREEMENT

If you decide to leave any of your music products on consignment at a store, draft a simple consignment agreement on your letterhead and include:

- *Date*
- *Contact information of store*
- *The items placed on consignment: quantity, name, description, and selling price*
- *The terms of the agreement including percentage of price going to the store (50 percent) and when the agreement ends (three months). Be sure to mention that you will pick up unsold goods at the end of the agreement and expect to be paid for sold goods at that time. Also, include a sentence that says damaged goods are considered sold and that you expect to be paid for them.*
- *You and a store representative should sign the agreement. Keep the original and make a copy for the store.*
- *You must follow up these agreements and pick up leftovers along with any money you are due. If the store wishes to keep selling your material, or if they run out before the agreement ends, issue another consignment agreement to cover the new items.*
- *Selling on consignment works best when your promote the store yourself. For example, tell people exactly where they can buy your CD. Even put the store's address on flyers, postcards, and on other promotional material you distribute.*

Sell through affiliates. You can join affiliate programs or sponsor dealer programs and pay commissions on the sales.

AMAZON.COM ADVANTAGE

This is a free, non-exclusive way to sell your music CDs (videos and books, too). Amazon stocks your product and processes orders for you. They take 55 percent of the retail price giving you the other 45 percent. Note: music CDs must have a bar-coded UPC readable on the outside of the package to be considered by Amazon.com. You get:

• An Amazon.com page with track samples, space for customer reviews, bios, cover art, and liner notes.
• MP3 downloads to help fans discover your music—and buy your CDs.
• Ability to earn money from your MP3 downloads with the Amazon Honor System.
• Free stocking, shipping, cover scanning, and sound encoding.
• Full access to your sales, inventory, and payment reports.
• Quick payment terms and automatic reordering.

Several other online stores offer similar programs such as CDBaby ***(www.cdbaby.com)****. They charge $35 to set up your account and take $4 for each CD sold (no matter what you charge). They stock 5 CDs at first, reordering when they sell, handle the transactions including shipping, and pay you regularly. You don't need a UPC to sell through CDBaby.*

CHAPTER 3

Money Making Music 102, or What You Need to Learn Fast

"Life itself is a great classroom. And the lessons we learn from it are the most significant. Indeed, we learn as much or more by intuition as by tuition."— Laurence Boldt

LEARN TO DEVELOP A SUCCESSFUL ATTITUDE

You must master certain mental skills. These attitudinal behaviors sometimes are even more important than your physical skills.

Dedicate yourself. Commit right now to doing everything in your power to make your music career what you want it to be. You must be willing to work hard and smart. Seize the opportunities and earmark your resources toward realizing your dreams.

Clear the clutter. You can't be distracted by too many obligations that interfere with your ultimate goals. Purge the excess stuff from your life by eliminating both physical clutter and mental baggage. Sell off the stuff you no longer want and question your beliefs, notions, and stances about people, places, events, and life. It can be hard to let go of these things, but this sacrifice is necessary. When you clean your closets, you usually end up making a bigger mess first. Life is like that. You might have to weather some chaos first before the true calm emerges.

Focus your efforts. You can't do everything, so concentrate where you are the most effective. Evaluate your strengths and weaknesses. Work your strengths hard while resolving to improve your weaker aspects through training or by getting help from an outside source. Your goal is to master your skills and art to such an extent that the work comes easily and naturally. This state of "effortless action" is what the Taoists call *Wei Wu Wei.* You become completely absorbed in a task and ignorant of the world around you. The next thing you know, hours have passed and you can't remember what happened. Most importantly, during this time you were focused, creative, enthusiastic, and productive. It came easy, right? Effortlessly? That is *Wei Wu Wei.* And it takes practice, hard work, and perseverance to reach it. You'll know when you've reached this state when you lose all track of time, accomplish more and of better quality because your work energizes and excites you, and your enthusiasm doesn't wane.

Understand your motivations. What drives you to pursue music? Is it creative expression? Money? Fame? Or is it some deeper feeling that manifests itself in some personal, unique manner? Your motivations should come from your core values. They establish your fundamental beliefs and therefore trigger your response to situations. Return to those beliefs when you suffer any setbacks and reach inside for the motivation you need to keep going. As Marilyn vos Savant said: "Being defeated is often a temporary condition. Giving up is what makes it permanent."

Kindle your fire. Have you ever noticed that when you are passionate about something you really care about, your entire mood changes? When you do the work you love, the energy comes from within. There's a fire in your belly that won't be quenched unless you pursue your dreams. Don't extinguish your blaze. Instead, harness that power and let it help you along the way. This passion is what you must bring to your career, as it can make the long, hard journey more palatable. Ron Rubin and Stuart Avery Gold, CEO and COO of the Republic of Tea, offered this insightful advice in their *success@life* book: "Passion provides you the best possible odds to successfully catch and live your dream."

Get excited. Even as you are passionate about what you do, make sure that passion shows on the outside. Your enthusiasm for what you create, and for your client's aspirations, will serve you well. It's contagious. People will notice your excitement and become equally exhilarated.

Confront your fears. Fear is not a four-letter word. It can be a powerful immobilizer when your worry stifles your inertia into inaction. On the other hand, fear can be a terrific ally and mobilizer when your fight or flight instinct kicks in. You may use fear as a motivation for fighting for what you believe in. Or, you may see a bad situation and decide to run away fast. Humans often have many fears, some rational, many irrational. We fear failure and the embarrassment that losing can bring. Many people fear success, too. Reaching a pinnacle can bring with it a fear of discontent. We dread we may get there and say: "Is that all there is?" More people have been paralyzed by their own cold feet than any other obstacle. Recognizing what you fear, and working to overcome these fears, is another important step when taking on your musical journey.

There are no guarantees. Even the most ardent, pragmatic search for the "sure thing" will be mostly in vain. Follow the ideas here with zeal and get-up-and-go, and you better your odds. Have no regrets either. No matter how everything turns out, you will be more content because you took the chances and went after what you thought you wanted.

Make mistakes. Part of the learning and growing process is failing. You didn't learn to walk without falling down a few times. You won't make your music career anything special without falling down once in a while either. "The greatest mistake you can make in life," says Elbert Hubbard, "is to be continually fearing you will make one." A mistake can be costly if you let it get the better of you. Mistakes can also be opportunities. You will know what doesn't work and can then arrange things so they come out as expected the second time. Always take full responsibility for your mistakes and also be humble about your success.

Challenge yourself. Don't rest on past success or fall into a rut. Motivate yourself in whatever ways work for you. Demand of yourself to do better. But don't impose unrealistic or harsh limits on yourself. If you are facing a roadblock, start asking the right questions. Why am I not selling enough CDs? Why can't I land another soundtrack? Why is my project studio empty?

Take the entrepreneurial view. The people with vision and courage who take the risks and start their own businesses comprise an elite group. When you make the mental shift to being in business for yourself, you join the club. With that membership comes certain obligations, but also new choices. You reduce, even eliminate, some restrictions in your life and free yourself to pursue your dreams with as much fortitude as you can muster.

Have some guts. Understand this business axiom: The more you have at stake, the more cautious you will be. Conversely, the less you risk, the more adventurous you may be. There is great risk in any venture. To be successful requires guts. However, if you have too much to lose, you will not proceed as aggressively as you may need. For example, if you have a steady job, mortgage, car payment, children, and more counting on you, it will not be easy to start your own music business. The pressure would be enormous because too much rides on your success. This stress would cloud your judgment and most certainly stifle your creativity. This situation requires a different tactic. Take calculated risks. Don't throw caution to the wind. You must lessen your risk through careful, methodical preparation. Make sure you "cover all the bases" first before plunging into those waters of uncertainty by making sure you've considered all the angles, good and bad. Proceed when it feels and looks right.

Diminish limiting behaviors. We all suffer from a little self-sabotage. We are our own worst enemies and sometimes stand in our own way of success. You may delude yourself into thinking that it's impossible to do something. You may tell yourself that you don't know how to do something. You may feel you don't deserve the acclaim, money, recognition, or whatever. Or you may decide you don't really want or need something (even when you really do). You may also mislead yourself by passing the buck and saying everything is beyond your control and not your responsibility. When you catch yourself falling into these traps, work hard to escape their ruinous hold. You can change the way you think, feel, and react. It *is* possible to achieve what you want. You *can* learn what you need to do it. You *do* deserve the fruits of your labors. You *do* need to live the life you want for yourself. And you *are* responsible for whatever happens to you, success or failure.

Get flexible. Learn to be open to change, because change is the only constant in our world. It's easy to become complacent or stubborn. It's the main reason many businesses fail when their competition overtakes them. You can't let that happen to you. You know that even the most carefully executed plan sometimes must be revised or dumped entirely. That flexibility can save the day and mean the difference between a lackluster existence and a thriving, vibrant life.

Be proactive and aggressive. There is no need or room to be timid or apologetic. You need to cultivate a take charge attitude that doesn't react to problems, but moves ahead of the pack before anybody else realizes what is happening. Be opportunistic by carefully studying the trends and moving fast. Remember that you are in control of your own career at all times. The burden to make contacts and sales falls to you. Never wait for the phone to ring. Pick it up and dial it yourself! You must go after what you want full-speed ahead with conviction and tenacity.

Put on a tough hide. You will face a lot of rejection in your career. How you handle those rebukes is important to your survival. You must learn to not take "no" so personally. Instead, find out all you can about the negative response and work to overcome those shortcomings in the future. Also, don't worry about the tire-kickers of the world who gladly waste your time and energy without ever buying from you. Once you've been doing things a little while, you'll recognize them easily and know how to courteously jettison them.

Find balance. Everything is good for you, in moderation. How many times have you heard that phrase? It is nonetheless true. Finding the fulcrum in your life and balancing all the differing aspects of it is a great challenge. Everything is not black and white or good and bad. And you can't be all work and no play. The Chinese Yin/Yang symbol represents balance. It comprises two, seemingly opposing forces each with the seed of its counterpart within. Therefore, the world is not made up of opposite forces, but rather *complementary* ones. For example, this implies that within all bad is some good and within all good is some bad. It is a concept that is difficult to grasp initially. However, once you understand what balance really means, you can integrate its basic tenet into your life.

Persist. Success rarely happens overnight. It takes time and effort. Yet, even in your darkest hours you must search deep down inside for the courage and energy to go forth. Just when things look the bleakest, depend on your steadfast resolve to continue in spite of whatever obstacles stand in your way.

Find inspiration and comfort. If you are having problems with your life and career, or if you just need some inspiration, consider studying other people who faced and overcame adversity in their lives. Pick up some biographies. You can grab music-related bios or choose other inspiring people. I specifically recommend the *Beatles Anthology* and Joe Jackson's *A Cure for Gravity*. Jackson's poignant musical journey captures his search for his life's purpose in his love for music. If you consider yourself a musical artist where music feeds your soul, you will find a certain kinship in this story.

I further suggest renting some movies with central themes where characters make major changes or transformations in their lives. You may find it inspiring to see these fictional people confront their demons, exorcise them, and move on, happier and healthier. *It's a Wonderful Life* with James Stewart is a classic metaphor for this exercise, as is its modern counterpart, *Family Man* with Nicholas Cage. Two other favorites are *Regarding Henry* with Harrison Ford and *Tender Mercies* with Robert Duvall. Movies have a way of feeding our voyeuristic tendencies, letting us experience alongside the characters, while getting the benefit of resolution that so often is lacking from our lives. The film ends and, usually, ties up all the loose ends. Life tends to be a little more messy and open-ended.

GETTING CREATIVE

When composing music, there are four main steps to the creative process.

- *Collect material. You usually jot ideas down, strum a few chords, maybe even the hint of a melody. This is often just playing around; the musical equivalent of doodling. You are usually unfocused and disorganized.*

- *Idleness. You appear to be doing little, if anything. You may feel frustrated at this point because you just can't seem to do anything good. However, this is often the crucial step that lets ideas swim around in your brain waiting for the spark. Though many great works have been given life through the constant nag of an imminent deadline, the secret to real inspiration and creative work is time. You need time to bring ideas to fruition. As author Carol Lloyd said: "Creativity takes time: time for doing the work, time to rest and replenish your imagination, time to study your craft, time to dream."*

- *Inspiration. Suddenly everything just starts flowing and you scribble down the lyrics, chords, melody, and perhaps start recording, too. This step is usually effortless and your work seems to come from beyond you.*

- *Perspiration. Now the hard work begins as you start pulling together what you did into a cohesive musical piece. You make something special out of your creation and give it the polish it needs to be real.*

Not every piece you do will follow these steps exactly, but what you may discover is that overall, most creative people follow this process unconsciously. Knowing this can help you get through the "writer's block" we often face during step two.

GETTING BETTER FAST

No matter what aspect of the music industry you pursue, you can improve your skills in just three easy steps.

- *Record your rehearsals*
- *Record your shows*
- *Listen, learn, and improve!*

While that's simple advice for a band, how does that apply to others? If you are a manager who needs help making sales, record your practice sales pitch (audio and/or video), record an actual meeting or two (audio), and use what you learn to become better at making sales.

LEARN BASIC PROFESSIONAL SKILLS

You need certain skills to run your own business and you need an education to make your music industry career a success. This section details the skills you need to cultivate and the education you need to acquire and from where. It also helps to possess a rudimentary general knowledge of history, art, science, etc. These liberal arts make you a more well-rounded individual. They serve to ground you and often provide jumping off points for new ideas and radically different approaches. Also, you obviously need whatever your music skills and talents are or other special knowledge you bring to the table.

Recently I received an e-mail that asked me how to start an indie record label. What surprised me the most was that this person had no clue how a record label worked or what its functions truly were, let along how to manage a successful one. It is rare that you'll be a success jumping into something you know little about. Research and actually doing the work is the path to understanding the demands of a particular business and what it takes to succeed with it. You probably learn about 70-80 percent on-the-job while the other 20-30 percent you get from formal education. Therefore, the people you work with, the experiences you acquire, and the challenges you face in the real world account for a significantly larger and more valuable portion of your education. More than books, more than college or other courses, experience teaches all of us. And this experience must be gained through study, formal education, and trial and error. Knowing that the tuition you pay for the School of Hard Knocks is usually more vital to your continued success, helps you better focus your resources.

People. You will deal with people and people will deal with you. Therefore, it is essential that you master your interpersonal skills. You need to be friendly and polite, able to take charge when necessary and acquiesce when required.

Sales. Selling is not some manipulative behavior that you use to exercise control over another. Selling is dream spinning, presenting your products and services so that a buyer can see, taste, feel, smell, and experience using, having, and benefiting from them. You exist to fulfill needs.

Research. You need a lot of information so you can make informed decisions about your business and your role in it. You must dig deep to find useful information. Access to the web and a good reference library are absolute essentials. Spend a day at the library and thumb through books and magazines for ideas and information. Spend a day on the Internet similarly, too. You need to know where to start, where to go, and how to sift through the often conflicting data and opinions to arrive at something advantageous. Also, your research should help you find the niche markets for what you sell and show you how to adjust what you sell effectively to increase your sales.

Critical thinking. Just because you can find out a lot of information doesn't mean you know what to do with it. Critical thinking requires using your head (your experience) and your gut (intuition) to make better decisions. You learn to trust your intuition through a track record of successes. And there is a direct correlation between success and confidence. The more you achieve, the more confidence you will have to set your goals higher.

Read. Hot on the heels of research is reading. Even when you are not specifically looking for information, you should take time to expand your knowledge through reading. Many of your best ideas will come from where you least expect it. Read as much as you can and work to gain a diverse look at the world. Read the newspaper, a major magazine or two, books, e-zines, Web sites, and industry-specific media that appeal to your clients. Also, read some material that is wholly unrelated to whatever it is you do or like. This fresh perspective can really spark your creativity, musically and business-wise.

Watch. Half the world is visually oriented, so you can't stay buried in words all the time. Turn on the TV, surf the Web, get out into the world to see what's going on.

Participate. Don't just slumber through life passively. Experience the world. Take an active role in matters that pertain to your music career and outside of it. Enroll in a class or two, travel to new locales, join a club or association, network, and volunteer for some worthy causes. Simply find ways to accumulate new experiences. Embrace the knowledge you acquire and apply it to your music career.

Listen. Since knowing what people want is so important, carefully listening to their demands and dreams helps you better tailor your music products and services. You must truly listen to what people tell you and to what is going on around you. The best rule is to talk less than one-third of the time. If you are meeting with a prospect, listen to what she says. She will usually tell you what she wants and then you can explain how you can deliver it through what you sell. Since music requires listening, make sure you open up your ears to all the music the world has to offer, too. Don't cement yourself in one genre or you'll become a musical snob. Instead listen to a variety of music to expand your mind and improve your musical skill.

Plan. Though we'll discuss this issue in greater detail later in the book, recognize now that careful planning will save you so much time and effort that would otherwise be wasted.

Write. You will do a lot of writing in your career—letters, promotional material, and e-mail. Knowing how to use words effectively is vital. Your writing must communicate simply and succinctly what you need to say. Your spelling, grammar, and structure must be correct, too. Practice writing simple prose—lean and to the point—and you won't go wrong.

Speak. You will talk a lot, too. You will connect with people by phone and in person. You will make sales presentations, even speeches. You may be on stage, too. Practice making sure your voice is pleasant to listen to, strong and clear, and free of annoying speech patterns.

Business literacy. You need to acquire more savvy on business matters. If you haven't a clue about what being in business is all about, this book should provide the basic knowledge you need. Also, look beyond these pages for additional business information that completes your education.

Broaden the depth of your knowledge by being a voracious student. The more you know, the better your chances of becoming and staying successful. There is so much information available today that can help you achieve your dreams. You need to find it, understand it, transform it to your situation, and own it. Set a goal to learn something valuable each and every day. And set a goal to experience something new, too. Use what you learn and experience to expand your music industry career options and opportunities.

Pro/Files—Marina V

Originally from Moscow, Russia. Currently lives in Los Angeles, CA
www.MarinaV.com—Marina@MarinaV.com

What do you do in the music industry? I am a pop/rock/alternative singer/songwriter/live performer/pianist with a band

What promotions work the best and why? Putting flyers around, telling people personally, e-mailing them in person and asking to come to my gigs, commercial radio appearances, small ads in the paper.

Where does the money come from? Day job, CD sales, gig pay

What were some of your past projects? Recorded 2 CDs independently

What has been your greatest achievement so far? 1. I opened for a great national act, Beth Hart (Atlantic Records). 2 & 3. Signed an artist endorsement contract with Audix Microphones (Alanis, Bruce Springsteen, Willie Nelson) and also with Sabine Tuners

(Johnny Cash, the Who, etc.). 4. Was a Spotlight/Feature Artist at least a dozen times on many music Web sites. 5. Appeared on the highest rated commercial radio station during their most popular program for 40 minutes (in Central, IL USA). 6. Within 1 year of doing music professionally, I was contacted by 3 major record labels (nothing for sure so far) before ever contacting them. For more, please visit my Web site.

How did you do it? Lots of hard work, persistence, talent, good music, intelligence, politeness, and hard work.

What lessons have you learned along the way? You have to be very strong and persistent and never give up. Try to learn everything about everything (and still be good at what you do best). Try to improve yourself all the time. Everyone wants to knock you down; don't let them! Appreciate every fan and every person who is nice to you and reply to everyone (short and polite).

What is your current project or next goal? Signing a publishing contract with a major publisher and then looking for a major label to work with.

LEARN HOW TO MAKE MONEY

You should take a concerted approach when it comes to making sales with your music products and services. Implement these guidelines in your daily business life.

Keep it simple. You do not need stacks of promotional material to make money with your music. You can do well with some simple, basic material that has a consistent look and feel. They should work together and share a common, cohesive theme, image, and look. Choosing the graphics, color, typestyle and so forth are critical as is using these design elements repeatedly. People start to associate a particular look with your music products and services and begin to recognize your "logo" which goes far beyond an actual icon-based logo (which you may or may not employ).

• Develop some basic promotional material, including sales letters, small brochures, business cards, flyers and postcards, newsletters, and a FAQ. Prepare this material so it can be sent by regular mail or e-mail, as well as posted on the Web.

• Produce a demo as a record of your music products and services. A band's demo may be its indie CD while a jingle composer may have a video demo reel of her TV spots.

• Create a simple Web site that both promotes your music products and services and gives people a way to purchase them.

• Use phone calls, e-mail, and in-person visits to promote and sell. Warm up otherwise cold calls through other promotions.

• Use publicity to get your message out.

• Cultivate referrals and word of mouth through specific actions that bring in more business.

• Approach the same kind of people with the successes you achieved working with *their* peers.

• Re-approach past clients regularly and make them special offers.

Make it easy for people to buy from you. Don't put up barriers to free and easy commerce. Accept all forms of payment: cash, checks, and credit cards and make it simple for people to buy. A Web store is open 24-7-365, ready to help when the buyer is ready. You also want to make it easy for people to buy from you by reducing or eliminating the risks. Remember, people are skeptical and you must reassure them that they are making the right choice.

• Push the benefits of what you sell.

• Explain all details carefully so the client knows exactly what she is getting

• Provide samples to further reassure the buyer.

• When you accept credit cards, make sure the processing in secure.

• Include testimonials by real people who share their experiences with you, your products, and your services. Prospects identify with their peers.

• Use endorsements from the media or other people in a similar manner to testimonials.

• Get referred. When someone recommends you to their friends and colleagues, you are in a terrific position to close a sale. People take these recommendations and referrals very seriously.

• Provide an extensive, no-questions-asked money-back guarantee.

Give something away up front to stimulate sales in the future. This sales tactic is the most used because it is the most successful. You can take two approaches: One, provide a loss leader or two, a free sample. A loss leader is selling a particular product or service at a greatly reduced price in the hopes of generating more business later. A free sample is giving something away that's indicative of the other items you sell in the hopes that people will love it and want to buy more. The free MP3 of your music is the ideal free sample. Using this strategy is effective on its own but is made more powerful when you know the lifetime value of a typical client. If the average client spends $10 with you, you can't afford to give away too much. However, if your average client spends $1000 with you, you can afford to give away much more because you know once you get them in the door, they'll keep coming back and buying more.

While you should include CDs of your music with publicity and other promotional kits and MP3s on your Web site, don't neglect making other short sample CDs. For example, put a couple of your songs on a CD and give them away to promote your act. This will always work better than any other promotion because people who get the CD can hear your music and decide if **a**) they want to come to your show and/or **b**) they want to buy your full CD. Make sure you have full contact information on the CD label including where to buy your regular CD, how to book your act, etc. You can also include a short card or flyer to profile upcoming gigs and other pertinent information. To keep the costs down, create the CDs in-house with a CD burner, a spindle of blank CD-Rs, some labels, and paper see-through envelopes. Distribute these promotional CDs as you would any other promotion: mail them, tack them on bulletin boards (why tack just a flyer when you can pin up a half-dozen CDs, too?), pass them out on the street, give them away at gigs (yours and *other people's* performances), hand them out while street performing, and any other creative ways you can think of.

THE NEW MEANING OF *FREE*

Prices are going down. With online delivery, it can cost virtually nothing to deliver music. Encode a track to MP3 or Real Audio, post it on the Web, and people download this intangible music for their listening pleasure. Though many fail to admit it, there has always been, and continues to be "free" music. Radio comes to mind. Giving away singles entices people to buy whole CDs (or additional songs). Netscape gave away millions of Internet browsers to build a solid base of users (and to find customers for their more expensive server software). This method of transacting business is not unusual. When you have a product or service line that fits together, you can give the main piece away and let people buy plug-ins and other ancillary products and services that work with the main piece. You can give even your CDs away, as long as people hire you to play live.

For example, Sonic Foundry makes an outstanding software music production tool called Acid. It is the basic engine that forms the foundation for several related products in the Acid family. They also make the sound loops that go with the products. This keeps you coming back and buying more after you've purchased the main software. In fact, they give away a scaled down version of Acid in the hopes you'll love it so much, you'll upgrade to the full version and also continue to buy loops to expand your musical and sound palette. Additionally, they've created a Web community ***(www.acidplanet.com)*** *for users to gather, share their work, ask and answer questions, and more. This business model works well in today's music business.*

Upsell and resell people. Your goal is never to make a single sale of a single item. You want people to increase the amount of money they spend right away. If 100 people spend just $5 more, you clear an extra $500. That's the real value of upselling; it generates more income for you.

Put together hard-to-resist package deals that save people money while at that same time get them to spend more money. If you are selling a main product for $15, have a few $5 items on hand that can get the sale to $20. For example, you could sell a studio produced CD for $15 and throw in a live album for $5 more. The studio release should be retail ready (graphics, packaging, etc.), but the live album can be a five-song "white-label." Also, selling in increments of $10 and $20 is terrific, especially for back-of-room sales because people usually have these bills in their wallets. Occasionally, put everything you offer on sale, as well. Discount everything 20 percent-30 percent for a limited time and make it up with a volume increase. Offer premiums and other incentives to increase your sales, too.

Service sellers usually have several anchor clients who contribute a large amount of your total sales. These people usually buy regularly, often without any effort on your part. However, don't wait for them to call. Stay in touch with these people and keep them buying what you sell. You might even offer them a special, exclusive discount as an incentive to buy from you again.

Also, get people to buy more often by releasing new items or new improved items regularly. If you haven't produced anything new lately, it's time to unleash another music product or service to your past clients. Since these people are usually already sold on you, generating new sales is a snap. After you've exhausted your past buyers, turn your attention to selling this new stuff to prospects who have yet to patronize you.

THE 10 PERCENT = 33 PERCENT SOLUTION

When you think about making more money from your music, the usual thing that pops into your head is to get more clients. In fact, there are two other ways that can put more money in your pocket. You can get people to spend more with you when they do buy and/or you can get them to buy more often.

What if I told you that you could increase your revenue 33 percent with only 10 percent more effort? Here'show it works: Let's say you have 100 people spend $10 with you twice each year. You'd make $2000. Now if you increase those numbers by a mere 10 percent (110 x $11 x 2.2), you'd clear $2662. That's a 33 percent increase in dollars. What can you do today to get 10 percent more clients to spend just a lousy 10 percent more, and repeat buy a little more often? Launch some promotions that land a few new buyers. Increase your prices or create package deals that entice people to buy more. Create new products and services regularly that get people to buy again faster.

Build mutually beneficial relationships with people. Treat every client as if that person is the only client you have. Sell one-to one and make sure that what you provide meets the client's needs exactly. Follow my often quoted formula: **Leads + Follow-up = $ales**.

Find people who need what you sell and get them interested in it. Stay in touch with them through carefully implemented promotions until they finally buy. People continue to tell me that the personal touch makes all the difference. Respond to those e-mails, return those phone calls, and get out and meet people face-to-face, these are the ways to generate loyal, repeat buyers for all that you sell. These relationships should extend to your vendors, the media, and any other people comprising your extended network.

Keep in touch, too. Your contact with a client can't begin and end with a sale. You want them to stay loyal and continue to buy from you for a long time to come. It's vital that you stay in contact with the people who do business with you. This includes your main or anchor clients, current clients, past clients, warm prospects, media contacts, vendors, affiliates, your network of people who aren't clients, key industry people, key clients' industry people, and others. Pick up the phone, send letters and e-mails, go to meetings and other functions, make special offers just for them, and more.

Practice good service. If you strive to focus on your clients you can't run away during or after the sale. Make sure you have policies in place to deal with client problems, such as product returns. Have a written money-back guarantee that goes with every product you sell. Provide remedies for situations when a client is unhappy with your services, too. You may need to revise something at your expense. Always respond fast to problems, too. Take the blame if it is your fault and take action immediately to satisfy the complaint. Your best tactic is to eliminate problems up front. Carefully spell out the goals and objectives of a given project and who is responsible for what actions. You clearly state and get the client to agree exactly what they get, when, and for what dollar amount *before* you start working. In short, use contracts to prevent things from spiraling out of control and costing you money.

CHAPTER 4

Map Your Musical Journey

"If you take too long in deciding what you will do with your life, you'll find you've done it."—George Bernard Shaw

All businesses start with a plan. Your music business is no different. Sometimes this plan is just an inkling while other times you have a detailed blueprint of what you want to accomplish. A business student recently called to ask me a few questions about my company. Her first question was if Fisher Creative Group had a formal business plan. "Yes we do," I replied. Then I added rather flippantly, "But we prefer to call it a To Do List around here!" Despite my initial levity, I told her that a solid business plan is a critical component to business success and something you can never neglect.

Planning means looking to the future. That future may be only a few days away or it may be several years down the line. While you don't need to plan your life to the nano-second, it does help to have a general idea of where you want to go. Planning really works when you take the time to make crucial decisions up front, leave in some contingencies, and detail the components that your plan requires.

These exercises might imply that you can only choose one thing for your music industry career. That's not true. While it is important to focus on one main niche, you need to also accommodate the related, spin-off ventures you will add to your central career/business theme. Choose a basic foundation and build on from there with the details you need to make your music industry structure.

Planning requires four steps: setting goals, determining what you need to reach those goals, implementing the plan by acquiring resources and moving through the planning steps, and reviewing the plan, adjusting it as needed.

You must have specific and reasonable goals and objectives for your life and career. You must also have directions for how you plan to achieve those goals and objectives.

Once you gather meaningful information about yourself, your clients and competition, and the basic facts about the music business, you can turn your attention toward planning your music career. Plans are road maps that help you establish goals, anticipate problems, overcome them, check your progress, and measure your success. Don't just *think* about your plans, goals, and aspirations. Write them down and make them real. Putting pen to paper establishes a permanent record. You create a sort of contract with yourself. And written contracts always work better than simple promises or daydreams.

Planning comes in two varieties: general and specific. While it is good to formulate an overall plan for your music career, the real power of planning comes from the details. The more specific you make your plans, the better your chances of achieving your ultimate goals. I'm always amazed by the sheer lack of planning that typifies most ventures. People jump in wholly unprepared and are then rightfully surprised when everything falls apart. Taking the time to plan carefully and consider alternatives is a step that you can't ignore.

What kind of person are you? Paul Ray and Sherry Anderson, authors of *The Cultural Creatives,* divide our culture into three distinct groups. In a *Chicago Tribune* article, penned by Keir Graff, they cite: "The Traditionals' world view includes nostalgia for simpler times. The Moderns, the dominant group, place high value on material gain, success, and technology. Cultural Creatives are more inclined to find meaning and prioritize their life. They prefer ecology, personal relationships, spirituality, and consistency between speech and deed. They better recognize that most humans want more beyond the basic food and shelter." What group do you fall into? You'll probably find that you are a little of each, but tend to lean toward one category.

Seriously evaluate your primary personality traits, too. Maybe consider asking another person to objectively help with your assessment. Your answers can help with your planning because you'll recognize your strengths and can then overcome your deficiencies by either getting better yourself or seeking help from other people. What is your personality?

- Introvert or extrovert?
- Dreamer or practical?
- Independent or a joiner?
- Leader or follower?
- Talker or listener?
- Logical or emotional?
- Organized or disorganized?
- Gregarious or reserved?

What do you value the most? Is it your relationships? Your sense of place in the world? The activities you pursue and experiences you chalk up? Is learning and gaining knowledge important to you? Or is collecting and owning stuff your thing? These questions help you establish your fundamental or core values. Knowing that you'd prefer being with and helping people over owning a mansion provides real insight into what you want for your life. The right path for your music career must align with your core values.

Where are you going to go? Before you started this book, you probably had a notion of what you'd like to pursue. With all the knowledge you accumulated here and elsewhere, that initial dream may have changed somewhat, disappeared completely, or held steadfast. Whatever your situation, now is the moment for you to make an educated, informed statement of where you want to head. Ask yourself these simple questions: What do you really want? What is the ultimate goal or direction for your life? As you consider your answers, remember all the data you gathered through the earlier exercises. You can't just focus on your dreams and aspirations without giving some thought to the practicalities of life. For this planning to be effective, you must set reasonable goals and objectives that can be achieved through *specific* means. Also, consider how your choices affect your personal and professional life, impact your family, and benefit the parochial and/or global community.

Now complete this sentence: *I will use my __________ (fill-in-the-blank with your music products and services) as the means to achieve my ultimate goal(s) of __________.*

• I will use my songwriting as the means to achieve my ultimate goal of supporting myself and my family with the money earned from the licensing of my music.

• I will use my project studio as the means to achieve my ultimate goal earning money by recording and producing music and sound productions.

How are you going to get there? Once you know what it is that you want, turn your attention to how you plan to achieve your goals. At this point, focus on generalities and basic concepts leaving the specific planning for later. Complete this sentence: *I plan to achieve my ultimate goal(s) through* __________.

• I plan to achieve my ultimate goal through creating salable songs and promoting my music ruthlessly.

• I plan to achieve my ultimate goal through establishing a creative, well-equipped recording environment that musicians and others want to record their work in.

DISCOVER WHAT YOU REALLY WANT TO DO

Knowing who you want to be and what you want to do goes far beyond simply making a choice. You need to uncover what it is through a journey of introspection and self-discovery. Sometimes you need to put on some other's shoes and walk around in them for a little while. Author Marsha Sinetar calls her four steps toward finding the real work you want to do "Positive Structuring." Most people follow these steps intuitively. If you review your past choices you may discover you did these steps without realizing their practical value.

First, play with the idea of your chosen work in your mind. Daydream your way to enlightenment. Cut out articles from magazines about what you'd like to work on. Clip articles about people you'd like to pattern your life after. Daydream what it would be like to do the work you feel is right for you. This playing with ideas helps you bring some order to your dream and helps you better clarify your vision. I feel Carl Jung put this lesson in perspective when he said, "Without this playing with fantasy, no creative work has ever come to birth. The debt we owe to the play of the imagination is incalculable."

Second, experiment with your new vocation. Do a mock-up of what you'd like to do. For example, a soundtrack composer could videotape a TV commercial and write new music for it. A songwriter could try to write a song. A performer could put on a show (in private or with a small gathering of friends and family). This step becomes the physical model for change in your life.

Third, begin to work part-time doing the work you'd like to do. This is a crucial step where you will really discover if what you want to do simply feels right. The way to really learn about any aspect of today's music business is to work in the industry first. Get a job on the inside or start on a small scale yourself and learn that way. Working part-time also doesn't take too much time or a major investment in cash. If it goes awry, you risk very little. At the same time, you may gain some truly helpful insight into what you really want to do.

Fourth, carefully evaluate the first three steps. If you feel that this is the right move for you, take the plunge. Start promoting to land the projects of your dreams. Take action today doing the work you feel you really want to do. If it doesn't work out as you expected, start the process again.

Refine your answers. Now it is time to create a formal structure for you to follow. After you prepared these two general statements, you should begin to add the specifics that make your planning more effective. Right now consider yourself at step A and the ultimate goal of your career as step Z. You know where you are right now and where you wish to end up, but you probably have few ideas on how to get there. Before you worry about step Z, think first about how you'll get from step A to step B on to C and so on. In other words, you have both short-term and long-term needs and goals. The short-term goals are immediate needs such as repairing the PA equipment before starting on a new tour. Long-term goals are those requiring longer time frames or more resources to complete. These long-term goals serve as milestones for your career as you take the journey toward your ultimate goal.

There are two ways you can establish these goals. One, you need to ask the right questions about your goal. What will it take to get you there? For example, you want to publish your own indie CD. You need the songs, the players, recording, mixing, mastering, duplicating, packaging, distribution, and promotion. Two, you can work backwards by first establishing the final goal and then working back to record what must happen just before each step.

Start by making two lists. One, list all your long-term goals. These goals should lead from your current position to the ultimate goal you defined above. Be specific. For example, an indie band might say they need to finish their first CD, launch a Web site and promotional tour, and complete a second CD within another year. Two, list your immediate needs. These short-term goals step you closer to completing the long-term goals in the other list. A project studio owner might need to buy a digital multitrack before looking for the next client, for instance.

Now test each item on both lists by asking these questions: Are you sure this is what you want? If not, you need to rethink this item. Is it realistic and possible? Let the pipe dreams go. Is it enough and will you be satisfied? Do your short-term goals lead logically and systematically to your long-term goals? If not, you need to fix them so they do.

Make the money real. It's crucial that you set specific income objectives that support the level of success and lifestyle you chose. Recognizing what it really means to earn an amount is often a sobering experience. One person told me in a survey on my Web site that, "People often get starry-eyed thinking about the gross receipts side of the ledger, without due consideration to the expenses, time, and effort required to generate those receipts."

Let's say you want to make $500 this month from your music. That means you must make $115.47 each week, $23.09 each day, $2.89 per hour (per eight-hour day) to meet your goal. That sounds easy enough. However, let's say you want to make $50,000 this year. That's $4166.67 each month, $961.54 each week, $192.31 each day, and $24.04 each hour of that day. Every sixty minutes you waste not bringing in new business is $24 that you lost. This exercise helps you focus clearly on your income objectives. Knowing what you need to earn puts you in a better position to make the right choices for all aspects of your music business career.

STUCK IN A RUT?

If you are unsure of the direction to take with your music business career, ask and answer these two questions:

• *What are the five most important things you must do to be successful? Once you write them down, start planning how you will accomplish these items and when.*

• *If you had $10,000 to invest in your music career today, how would you spend it and why? Once you figure this out, start using whatever resources you* ***do have*** *to acquire what you feel you need.*

How much money do you need? When you bring home a steady check, doing your finances can be rather easy. You deposit the check, pay all your bills, and whatever is left is your spending money (or savings if you are especially forward-looking). You don't need to plan much in this situation. However, when you go into business for yourself, you need to take the opposite approach. If you don't know how much money you need to support your current lifestyle, you'll never be able to determine how much money you really need to make. Earning more than you spend is what keeps you *in* business.

What are your personal expenses? Grab up your bills and check stubs and record what you pay for rent or mortgage, utilities, food, entertainment, and so forth. First, total your yearly expenses. Some bills you may only pay intermittently (such as semi-annual insurance premiums), so you want to make sure you don't exclude these expenditures. With the yearly total complete, divide that by twelve to arrive at your typical monthly expenses. If you have no clue where your money goes, record your spending for a few months and then return to this exercise.

Housing
• Rent or mortgage
• Property taxes
• Maintenance
• Insurance
• Utilities (gas, electric, water, sewer, garbage, etc.)
• Telephone

Car
• Loans
• Maintenance
• Gas, tolls, parking
• Insurance

Credit card or other loan debt

Living expenses
• Food (groceries and dining out)

- Entertainment
- Clothing (bought, laundered and dry cleaned)
- Personal care
- Medical costs
- Insurance (health, life, etc.)
- Miscellany

Income taxes
- Federal
- State
- Local
- Self-employment

If you are already in business, do this same exercise with your business expenses. Here you want to both arrive at the typical monthly figures (for setting income goals) and look for excessive waste that you can cut out. Typical expenses include payroll, rent, telephone, utilities, equipment, furniture, supplies, license fees, dues, insurance, taxes, promotional expenses, adviser fees, and more. If you've never been in business for yourself before, you'll have to make some guesses. If you've been in business for a little while, you probably already know the basic costs incurred through your business practices.

TIME/MONEY DIARY

Keep a diary of both your time and money. Record your day and how you spent it. This journal is more insightful when you record your thoughts and feeling along with these highlights. For example, "9:00-11:00 wasted two hours surfing the Net looking for free DirectX plug-ins. Felt guilty when I should have been working."

For the money diary, keep detailed records of both your compulsory and discretionary spending. Compulsory bills include mortgage and rent, utilities, insurance, food, and so forth. Discretionary spending is what you spend on things like leisure, designer coffee, and so forth. Write down every single dollar you get and every purchase you make.

Diligently record both diaries for three months and review them at the period's close. This will bring up some unexpected expenses and provide a truer picture of how you spend your time and money. You will be surprised by these diary results. You'll see how you manage your time, good and bad. You'll see where every penny goes and what you have to show for it. Once you see the numbers, find some ways to cut out frivolous spending and reduce regular expenses. You should look for waste—time wasted and money wasted. You should also, hopefully, see some triumphs, too. Now put a specific plan of action in place that lets you decrease the waste and increase those triumphs. When you give your time and expenses this kind of scrutiny, you will stop wasting your precious resources on junk that doesn't really contribute toward making your life better or happier. You will be frugal, not a miser.

With your expenses documented, turn your attention to income. Again, arrive at a yearly total and divide by twelve to get the average monthly dollars. Compare the results to your expenses: **Income - Expenses = Savings**. Are you earning enough to cover your lifestyle? If not, you'd better both increase your income and reduce your expenses to bring them in line. Hold on to that savings figure; it will be important later on.

This exercise concentrates on your past earnings and spending. You may have had to estimate (even guess) some of figures. From this point on you should start tracking your *actual* income and expenses. This scrutiny is key to measuring and achieving your financial success. There are specific money management strategies later in this book.

If you are just starting out or pursue music activities part-time, you probably earn more through other activities besides music. If your goal is to make music your full-time career, start keeping track of music and non-music income separately. When your musical income exceeds your job money, you can make the leap to full-time. Here's how to chart your progress. Get a large piece of graph paper and three different color pens. Draw one vertical and one horizontal line that intersect in the bottom left corner. Label the vertical axis with dollar amounts starting at $0 and moving in $100 increments, topping out at several hundred above your highest monthly income/expenses. Label the horizontal axis with months starting with the current and moving ahead as many months as fit. Use one color pen to put a large dot in the first month that corresponds to your expenses, say $2000. Next, use a different color pen to place a dot at your non-musical income amount, say $2250. Finally, use the third pen to put a dot in the space that shows your music income, say $150. Record these amounts diligently, connecting the corresponding dots with lines. While your expenses and income may fluctuate, hopefully your music income will rise steadily. Over time, your music income may surpass your other non-musical income. This is when you can safely afford to quit the day job and pursue your music full-time!

This chart serves two functions. One, it forces you to carefully document your income and expenses. You'll always have a clear picture of where your music industry career is financially. And two, the chart is a reminder of where you were, are, and heading toward. You'll see your progress (or any setbacks) and that visual reminder can help you stay on track. By the way, you can do this charting on your computer using a spreadsheet program, however, this physical version, posted above your desk, is often more compelling. The very act of writing down your numbers can make the effort starkly real.

Example Chart

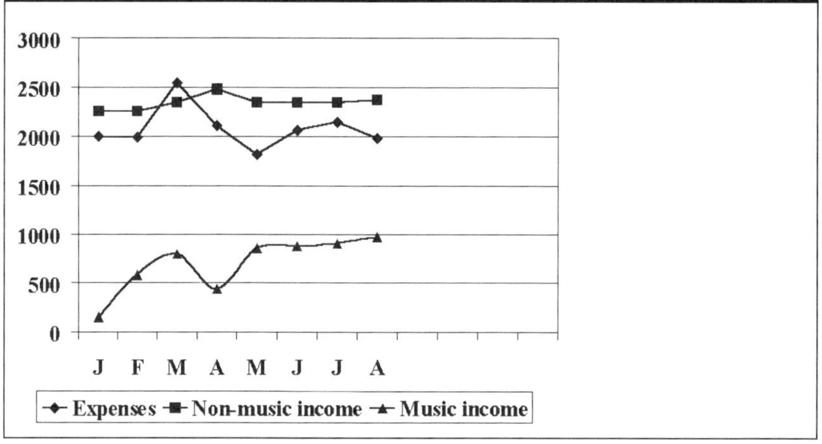

EMERGENCY PLANS

Put in place an alternative plan to cover unexpected circumstances. These contingencies are especially useful should everything go awry. You implement this plan to buffer your career while you work to get back on track. Have an alternative way to make money by either grabbing a job quick or capitalizing on some other skills you possess. Have some emergency cash set aside to pay your bills for a few months (see below). Prepare some promotions to appeal to both new and past clients so that initial sales bring down some much needed change. In other words, get creative by considering the downside to any of your music activities and preparing for the worst in advance.

Also, make sure you have enough money in savings to cover three months of your average monthly personal expenses in a liquid, high-interest money market account. This amount should help you through a lean month or two or help you pay for an unexpected problem. If you do tap the cash, make sure you contribute back to it when your situation improves so that you're ready for other emergencies. This financial cushion gives you the peace of mind you need to concentrate on your career without worrying about the bills. If you plan to keep a part-time or day job while pursuing your music career, you can get by with less in savings. Many up-and-comers use their part-time job to pay their expenses while letting their music income create extra money.

Pro/Files—Dave Anderson

Millgrove, Ontario, Canada
www.daveanderson.ca—nicetry@sympatico.ca

What do you do in the music industry? Singer/songwriter/indie artist

What promotions work the best and why? So far, using radio promotion people.

Where does the money come from? I own a successful business. My studio and business run out of the same office building located on my farm.

What were some of your past projects? I released a Christmas single called "Mrs. Santa Claus" last winter and received some airplay in various pockets in Canada.

What has been your greatest achievement so far? Growing my business to a point where I can now afford to spend two days a week in my studio. That was my plan 5 years ago and six months ago it became reality. I now look forward to releasing 10 CDs over the next 15-20 years from my 400-song catalogue (which grows weekly) and learning the marketing and promotional side of the business which I look upon as an adventure in fun.

How did you do it? By setting 10-, 5-, 2-, and 1-year goals annually and reviewing them weekly. Also by putting achievement of lifestyle above pure monetary achievement. I trusted that the hard work put into my day gig would bring about the freedom to allow me to breathe life into my musical dreams. And by being internally driven to write and sing.

What lessons have you learned along the way? I think that because I started to plan 10 years out about 10 years ago, and have achieved so many of my goals, I have gained confidence in my abilities and it has given me the perspective to look 20 years down the road and know that what I can see is very possible. I have always believed that music is timeless and that a great song will always be a great song. That was my original goal, to become a great songwriter. After having studied the greats and honed my craft, I realized that it is not enough to have great product, you must have great promotion. There are many amazing, talented artists living in complete anonymity in the world waiting to be discovered and it just isn't going to happen. The skills I picked up in taking a one man business enterprise to one with 30 people on the payroll is the fuel for my next business project "To Ruthlessly Self-Promote Dave Anderson." (I bought your other book)

What is your current project or next goal? We have just started to mix the 14 tracks which will be on my first CD entitled "It's Just About Time." I am also currently working on setting up my web site to be ready for the CD release date. I will also be working to better promote "Mrs. Santa Claus" for this Christmas season and many more to come.

DETERMINING WHAT YOU NEED TO ACCOMPLISH YOUR GOALS

The next step is to consider what needs to happen in order for you to complete the items on your lists. What resources do you need in place? These resources typically include skills, equipment, places, money, and people. Some resources you may already have, others you may have to acquire in various amounts and combinations. Go through your lists and further define the specific resources you need to check off each item on the plan.

For example, what resources comprise a CD project? There are the people (creative team), a place (the recording studio), and the money (to pay for the expenses). The writers provide the content when they compose the music and lyrics. The musicians play on the tracks. There may be a producer who helps the creative team realize their vision for the CD. Of course, the recording, mixing, and mastering engineers are responsible for getting the sound in a presentable form. Throughout this whole creative process there are business issues that require attention.

HAVE DAILY GOALS

A to-do list is important to planning, but some items on your list may be vague. "Finish CD" is too broad a notion to have any real meaning. Break these larger tasks down into smaller chunks. Establish quotas, too. For example, when writing books I strive for 1000 words each writing day. When recording music, I separate songs into distinct steps: basic tracks, lead overdubs, re-recordings, extra ear candy, and mixing. This approach to your daily planning keeps you on track and also helps you feel as if you are making some progress, especially when facing major undertakings.

You need to acquire certain resources before putting your plan into action. These resources come in five varieties: content, people, equipment, location, and money. You need some *thing* to sell. You need people both to provide and buy the content, and you need people to help you conduct your music business. You may need some equipment such as musical instruments or a PA system. You need a place to work. You need some money to get started and you may need additional cash in certain circumstances. Finding all these resources can be either an all-at-once or gradual proposition.

Content. What musical products and services are you planning to market? Where will they come from? Who will do the work? What are your specific musical skills? Who would buy these skills? How can you sell yourself to these people? These are basic questions you must ask and answer. Other chapters help you determine the specifics of what you will sell.

People. You will be the central figure in your music business career, but you can't go it alone. You may need help from other people to develop the musical content that you sell. This may take the form of others with whom you collaborate, such as band members. You may also depend on a supplier to send you products that you in turn sell or a designer who does the artwork for your CDs. You may need additional help managing various aspects of your business such as hiring a manager, booking agent, bookkeeper, attorney, and so forth. All these key people may be employees, partners, or independent contractors. You may occasionally hire temporary staff or other vendors who will come in and do a single job and then leave. Also, you definitely need contacts inside the industry and in the media. These people help you build your career through both networking and promotion. Lastly, you need people who are interested in what you do and will buy the music products and services that you offer.

Take time to fully assess your skills and know what you can do and what you can't. What are your skills? In what areas do you need help? Who can help you in these areas and where can you find these people? Don't just concentrate on your strengths. What are your real shortcomings? If you don't feel you can answer that question yourself, ask a trusted friend or significant other for insight. The point of this question is not to undermine your confidence. You want to discover gaps in your skills that you can fill either through education or by hiring internal or external expertise. For example, I'm not a team worker as I prefer to do as much as I can by myself. What have I done to beat this weakness? I hire other people and delegate some tasks to them instead of handling it myself. For example, I used to do some design work myself (brochures, ads, and so forth) and now I let some far more talented people do the work for me.

GETTING HELP

One drawback to being self-employed and running your music career as a business is that there is only so much time available. That means you can only make so much money. With a typical year yielding about 2000 working hours (40 hours/week x 50 weeks), you have a finite time frame within which you can earn income. How can you make more money in the same time allotment?

• *Partner. You can team up with another and go into business together. Partnerships usually work best when each partner's skills complement the other's.*

• *Employees. If one person can generate so much income, then two people can generate twice as much. Indeed, this is the principal reason companies add employees. While the misguided often see payroll expenditures as expenses, the enlightened see these costs as investments in the company's success. Adding employees brings new challenges to your business. However, there are alternatives.*

• *Independent contractors. Instead of hiring employees, you should first consider selecting and retaining other service providers and product suppliers to handle specific tasks. You probably already do this without realizing it. Your accountant is an obvious example; another might be the copy shop that prints your business cards, brochures, and other promotional material. Following this model allows you to complete the tasks you are most adept at handling while leaving certain professional services and some mundane matters to others you retain, regularly or as needed.*

• *Interns. Both high schools and colleges sometimes offer internship programs that let you get either free or low-cost help for business. One colleague told me that students are lining up to get a chance at working in the music industry. He found their help as a great way to get the little time consuming tasks done. The kids learn the reality of the music industry at the same time.*

• *Family. Take advantage of the extra hands provided by your spouse, children, and other relatives and make your career a family business. My wife pitches in occasionally and I've hired nieces and nephews to address and affix postage to promotional campaigns, build name and address databases, and other tasks.*

Equipment. The music industry is obsessed with gear. At least once each month a catalog arrives with hundreds of pages of music and recording gear for sale. As a whole, our industry focuses more on the mechanics of making music rather than actually making music itself. This onslaught seems to say that without the latest, greatest toys, you'll never be successful. This of course is rubbish. People make the music. The gear is just a tool. Make sure *you* treat gear as a means to an end.

Ask and answer these questions: What equipment do you need to enable you to create and deliver your music products and services? What are the minimum requirements? What do you have in your possession right now? What do you still need to get? How and where will you get what you need? Follow this five-step process.

• Objectively evaluate your particular wants and needs. Don't just buy something because you think it's cool. Have real reasons to open your wallet. Will this gear allow you to make money? What will happen (if anything) should you not buy the gear?

• Research possible equipment carefully. Go to manufacturer's Web sites, read reviews (magazines and on-line), and ask other musicians for their opinions. Recently, a colleague suggested using the 90/50 rule. You don't have to buy the best gear to get a good value. Chances are there is something that does 90 percent of what the top-of-the-line equipment does for about 50 percent of its cost. This less expensive choice may be a better choice. Also, consider renting the gear first to see if it will meet your needs. You may be surprised when you discover that the gear isn't worth the price or that you need to take a different approach entirely.

• Put together a basic plan for the equipment. Include when you will buy it, how you will use it, and how much you'll charge clients for it or how you will earn back the cost. I recently needed some gear and was prepared to rent it for about $600. I decided to buy the gear for about double that and figured I'd recoup my costs with a second use. I was right, and the gear is still making me money.

• Determine how you will pay for the gear: raise the cash, finance it, lease or rent it, and so on. I suggest saving and paying cash for most equipment purchases. Whipping out the credit card can be oh-so-tempting, but the additional interest can really squeeze your finances in the long run. That said, look for other creative ways to finance your gear needs. Some companies offer no-interest payment plans such as three payments of $99. Best Buy offers a six months same-as-cash deal (you pay 1/6 of the amount each month with no interest or finance charges) and sometimes offers a twelve months same-as-cash deal. If you know you'll be generating the income you need to pay these installments, this kind of financing can be a terrific scheme.

• Finally, after you complete these steps, make your decision. If yes, go ahead and buy the gear; otherwise, don't do it. The Internet makes shopping for equipment easy. You can visit Web sites of the companies that make what you're considering. You can read reviews by the media and by people who actually use what you need ***(www.epinions.com)***. You can shop around for the best deals and compare prices with just a few mouse clicks ***(www.gearbeat.com)***. And, you can buy used gear at greatly reduced prices, too ***(www.digibid.com)***.

CONFESSIONS OF A FORMER GEAR JUNKIE

I used to have a substantial investment in gear. Not anymore. Technology has allowed me to dump most of my hardware in favor of computer-based counterparts. A couple of good mics and mic preamps, guitar amp simula-

tor, MIDI keyboard, and my guitars are the only sound gear outside of the "box." Software provides the rest of what I need to do my work from my project studio. I've found that stripping away the unnecessary layers and simplifying my approach to composing and recording has made me more creative and productive. Not keeping up with the horrible "gear acquisition syndrome"—as one associate quipped—saves time, money, and sanity. And should I need something that I don't possess, I rent it. My suggestion: find the tools you need to realize your music and learn to use those resources to your greatest advantage. Don't worry about the rest.

Location. Your music business must have a base of operations. Where will yours be? You can work from your home or rent an office, warehouse, or retail space. Use these tests. If you work mostly alone, stay home. If you work mostly at other locations, such as a gigging band playing clubs, locate your main office at home. If you need partners and employees, consider outside space. If you will have clients coming and going all day (and night), consider outside space. If you sell retail to the public, you must get an outside store.

Don't overlook your need for rehearsal space. Depending on your musical act, you may need an additional place to practice. Options to explore include renting space at commercial rehearsal studios that cater to band needs, striking a deal with a club owner to use the stage when the venue is closed, and asking friends and relatives if they have any space available such as a warehouse, secluded garage, or other suitable location. Consider using this space as needed and running your daily business from a home office. You'll save a lot of scratch in the long run.

Working from home is particularly suitable to most musical work, and probably 99 percent of you will choose this route. You can easily manage and promote a band, record label, and publishing company with a computer and telephone on a desk in a spare bedroom, even a corner of your living room. An Internet-based retail music site can work this way, too. An unused room or basement can house a small project studio for music and sound production (record production and/or soundtracks and jingles).

There are two main advantages of working from home: You save money and you save time. You won't need to shell out monthly rent for your workspace. In fact, some of your personal housing expenses may be deductible from your business income, reducing your income taxes substantially (discussed later in this book). You won't have to commute to some distant office either. You can be working as fast as it takes you to walk from your bedroom to your office. My project studio commute is two flights of stairs. The downside to having your office in your home is the constant lure of work. It's far too easy to put in long hours because the work is always right there beckoning you. Another disadvantage, depending on the work you do, is having clients parading about your living space. For some, this is a blessing; for others, it's a curse. Additionally, your local government may have strict zoning laws that can limit the kind of work you do in your home.

Technology enables completely mobile offices, too. Armed with a laptop computer or personal digital assistance, a wireless modem, and a wireless phone, your music business can go and be anywhere. For a touring band, this can be an ideal solution. It can also work for someone who still works a day job. You can use breaks to manage your music business with your mobile office.

SETTING UP YOUR MUSIC OFFICE

While you may need a place to rehearse or to house all your music making and production gear, you also need a simple office to handle your daily career and business demands. This space should be set up for handling correspondence, phone calls, managing activities, bookkeeping, meetings, and so forth.

- *Find the ideal location for your office in your home or at any space you rent. If you work alone, any quiet, functional space will do. If you have regular visitors, you'll want to separate your home office from your personal living space. Have a bathroom nearby in this case, too.*

- *Get a good desk with plenty of room for papers, computer, printer, and more. A separate conference table or seating area is handy when clients or associates arrive.*

- *Invest in a quality chair as you'll be spending a lot of time parked in it.*

- *Install the proper telephone lines or have an extra wireless phone that stays on the desk. Deliver the right amount of electricity to the space as your equipment demands, too.*

- *Proper lighting is conducive to work. Natural light works best; add other task lighting.*

• *Storage is essential, too. Get filing cabinets for short-term needs and boxes for long-term file storage. A fireproof box is great for storing critical files, CD masters, and more (though you may prefer an off-site safety deposit box for these purposes). Bookcases, credenzas, and other furniture serve double-duty—storage and aesthetics.*

• *Combine a good wastebasket with a shredder to take care of junk mail and other office overflow.*

Money. You can't launch even the humblest business without some idea of the money issue. Money is often the primary resource most fledgling businesses fail to have enough of. It costs money to start and stay in business. And it takes time to build a business that generates sufficient cash flow. How much money do you need to get started? How much money will each item on your plan require? How much money do you have already and are willing to earmark for the business? How much do you need to get and how do you plan to get it? There are more suggestions on this issue in a later chapter.

IMPLEMENTING THE PLAN

With goals in place and resources determined, now you can finally start working your plan. Implementing the plan means working through its steps, acquiring the resources you need along the way, and achieving the milestones you set for yourself. Plans are most effective when they include a deadline. Get a 16-month calendar and start plotting out your specific short-term plans. Alternately, use calendar software or a word processing file for long-term plans (I use my Palm programs). Start indicating the dates when the items on your list are due.

It might be helpful to work backwards in some cases. You might pick a deadline for your CD release and then drop in the steps leading up to that date in the weeks and months prior. Start small, too. You do not need to launch full tilt into a big project. A CD is a major undertaking. However, you can start with a single song. Four songs make an EP. And ten songs complete the project. It may take a year, but you'll get there eventually. Remember to always work hard and take steps toward your goals every single day. Don't let sloth or procrastination interfere with your journey. Slip on some comfortable shoes and step into action.

DRAFTING A BUSINESS PLAN

Planning your success is central to achieving your success. While your personal plan can be informal, if you decide to seek funding from a bank or investor, you will need a formal business plan. Here are the typical ingredients to a solid business plan.

• *Introduction or executive summary. You need to briefly discuss your business idea and ask for what you require such as a loan to accomplish certain tasks. Be sure to include your business name, your vision of the business, and an indication of your core beliefs and competencies.*

• *Financial plan. The bank or investor will need to know how you plan to make money, how much you plan to make, and what your expenses will be. This analysis shows that you can pay back the amount you borrow. Show the money you need to cover your start-up costs. If you are bringing your own money to the venture, indicate how much. Banks usually require detailed cash flow projections. You need to make sales and expense projections for the first five years.*

• *Marketing plan. Start with your strategic goals and an action plan to achieve each one. Include descriptions of all your music products and services. Profile your competition and indicate how you differ. Next, show that you understand the people who will buy your music products and services by indicating your research findings. Show how you will organize and operate your business. Don't forget production and distribution methods, too.*

• *Growth plan. Nobody wants to loan money to a business that is going nowhere. Clearly show how you plan to expand your business during the next five years.*

• *Personal information. Include detailed résumés of the key people involved in the business. Don't forget to include your personal assets and liabilities. You may also be asked to include copies of your tax returns. If you have letters of recommendation from credible sources, attach copies.*

• *Other items. You can make your business plan better by including product and/or service samples, pictures, promotional material, and other goodies that serve to reinforce your vision.*

REVIEWING AND REVISING YOUR PLANS

This is the final part of planning that too many people forget. All this planning is wasted if you don't follow your map and adjust it as situations arise. Consult your plan regularly and set aside time to revise it, if necessary, and expand it as you continue to check off your accomplishments. This review keeps you on track with your long-term and ultimate goals. Your plan should be organic and adapt to changing circumstances. You'll get a great feeling when you discover how all this planning helped you progress and achieve.

Also, during this review process, ask yourself this question: What do you need to do to make your music business better (or the best) this year? This is the big picture question, not a trifle. You may not be able to accomplish what you dream, but that's not the point. You have to know where the finish line is before you can start.

PART TWO:
FIND THE MUSIC MONEY

"Never tell people how to do things. Tell them what to do and they will surprise you with the ingenuity."—George Patton

No matter what music products and services you sell, you must first possess a keen understanding of how today's music industry works. Remember that there are only five methods to make money on something musical: create, perform, package, sell, and support.

Don't think too narrowly about your work. Playing music in a band is only one path. What should become clear as you read through the following discussion is this: The real path to making money from your music products and services is to pursue all these methods as a performer, writer/composer, label, publisher, retailer, production studio, and more. There are many other music-related activities you can incorporate in your life; study the many possibilities, choose the ones that fit your interests and personality, and then look for ways to combine, transform, and ultimately create your unique and specific music industry career vision.

CHAPTER 5

Create Something Musical

"Learning music by reading about it is like making love by mail." — Luciano Pavarotti

The song is the driving force of the music industry. Opportunities abound for writing and publishing original songs for yourself and other people to record and play. You either start your own publishing company or link up with a major publisher who promotes your work. Today, some songwriters build their reputation with their own act and CDs. Other recording artists hear this music work and want to cover the songs with their own CDs. Some of your musical income can come from the royalties earned by your songs.

SONG ROYALTIES

Songs have specific mechanical, performance, and print rights. You earn money by licensing (basically renting) the rights to use your songs. Songs earn royalties by collecting on these licenses.

Mechanical rights. When a song is reproduced on CD and/or other media, it earns a royalty that is 8 cents per unit sold. For example, if a song appears on a record that goes on to sell 100,000 copies, the song earns $8000. The money earned from mechanical rights gets split 50-50 between the song's writer(s) and publisher. Once a song is first released, any person can record their own version of it as long as they pay this statutory mechanical license rate. In other words, you can cover any song on your own CD legally if you pay the license fee. Anybody else can cover your songs if they pay you (or your publisher) the license fee as well. This compulsory mechanical license and rate are part of U.S. Copyright law.

The Harry Fox Agency *(www.harryfox.com)* represents over 20,000 publishers and licenses music on their behalf. Harry Fox collects all these mechanical royalties and distributes them accordingly. They take about 5 percent of what you earn as their administrative fee. They also help license songs to film, TV, and commercials. If you wish to license songs (as your own publishing company) or make sure your songs are licensed correctly, contact Harry Fox for membership information. If you "cover" other people's copyrighted material on a recording, you *must* pay the mechanical royalty, too. Grab the "Mechanical License Request Form" from Harry Fox and follow their instructions.

Performance rights. Every time a song gets publicly performed on radio, TV, or in a restaurant or club, the song earns a royalty. These royalties are administered by two major performing rights organizations: ASCAP and BMI. They collect about a billion dollars each year and distribute the money to their members. Together they monitor about 97 percent of all American musical works. (A third organization, SESAC, administers less than 3 percent). Performing rights organizations collect money by issuing both broadcast and non-broadcast licenses. The broadcast licenses include the major television networks, public television, cable networks, the local TV stations, and all the radio stations. Non-broadcast licenses include orchestras, concert venues, restaurants and bars, and other public entertainment locations.

While TV stations must provide accurate logs (called cue sheets) of all music played, radio performances are determined by statistical sampling using a computer system called Broadcast Data Systems. Non-broadcast performances are tracked by issuing blanket licenses to cover the venue's specific music use. All the money collected from these licenses is distributed to the song's writer(s) and publisher based on either the actual performances (TV) or a statistical representation (radio airplay). In short, the more a song gets performed, the more money its writer(s) and publisher earn. Writer(s) and publisher split this money 50-50.

You should join either ASCAP *(www.ascap.com)*, BMI *(www.bmi.com)*, or SESAC *(www.sesac.com)* as a songwriter (you can belong to only one). If you decide to start your own publishing company, you should join the same organization as a publisher as you did as a songwriter.

Synchronization rights. When a song is used in conjunction with images in a commercial, film, or TV show, the song earns a royalty. Fees for synchronization rights are negotiated and based on the song's use. Again, the Harry Fox Agency handles much of this licensing. There are two different synchronization rights: one for the song itself and the other for the actual sound recording as performed by an artist. When the song is "covered" and used in a film or on TV, the negotiated rates are much lower. When an actual recording by an artist gets used, the rates can be much higher. For example, Microsoft reportedly paid one million dollars to use the Rolling Stones' recording of "Start Me Up" when they launched Windows 95. Money earned from synchronization rights are split 50-50 between the writer(s) and publisher. The synchronization rights are above and beyond other royalties earned. In other words, the song still earns performance rights when a TV show also licenses the sync rights.

Print rights. When a song is reproduced as sheet music, the song earns a royalty. The standard royalty for sheet music sales is between 10-15 percent of the retail price. However, magazines that reproduce music and lyrics usually pay a flat rate between $250-$500 per song. Any sheet music royalties are split 50-50 between the song's writer(s) and publisher.

Download rights. The next area for writers to earn money is from electronic rights. Though these royalties are still not completely decided, there are two parts to this issue: music played on Internet radio stations and music downloaded to computers and other players. Music played on Internet radio stations will probably be part of the statistical sample used by ASCAP and BMI to document performance royalties. Downloaded material will probably be similar to the mechanical rights payments made for existing media. Watch this area closely to see how it affects you.

Foreign rights. All of the above rights pertain to the United States. Thankfully, all of these royalties can also be collected through the International uses of a song. The international publisher will usually keep 50 percent of the licensing fees and return 50 percent to you which is then, as usual, split between the writer(s) and domestic publisher.

HOW A SONGWRITER MAKES MONEY

*Songwriters collect their royalties as detailed in the text for the music they write and license. Here's a real-world example. Billy Mann (**www.billymann.com**) released his self-titled debut album in 1995. He earned royalties (artist, mechanical, performance, etc.) for his effort. His songwriting chops also caught the ear of many people and he went on to pen songs for several big names. One of his songs was covered by Celine Dion on an album that went on to sell 30 million copies. Obviously, Mr. Mann saw some huge royalty checks. His share of the mechanical rights alone on Ms. Dion's CD were worth seven figures! Other songs by Mann have done well for other artists even as his own performing career has stagnated somewhat. Why bother recording your own stuff and touring when songwriting pays the freight so handsomely?*

HOW A FILM AND TV SOUNDTRACK COMPOSER MAKES MONEY

Commercial music composers make money by either licensing their music, selling it outright (called a copyright buy-out), or some hybrid of the two. Music can be licensed (or rented) for a specific use. The composer keeps all rights and can license the music repeatedly. The buy-out means the composer gets one fee for the music and realizes no additional royalties. This is typical for national jingles. Hybrids are when a composer may sell the copyright like a buy-out, but retains performance royalties.

Most scores and jingles are produced as a package deal. That means the composer charges one fee and must pay all the recording costs from that fee, keeping what's left as the fee for the music. Composers can join with a publisher or self-publish. Their music can earn mechanical (CD, VHS, and DVD), performance (radio/TV), and sheet music royalties just as any song. Performance royalties for music scores played on network TV can be substantial, approximately $200 a minute. Additional money can be earned through reruns and syndication.

WRITERS AND PUBLISHERS

The royalties earned by a song get split 50-50 between the song's writer(s) and publisher. If a song earns $8000, $4000 would go to the writer and the remaining $4000 would go to the publisher. In the case of a song with multiple writers, the royalties paid to each writer come from the *writer's share only*. If two writers contributed equally to the example song above, each would receive only $2000. The remaining $4000 still goes to the publisher.

You can choose to either sign with a traditional publisher or form your own publishing company. What does a publishing company do? A publisher tries to sell your songs for other artists to record and for use in TV, films, and radio and TV advertising. They also work on your behalf to take care of the administrative duties such as handling contracts, registering copyrights, filing paperwork with ASCAP and BMI, and, of course, collecting royalties. In exchange for their services, you usually agree to give them the copyright to your songs and split all revenue received 50-50. Giving up your copyright is a big deal because the copyright owner has complete control over the song. They can do what they want with it as long as they pay your fair writer's share.

Most publishing deals come with an advance of some kind. Publishers base this up front money on what they expect to earn from a song within a specific amount of time (say a year or two). Publishers typically sign song writers in these ways:

• One song. They select one song that they feel has potential and secure the copyright to the song offering you a 50-50 split of future revenues.

• Exclusive songwriter contract. You sign with the publisher for a specific number of years and they get every song you write during that time. Alternately, you may sign for a specific number of songs that you agree to deliver by a certain deadline date. Instead of taking a lump sum advance, you can sometimes take a writer's draw, which is really just a monthly income based on future royalties. Having this steady income can let you concentrate on your music without having to make money to pay the bills.

• Development deals. When a publisher finds a band that it thinks is poised to do better, they may offer this scenario. Essentially the publisher agrees to help the band make and shop demos in order to land a recording contract. The publisher gambles on the band, but still gets the potential to earn more (by owning the copyright to songs and through the 50-50 revenue split).

• Co-publishing. This deal essentially cuts the other deals in half. You split the copyright 50-50 and give the publisher only 25 percent of the revenue with the writer(s) keeping the other 75 percent.

• Administrative. You can simply hire the publishing company to administer your songs and pay them 10-15 percent of income generated for their services.

While signing with a major publisher, and getting a nice, fat advance can be enticing, never forget that you lose some, if not all, of your copyrights. You also stand the chance of earning far less money in the long term. Consider forming your own publishing company and administering it yourself. With help from the Harry Fox Agency and perhaps hiring a firm to oversee the administrative functions, you will keep control of your work and keep most of the money, too. The same advice you find in these pages about setting up your initial music business applies to your publishing division as well. It should be a separate business, with a different name dedicated only to this part of your music business career.

HOW A PUBLISHER MAKES MONEY

Publishers license the songs written by the writers they retain. These songs earn mechanical, performance, synchronization, and sheet music royalties. The publisher keeps 50 percent of all the revenue these songs generate.

Commercial music. A subset of songwriting is the commercial music industry: soundtracks and jingles. Working from a well-equipped home project studio, you can earn core service income, full or part time, composing scores and jingles. The traditional music users like TV/radio advertisers, TV programs, and motion pictures are not the only companies needing original music, though. Corporations make audio-visual presentations for sales, training, and other communications. Local broadcast and cable TV shows offer countless opportunities for jingles and catchy music scores. Computer games and software use music to support their images, too. These outlets are all prospects for your original music scores and jingles.

There are essentially four places to sell original music: Advertising agencies, radio and TV stations, production companies, and direct to businesses. Ad agencies buy music for the radio and TV commercials their clients need. Radio and TV stations buy music for their on-air promos, including commercial spots they produce for their advertisers. Production companies include film, video, multimedia, game, and software companies that need music to accompany the audio-visual productions they produce. Some businesses buy music for the AV productions they put together in-house, too.

Commercial music is an R&R business: relationships and reputation. The production world is full of hard-to-penetrate cliques that make it difficult for the ingenue music house. At the same time, most people are not willing to take a chance on an unknown which makes building a track record of success vitally important.

• If you want to pursue the commercial music scene and you aren't using my book, *How to Make Money Scoring Soundtracks and Jingles*, run, don't walk, and get your copy of this essential reference right away. It has the crucial details you need to succeed in this lucrative industry.

Arranging. If you have the orchestration chops, you could offer your services creating new arrangements to music. You might be needed to adapt a popular song for a school marching band, for example.

CHAPTER 6

Perform Something Musical

"A great deal of talent is lost to the world for want of a little courage."— Sydney Smith

There are two ways to make money performing music. You can play live and/or you can capture your performance in a recording and sell it.

LIVE PERFORMANCES

Playing music for other people is the whole reason most of us create it in the first place. There are few things in life better than performing in front of an appreciative audience. It can make all the toil that comes before worthwhile and satisfying. Whether you are a solo artist, duo, or band, playing live is a crucial moneymaker for you. How much you make depends on several factors including your act, the music you play, the venues where you perform, and so forth. Don't forget that live performances also let you leverage other sales of your music products and services.

When you plan to play live, make sure you consider venues outside what you might associate with the usual music scene. Besides clubs, festivals and wedding receptions, there are other possible audiences including private parties, corporate gigs, churches, schools, and more. You need to find the person who hires entertainment (corporate gigs usually come through meeting planners) and get them your most persuasive promotional material. Also, work to build your audience in specific areas and leverage that to play other places in the same area.

Band, duo, solo. Putting together your live act and touring/gigging is the place most musicians start. It forms the basis for a core service income. You have essentially two approaches that you can take: be either an original act or a cover band. An original act performs almost entirely its own material. Even the staunchest original band should still do some covers that show their musical heritage and roots. The idea here is to build a fan base and reputation within a specific musical genre and, hopefully, build a wider audience from there. Some club venues and private parties will be closed to original acts as these outlets want to provide broader appeal. However, certain venues celebrate original artists, especially folk, and there are additional opportunities in those areas.

The ubiquitous cover band plays either a wide range of music or focuses on one particular genre, even a single artist (called a tribute band). Good cover bands that can get people on the dance floor (sweaty and ultimately thirsty) are much sought after by certain venues and parties. Even the best cover bands often try to sneak an original number or two in during their sets.

Don't ignore the fact that you can be two acts. You could, for instance, establish an all original act under one name and image and pursue those gigs. You could also put together a cover band with a different name and image and land the often more lucrative private parties, wedding receptions, festivals, colleges, and other gigs. These two separate entities can even comprise the same band members. Individual members should grab other work, too. For example, a talented keyboard player could play a lounge gig during the week, freeing up time for the band on the weekend. Additionally, a guitarist could play sessions (jingle, album, and other projects).

PLAY FOR PAY

Where can your musical act find places to play? Here's a list to spark your imagination. Use these broad categories as stepping stones to specific venues available to you.

- Amusement parks
- Battles of the bands
- Bookstores
- Business parties, receptions, meetings, and other corporate events
- Cafes and restaurants
- Churches, choirs

- Clubs (playing covers and/or originals)
- Coffeehouses
- Cruise ships
- Festivals, fairs, and special events
- Fraternity and Sorority houses
- Fund-raisers
- Hotels
- Lounges
- Military bases
- On-call substitute (when another act/venue needs a player/band)
- Opening act for bigger names
- Prisons
- Private parties
- Retirement homes and nursing facilities
- Reunions (family, schools, alumni)
- Schools (grade, middle, HS, and college giving programs/ presentations, dances)
- Self-sponsored concerts
- Sessions
- Side player (vocalist hires you as an accompanist for her gigs)
- Stores and malls
- Street performances
- Theater
- Talent showcase
- Weddings and wedding receptions

HOW A SIGNED BAND (OR ARTIST) MAKES MONEY

The band earns an artist royalty on the sales of their CDs. If the band members also write their own songs, they either belong to a publishing company or run their own publishing company. In either case, the publisher and writer(s) earn mechanical, performance, synchronization, and sheet music royalties on the songs. The band also earns money from live performances. The band may sell or license merchandise and receive money for the sales of these products, too.

HOW AN INDEPENDENT BAND (OR ARTIST) MAKES MONEY

Live performing is the bread and butter for any unsigned act. CD and swag sales are the icing on the cake. Through back of room sales, the band's Web site, and any distribution deals (wholesale and retail), the band's CD generates cash. Setting up their own publishing company and administering their rights legitimately will put additional money in the hands of the band's song writer(s).

Pro/Files—Michael St. James

SoulThieves, LLC, Denver, CO USA.
www.soulthieves.com—soulthieves@yahoo.com

What do you do in the music industry? In the band: Songwriter, arranger, Vocalist, Guitar. Out of the band: Co-Manager of SoulThieves, Principal of SoulTone Records LLC and SoulTunes Publishing Ltd.

What promotions work the best and why? Something "culture" oriented. For instance, we did a hockey song called "Red Wings Suck!" In Denver, the Detroit Red Wings are absolutely hated and it caught on well. In fact, it's catching on in other states now. Radio play, network play and much free publicity.

Where does the money come from? The band is a business and we have played tirelessly for 2 years straight, 3-4 times a week, with every dime going back to the business of the band, while the players still have day jobs. We also went after small private investment from outside and within the band.

What were some of your past projects? Solo work, Songwriting. Jingle writing, Voice-overs. Ad Copy and development. Band Management. Various band projects including an acoustic duo and some studio work.

What has been your greatest achievement so far? Staying on target for our first major release. Overall, I would say, the greatest achievement is keeping a healthy business growing while maintaining artistry. It can be awfully hard to do both.

How did you do it? By basically forgoing everything else in our lives. Working from 7 AM to 5 PM and then 7 PM to midnight on band stuff. We also have really concentrated on associating ourselves with people in the music community who are interested in professional bands and helping them get to the next level.

Great press and promo people, great producers, studios, good club managers. Relationships are key in this business.

What lessons have you learned along the way? You must have a strong band, with strong relationships. That means: Is everyone willing to do what it takes to make it? Are you willing to play as much as possible? Are you willing to drag ass into work because you had a gig 125 miles away the night before? Is your family (wives, girlfriends) willing to sacrifice time with you and you them? If you don't work hard at the business the business will never work for you. There are thousands of brilliant musicians that you will never hear of because they have no idea about the business of music. And you must work at your craft. If the music isn't good, none of this matters. Work hard, be honest with yourself, and move toward your dreams.

What is your current project or next goal? Release of "Microphone in the SugarBowl" by The SoulThieves. The goal is to gain college airplay followed by a distribution deal. We are also actively seeking licensing and synch right deals for many of our songs. In the near future, plenty of touring in support of the album and hopefully an opening slot on a major tour.

Union royalties. Is it possible to earn a royalty through performing? Yes, if you perform on TV, radio, and other situations and are a member of the American Federation of Television and Radio Artists (AFTRA, ***www.aftra.com***) and/or the American Federation of Musicians (AFM, ***www.afm.com***) unions. When union members get hired to work on projects, they are paid according to prenegotiated wage scales that include an hourly wage, retirement contributions, health benefits, and often royalties for repeated use (depending on the project and the union member's contribution). When a band plays on a television variety show, for example, the union members will be paid accordingly. Also note, the songwriter will also get performance royalties when the song plays on TV, too.

There are many benefits to joining a union such as guaranteed wage scales, standard contracts, retirement benefits, access to lower cost health insurance, networking and gig opportunities, career help, and so much more.

DJs. There are two divisions of labor on the DJ front: The DJs who build reputations spinning at clubs, remixing, and such and the DJs who spin at parties and wedding receptions. The former are seen as part of the music scene while the latter are not. That said, if you have a good record collection (and are willing to play the *Hokey-pokey* every week), you can make money as a party DJ. The club DJs should pursue their careers much like a band or other act would.

RELEASE A CD

Products allow you to package your performance once and resell it over and over. You spend the time to record your CD initially and then collect the money as you continue to sell it to others. You can be working on a new CD while the other one continues to put money in your pocket. This is the real advantage to products. They allow you to constantly make income without zapping up your valuable time. Products can serve multiple purposes, too. For example, I created my *Melomania* music library to sell to people who needed music, but had minuscule budgets. These CDs also serve as my promotional demo for my original music services when prospecting for new business. Lastly, I use the music myself for projects where time and money are short.

When it comes to releasing a CD of your musical performances, you have two choices: sign with a record label or do it yourself. For many, the pinnacle of the music industry is getting signed to a major label. Many think their only path to fame and fortune is through this route. Well, that's all changed and more and more musicians are taking the independent path instead.

Let's face it. The music industry is a business, and the point of business is to make money. Record labels are no different; they are in the business to make money. This is why they prefer known quantities, bands that have already proven themselves to pack houses and move CDs, over unknown, unproven talent. Labels want to find the next superstar who will sell millions of records. They aren't as willing to take chances on a band that may only sell 50,000 copies. As long as a band continues to do well, they'll get support. But as sales drop off, or other acts jump in and steal the band's fire, the band will be summarily dropped. However, that same band selling 50,000 copies on their own would be phenomenally successful.

Record or artists royalties. In addition to live performance income, an act signed to a label earns record or artist royalties. The record label pays an artist royalty of 12-15 percent of the retail price of the CD minus certain costs as spelled out in the contract. These royalties are *only* for CD sales. The writer(s) of the songs still earn mechanical, performance, synchronization, and sheet music royalties as explained earlier.

Record or artist royalty arrangements are preceded by what is called an advance. A record label advance is really a thinly disguised loan—of your *own* money, a down payment of sorts for work that you will deliver in the future. What many people fail to realize is that an advance is really an *advance against royalties.* In other words, this is not some bonus; this is money that you have to earn back before you get any additional royalties. You'll never see another dollar until you earn back the advance and all the costs you agree to in your contract. While it can be wonderful to get a large advance from a record company, it may take a long time before you earn that money back and start to get additional royalties. In some cases, you may *never* get any more money beyond the advance, or the amount may be so small as to be insignificant. Here's the sad truth: 95 percent of all recording artists never earn any record royalties beyond that advance! They make most of their money playing live, selling merchandise, and through song royalties, if they write their own material.

Artist Joe Jackson offered especially poignant advice in his book, *A Cure for Gravity*. Instead of taking a sizable advance on his first record (*Look Sharp!*) he opted for just enough money for he and his band mates to quit their day jobs. They essentially took a monthly draw against future royalties. They had enough money to live on, yet didn't owe the record label a substantial sum. Consequently, the album sales took off quickly and Jackson ended up getting much more royalty money. He claims he's never "owed" a record label since.

RECORDING COST WAKE-UP CALL

Up-and-coming bands perpetually complain about having to pay for studio time. They usually cite some music industry myth: "The Stones used to lock themselves in the studio and emerge a few months later with an album. When we're famous our record label will pick up the tab and we can record for days for free!" Unfortunately, what most amateurs don't realize is that recording costs are often recouped by the record label from artist royalties. The band pays for their own studio time, not the record label. They typically pay about 75% of their music video's costs as well.

WHO TRACKS MUSIC SALES?

You know that little bar code on the back of CDs? It serves another purpose beyond just inventory tracking and an easy way to check out—beep! That Universal Product Code (UPC) is also the way the music industry tracks sales. All the major retailers of music (including the top on-line sites) use this system, called Soundscan. Billboard's music charts are also a result of the data gathered through these bar-coded UPCs.

You want to get a UPC and bar code for your indie CD releases, too. It's the way to start showing up on Soundscan as your sales start racking up. With real numbers on Soundscan, wholesalers, distributors, and even record labels will sit up and take notice of your sales. It is the path to wider distribution for your music.

You obtain your UPC number from the Uniform Code Council ***(www.uc-council.org)***. The number assigned will identify your company, the product, and the products' medium (CD, for instance). You'll need to have bar code art prepared for this number and included when you package your CDs. Securing a UPC can be a little expensive, but there is an alternative. Many duplicators will include a unique UPC on your CDs when you order from them.

Take the independent route. The act that creates and sells CDs can build a solid product core income, too. Though you might feel that people will only buy new, original music from a band, it is still possible for cover acts to sell CDs, too. If your interpretations of other people's songs are particularly interesting, you may generate some sales.

When you release your own CD, you take on all the risk yourself. You must pay for the recording and duplication and you must administer the sales. However, you stand to make much more money, too. Instead of 15 percent of the CD price, you can earn between 40 percent-100 percent of the CD price (minus your costs).

You'll get full price at gig sales and smaller percentages through sales at stores or through distributors. Taking the independent route forces you to work hard for distribution and for promotional and tour support money. You have to do much yourself, but at least you don't owe your record label any money.

Of course, the need to physically reproduce CDs may go the way of the dinosaur. The well-known Payback for Playback program on MP3.com puts cash in artist's pockets when their tunes are downloaded. However, I suspect that most acts still make their money selling physical CDs. Live performers always do better selling CDs to their fans over downloads alone. Even bands with heavy downloads that catch the attention of labels end up putting out regular CDs eventually.

HOW AN INDEPENDENT CD MAKES MONEY

For groups with already established followings, it makes real financial sense to make and sell your own independent recordings. Let's say your act spends $2000 to package 1000 CDs (recording in your personal project studio and farming out duplication). You decide to use 100 copies for promotion leaving you with 900 to sell. Your unit cost is $2.23 per CD (2000 /900 = 2.23). Some CDs you will sell at full price ($15), the rest at various discounts (direct to retailers, through distributors, and so on).

- *No discount is 15.00 - 2.23 = 12.77 x 900 = $11,493*

- *40 percent discount is 9.00 - 2.23 = 6.77 x 900 = $6093*

- *50 percent discount is 7.50 - 2.23 = 5.27 x 900 = $4743*

- *60 percent discount is 6.00 - 2.23 = 3.77 x 900 = $3393*

Your gross profit can be as high as $11,493 or as low as $3393, and will in reality fall somewhere in between. The key is to keep your recording, duplicating, and packaging costs down thereby increasing your profit margin and making it easier to recoup your investment. The more you spend, the more CDs you will have to sell to make any profit at all. Breaking even at 134 full-priced units is more realistic and potentially more profitable.

You can also sell your recording to international record labels. You can negotiate royalty deals or joint ventures. With the royalty deal, they'll handle the manufacturing themselves and pay you based on sales. The joint venture would have you pay the duplication and packaging costs with the foreign label buying finished CDs from you.

There are two dates that apply when promoting your music CD. The add date tells radio stations to start playing your CD. Contact radio station a few weeks before the add date with promotions designed to get them to listen and consider adding the record to their playlist. The street date is when your CD will be available in stores. Promote to stores (Internet and brick and mortar) several weeks before the street date to let them know what is coming or to get them interested in stocking (either wholesale or consignment) your CD release. If you plan to pursue retail sales of any kind for your indie CD, don't forget to include a UPC bar-code on the package and also shrink-wrap it.

If your sales really skyrocket, record labels may come knocking on your door. Instead of signing a standard deal, you can sign a distribution deal that lets you keep control of your music (and most of the money) while the record company gets 15 percent or less for using their clout to get your CD better distribution. Paul Carrack took this route by licensing his "Satisfy My Soul" CD to Compass Records.

If you do decide to release your own CD, do it legitimately by setting up your own label. Pay the artist (even if that's you) an artist royalty. Pay the necessary mechanical royalties to the publisher (even if that's your own publishing company), and distribute any other royalties as usual. Your label will have costs to pay and anything that's left over is the profit for the CD that would go to the label owners—you!

Sample CDs. While library CDs are complete musical performances available for use, sample CDs are snippets of performances and instruments that other composers can use in their work. You could choose to offer instrument sample CDs (for samplers), music loops (for use in Acid software), MIDI files, sound effects, and sound design for specific musical gear (synth patches, for instance). Providing the raw elements of music production is just another way to package your expertise. Follow the same basic advice on creating your own music library should you decide to include this moneymaking venture in your business plans.

Library music. The core product counterpart to commercial music is library music. Not every production company has the budget to buy all original music. They turn to pre-recorded music that is sold specifically to audio-visual content providers. By paying certain license fees, a production company, radio or TV station, or others can use the music non-exclusively in their productions. If you're like me you probably have many songs, sketches, mini-scores, and more sitting on tape or disk somewhere. There is no sense letting all that music gather dust when you could turn those old tracks into cash. By simply recycling existing music tracks, you too can keep money coming in.

YOUR OWN MUSIC LIBRARY CAN MAKE DOLLARS AND SENSE

Many of the same people who buy custom music may also have a need for library music. These primary buyers include film, video, and multimedia production and postproduction houses and radio, cable, and television stations. However, let's face it, some people will never buy an original composition from you even if it makes their program better. They may buy a collection of your work though. All those prospects who never became clients can be another ideal market for your music library. Since you can't rely on prospects and clients asking you for this service, follow this five-step process.

Select appropriate music from your past work. All unused music tracks and original tracks where you retain the rights can put some extra money in your pocket. You need about 15-20 cuts or 60 minutes of music to make a single music library CD. The best approach is to offer a mix of the most popular music styles to give clients a wider choice. That usually translates into more sales. A CD of music in one particular style can be attractive, too. Perhaps you specialize in orchestral music or solo piano and want to sell just that music style. Make sure you understand that you may limit your potential market, though.

Decide the rights issue. You make money with your music library by licensing the same music over and over to different people. Unlike a traditional music CD, buyers of your library are free to use the music in any way non-exclusively. You can set up your music library in one of two systems: per use or buyout. With per use, often called needle-drop, your client pays you only when they use a cut from your library. The per use method shifts the burden of reporting to your clients and can be difficult to administer effectively. The better choice for most of us is to offer the buyout, royalty-free music library CD. The buyout agreement lets clients pay one up front fee and then use the music however they want. Typical buyout CDs sell from $49-$199 each.

If you choose to sell a buyout music library CD, draft a royalty-free license to accompany the finished CD. This simple agreement should clearly grant buyers non-exclusive rights to the music. For example:

"By purchasing this music library, [Your Name Here] *grants you a non-exclusive, single-site, lifetime license to use any of the music on the CD within your own audio-visual productions. This music is protected by the copyright laws of the United States and other countries. You are in no way permitted to reproduce, re-sell, share, or otherwise transfer the music itself to another individual or company. Any attempt to will be subject to criminal prosecution including fines, imprisonment and injunctive relief."*

Create a demo of the tracks. Prepare both a demo CD and online demos of your tracks. For the CD, select a short snippet from each track (lasting about 10-20 seconds) and weave these together into a single montage. Follow the concept of those late night TV promotions and create your own library music commercial. For the on-line demos, encode the clips to low-resolution files, such as Real Audio.

Promote your library. Create a flyer to accompany the demo CD and include both with your standard promotional material. Use the flyer to highlight the music library CD, detail the music tracks, and ask for the order. When you approach a new prospect with your original composition services, you can pitch the music library as an alternative. You can focus on selling just the library, too. It will be especially attractive to companies with smaller budgets. After developing the printed promotion piece, adapt it to a Web page and post it, along with the demo clips, to your Web site. Promoting your library on the Web let's you sell your music to anyone in the world.

Make and sell the library. With your tracks selected and promotional material in place, put together the final library CD. Typical tracks last between two and four minutes long. For the radio and

TV commercial crowd, you can also create 59 and 29 second versions from that master track along with a short 5-second stinger. You can also provide alternative mixes of some music tracks, rhythm section only, for instance. Title each cut and write a description about the music including instrumentation, tempo, musical genre, and accurate track timings. Include this information in the CD booklet and tray card. You might also consider offering your library as .wav and .aiff files. This way, end users can open your music tracks in their computer-based A/V software.

It really doesn't make sense to mass-produce your library. With a color printer and CD burner, you can manufacture your library CDs on demand. Make a half-dozen at a time, and when you sell the fifth one, make another six. When you sell your music library on-line, you need to accept credit card orders.

I followed the steps discussed here to create my own *Melomania* music library. Go to ***www.jeffreypfisher.com/melo.html*** and see first-hand how you, too, can create, promote, and sell your own music library. After you've studied my example, get started yourself right away. Gather up a few tracks, create a demo, put together a promotion, master your final CD, and start making sales.

CHAPTER 7

Package Something Musical

"The price one pays for pursuing any profession or calling is an intimate knowledge of its ugly side."—James Baldwin

The next way to make money in the music industry is to be part of the music production side essentially recording and producing music in a commercial or project recording studio, providing duplication services, or running a record label or publishing house.

AUDIO PRODUCTION

Recording studios and mastering labs earn money by charging for the room, the equipment, and the people who run it as one bundled per hour fee. These fees are paid as incurred with the studio earning no royalties from the work they do. Small project studios may charge only $25 an hour while a large commercial studio may charge several thousand dollars per day.

Personal project studio. Technology has brought high-quality recording to anybody willing to invest in the proper gear. The low cost and high quality of digital recording equipment has made it easy for many to use their personal project studios for music and sound recording. There are a lot of choices in recording equipment today, such as all-in-one boxes like Roland VS series, digital hard-disk recorders and mixers, and virtual studios built around a computer and software (my particular project studio). With a well-equipped project studio, you can handle a variety of personal audio projects along with projects for other individuals and companies. Many people lay down basic tracks, overdub, and track vocals at home and then visit the expensive commercial space for mixing and mastering. Many other low to medium budget audio-visual productions can be recorded, mixed, mastered, duplicated, and delivered using a well-equipped project studio.

A project studio can accommodate both music and sound recordings. You can use your project studio to record demos of your songs to sell to publishers or to help other band members learn their parts. You can also produce your own indie CDs in-house and either sell them yourself or shop it around to record labels. You can help other bands and songwriters produce their demos and finished CDs, too. Many soundtrack and jingle composers have their own production spaces and use it for the majority of their work, too. A composer's project studio can handle much of the composition and demo process and often produce the final music scores, too. Many TV composers work exclusively from their personal project studios.

On the sound recording side, you can handle production duties for companies needing voice-overs, spoken word recordings, radio spots, on-hold messages, and more. You might produce demos for actors looking to land voice over work, too. There is also work handling sound design and mixing for video/DVD, multimedia, computer software and games, and the Internet.

• I've written an exhaustive book on this subject, *Profiting from Your Music and Sound Project Studio*, and I suggest you study its advice. Musicians, composers, producers, engineers, sound designers, voice-over actors, and other audio professionals learn how to set up, manage, promote, and sell personal music and sound project studio activities.

Production royalties. Music producers, mixers, and sound engineers have emerged as celebrities in the music world. Many command high fees and demand royalties on the records they work on. The typical in-demand, name producer can earn as much as a 5 percent royalty on the sales of these albums. Hot mixers and increasingly sound engineers are getting royalty deals along with their day's wages, too.

HOW A PROJECT STUDIO MAKES MONEY

A studio makes money by selling recording time to people and companies who need audio production services. They may make some additional money selling supplies or other products produced in-house or by others. For example, you might sell the CDs produced by the acts that record at your studio. Contrary to what most people do, consider charging for your professional services and not the project studio itself. In other words, people hire you for your expertise and get the studio for free. You'll be able to command much higher overall fees than what you could possibly get for the room alone.

Remote recording. Closely related to the personal project studio is putting together a portable recording rig. You could use your gear to record live acts in concert, school and church groups, and any number of music and sound productions.

Live sound mixer. Alternately, you could make money providing sound for live acts. You could install PA equipment (either permanently or as needed) and mix for bands, other performers, and for specific venues such as theaters, schools, churches, and others.

Technician (keys, guitar, or drum). Larger acts sometimes need a specialized roadie to manage their gear. You'd be responsible for the equipment setup and maintenance, usually getting everything ready before the act comes to the soundcheck. There isn't a major performer out today who doesn't have his own technician. Perhaps that's in your future.

Audio duplication, restoration, and encoding. Once the master tapes are finished, the CDs must be duplicated and packaged. Graphic designers work on the look of the packaging while the duplication house creates the CD copies, prints the booklets and tray cards, and assembles the final package. Some duplication houses even provide warehousing and fulfillment services—storing CDs and shipping them to distributors, stores, and individuals when purchased.

You can master final CDs—the last sweetening step before copies are made. Some people may pay you to restore old recordings, even create CDs from old records. You could start a duplication business and sell graphic design, replication, packaging, and distribution services. Business clients need these services along with performers. Another adjunct to duplication is digital encoding by turning music and sound recordings into MP3s or other formats for distribution online. Duplication service companies are paid for their services and realize no future royalties for their work.

Video/multimedia services. Though not strictly a music venture, video production work is a nice adjunct to audio production services. You could, for instance, handle not only the audio side of a video, you could supply the visual content as well. Related to video services would be to provide multimedia and Internet content design and production services. Join with video producers and graphic designers and offer a turnkey package. You could also produce videos for musical acts, even shoot rehearsals so performers can hone their onstage presence.

Gear rental. Have a lot of music and sound equipment sitting around gathering dust? Consider renting it to others. You could rent PAs, music gear, mics, recording equipment, and more. This service is an ideal complement to either a project or commercial studio venture, retail music store, or live sound engineer/technician.

Pro/Files—John Bartus

Radio Active Productions, Marathon, Florida Keys USA
www.radioactivedigital.com—jebartus@bellsouth.net

What do you do in the music industry? Jingle and creative radio production; marketing on-hold; voiceover talent for radio and TV; copywriting; compose, record, and perform original music (and covers); demo/CD production for local bands, artists, and songwriters.

What promotions work the best and why? Word-of-mouth and referral. Locally, I'm reasonably well-known. Mostly, it's an advantage, because people know the quality of my work.

Where does the money come from? Satisfied clients! It varies, actually: a mix of radio spot production, MOH production, and music recording, with live performance income and a live morning radio show paycheck as well.

What were some of your past projects? Voiceover work for the "Saltwater Flyfishing From A to Z" video series, releasing Velvet Elvis (album of original music) in 1995, plus radio spots and jingles in states from Florida to Indiana, and New York to California.

What has been your greatest achievement so far? Being named a National Winner in the Silver Microphone Awards for a radio spot campaign.

How did you do it? Loads and loads of hard work.

What lessons have you learned along the way? You can sleep when you're dead! The biggest lesson is not to let any one thing overwhelm one's life, and try to maintain some semblance of balance and perspective—not that I always succeed. I still have lessons to complete in the area of time management. My City Council position takes valuable time away from studio pursuits and relegates time management to deadlines and crises.

What is your current project or next goal? Current: MOH programs for a local real estate office and local law firm. Next: attract more lucrative projects through effective marketing, and update my Web site.

RECORD LABEL

Essentially, record labels discover, produce, and distribute musical acts. Labels usually take on most of the financial risk by paying for both an act's CD production, including recording and duplicating costs, and for promoting and selling the finished CDs. Some of these expenses are recouped from the artist's royalties. Of course, they pay artists the aforementioned record royalty on CD sales along with the mechanical license fees to the song publishers. Whatever is left over after all the bills are paid is the record company's profits. Record companies rarely receive the retail price for the CDs they sell (unless they sell from their own Web site). Their entire business model is based upon half or less of that amount.

Labels sell to distributors who in turn sell to retailers. Occasionally a label may sell direct to consumers. Product distribution divides into three main areas: wholesalers, retailers, and independent dealers. Wholesalers buy merchandise at greatly reduced prices and in turn sell the material to retail outlets. A $10 item would be bought by a wholesaler for $4 to $5 and sold to the retailer for $5 to $6. The difference would be the money they make. The retailer sells the item for $10, making their $4 to $5 on every sale. The product producer must pay all royalties, production, and duplication costs from the $4 to $5 they receive from the wholesaler.

Another possible distribution situation would be direct to a dealer of some kind, even to a retailer, bypassing the wholesaler. The retailer would probably want the same 40-50 percent discount they get from the wholesaler, but the product producer cuts out the middle and makes a little bit more money. However, they have to deal with individual retailers as opposed to just one wholesaler who gets it in the stores without additional help. Alternately, you might set up partnerships with other people and companies ranging from 10-15 percent commission to simple 50-50 splits of revenues. For example, bands sometimes split merchandise sales with the clubs they perform at, too.

Realistically, the record label will have a multitude of sales agreements with different companies. They may sell direct from their Web site, through a wholesaler or distributor, to individual chains or stores, and to other outlets such as specialty stores, catalogs, online stores, and so forth. The label may even sell CDs to its artists letting them in turn sell them at gigs (see below).

You can run your own record label that just features your work or you can decide to help other musical acts get heard. You'll need to find suitable acts and work with them to create and sell their CDs. You may set up royalty deals or simply joint venture and split the profits 50-50. You can create and run your own record label with little capital investment. When you only make 1000 copies of your own or another act's indie release, you do not risk a lot of cash. Running lean means you don't have a staff to support (in fact, much of the work can be farmed out to other independents and paid as services are rendered). Keeping those costs down means you can take chances with your career (or the music of other bands if you decide to start a label). You can work on your career, hone your chops, and ultimately find your voice—what you are about musically and professionally.

YOUR FUNDRAISING LABEL

Although this concept is a terrific fund-raiser you can also use the model for straight profit-taking, too. Your label can also provide a unique way for non-profits to raise funds. For example, you could record a school band or chorus, theater group, church choir, or other community organization and release their album. The group agrees to sell these CDs as a fundraiser. You function as a record label by paying the recording and duplication expenses. Typically, you also pay the group a royalty (say 25 percent) on *their sales with your record label keeping the rest. As an example, you make 100 CDs to sell at $15 each.*

- *Royalty to non-profit: $3.75 per CD ($375 total)*
- *Production/duplication costs: $3.25 per unit ($325 total)*
- *Your profit: $8.00 per CD ($800 total)*

Even with paying the organization a large royalty, you make almost 2 times your production expenses. If you are especially noble, you could take the smaller royalty and give the non-profit the larger figure.

The keys to this venture are to keep the production and duplication costs low and make sure the group can sell a minimum number of CDs. To save money, record the group live at their venue (auditorium, church, etc.) and keep the CD packaging simple (print labels and booklets in-house or at Kinko's). Most school bands, church choirs, and others have a built-in market. After buying CDs for themselves, they can easily reach a very modest sales goal of 100 CDs. If more units get sold, everybody earns even more money. To make these sales, produce the CDs and have them ready to sell at the group's next concert (for example, a school holiday concert). The group may ask local retail stores to carry their CD, too. One caveat: if the group records copyrighted material, such as a popular song, your record label will have to pay mechanical royalties (8 cents per song per copy). You'll need to plug those numbers into the cost formula above. If the group sticks to public domain music, this doesn't apply.

PUBLISHING

Packaging songs and getting them recorded by artists and printed as sheet music is the way publishers make their money. As mentioned earlier, publishers keep 50 percent of all the revenue generated by the songs they represent. Their costs can be quite minimal, mainly promotional expenses incurred shopping the songs around and administrative expenses. While you can self-publish your music, you can also publish other writer's works and run your own publishing company.

CHAPTER 8

Sell Something Musical

"Unhappiness is best defined as the difference between our talents and our expectations."—Edward de Bono

You do not need to be a writer or performer to make money wholesaling and/or retailing music-related content. You can start your own music store, brick and mortar or online, and earn money selling other people's music products and services.

RETAIL

You could sell music (CDs) and/or music gear such as instruments, PAs, and recording equipment with your own store. While it probably doesn't make sense to compete with the big names in these industries, you may carve out a niche in a smaller town where there is little or no competition. Of course, you can start an online version of these ideas, but you'll need to offer something unique to set yourself apart from all the competition.

You should work to buy products that you don't make yourself at significant discounts off their retail price. This lets you charge your clients the retail price and earn your money on the difference. Your profit is what's left over after paying any expenses. For example, a band signed to a record label can usually buy their CDs at wholesale prices and sell them at gigs, from the Web, and so forth. They may even get their royalty on these sales, too. The precise terms will be laid out in the record contract.

Setting up purchase agreements is rather easy. Once you determine a product you'd like to sell, draft a letter to the product producer that indicates your terms. Typically, the most discount you can get is between 40-50 percent. I suggest asking for a higher percentage with two incentives. Offer to not return the merchandise (even if it doesn't sell) and pay with your order. Most product producers will accept these terms. Of course, you'd better be very confident that you can sell the products and that you have the cash flow to float your costs in advance of future sales. Here's a brief example:

My company is interested in selling your [name of product] through our Web site. Our terms our 55 percent discount (plus shipping to our location). The products will be non-returnable, bought twelve at a time, and we will pay in advance by check.

MERCHANDISING

Virtually any music business can expand upon its central products by offering related merchandise. The best example of this concept is when a band sells T-shirts at their gigs. They pay to have these manufactured and sell them above their costs, earning money on the sale.

WHOLESALING

Instead of selling direct to the public, your business can function as the intermediary between product producers and retail sellers. This is essentially a sales business, buying up lots of products and selling them to the retailers.

HOW TO MAKE MUSIC MONEY ON THE WEB

Don't limit yourself to selling only your own music online. You can also recommend other music and music-related products and earn a little pocket change on the side.

Sell your own music products. *It doesn't really make sense to pursue this income-producing idea unless you already have something to sell. Bands and artists should have CDs ready to go. I sell my music books and CDs along with my own music library from my site. When you sell your own products on-line, you will need to accept credit card orders (discussed later in the book).*

Sell other music products. *Brainstorm and choose other items that complement or augment your own products. Buy them at a discount and sell them at full price. Additionally, join the free Amazon.com Associates program* ***(www.amazon.com)*** *and just place order links on your Web site and in your e-mail. Amazon pays up to 15 percent on orders that you orig-*

inate through a "click-through" system. The best part? Amazon processes these orders and handles everything! You just get people to click from your site and sit back to collect the checks.

The best way to make such a program work is to closely tie in the products you recommend—and therefore sell—with the content on your site. Don't just plaster your site with ads for products. Write a music review and include a link to buy the CD from the review. Write a tips article about a software product you use and provide a link to buy the software within the article. Text links are usually more effective than graphical links in these cases.

How you make money. You make your money in two ways: One, people see your products, place orders at your site, you ship them, and collect your money. And two, people read your reviews and recommendations, click through to Amazon, and place their orders. Amazon sends you commission checks on the orders placed from your site. I follow this specific advice with my Web site, ***www.jeffreypfisher.com/success.html****, and send you there for a real-world example of these concepts.*

Hardware and software. You can develop musical products, too. You can make instruments, even electronic noise-making gear. I bought a handmade bamboo flute from an artisan in Florida. Code writers can create new music software from databases, utilities, plug-ins, to recording, editing, and mixing software.

CHAPTER 9

Support Something Musical

"Anyone can hold the helm when the sea is calm."—Publilius Syrus

Perhaps you are better suited taking care of business for other people. If you have industry contacts you could work managing the affairs of other bands. You may be a business manager or a booking agent. In either case, your function is to make the music act more successful by landing gigs, even label and/or distributions deals, and more.

MANAGEMENT

Many musical acts need help running their careers. These helpers include agents, managers, booking agents, and publicists. Agents and managers function similarly in that they work to get their clients more business. A soundtrack composer's agent secures new films for her client. A band manager tries to land the elusive record deal. Booking agents work to get live gigs for their clients. While a publicist uses her skills to get airplay and press coverage. Agents, managers, and booking agents typically earn 10-15 percent of the revenue they generate for their clients. Publicists usually work on a monthly retainer that pays them a certain fee for working to promote a company, act, etc.

Booking agent. When you have the local contacts that can help you help other acts get gigs, start charging for your services as a professional booking agent.

Publicist. Is promotion your strength? Consider helping other acts get their promotional material together and using it to get airplay, media reviews, gigs, and more.

CLUBS AND OTHER VENUES

The people who book musical acts and put together shows are also part of the music industry. Though most club owners would consider themselves in the "restaurant business," they are, nevertheless, and integral part of the music scene. Colleges also support bands that come in and play for the student body. Of course, concert promoters work to bring name acts into their cities taking their cut from the box office receipts.

TEACHING

Beginners and pros alike benefit from ongoing training. The different between a mediocre player and a good player is often the level of instruction the latter received. You can teach private lessons or in a school situation. If you have the chops and the patience, you can earn scratch helping other musicians master their instruments. Just a few students each week can add up nicely. Lessons are not strictly for kids as adults and seniors also want to expand their horizons through playing. Closely related to lessons is producing an instructional book, video, or software. It's the natural product to complement your lesson service. Teachers usually charge by the lesson (half- to full-hour).

Music Director. Theater groups, churches, and schools often require the services of a professional music director. Part band leader, part teacher, and part organizer is the list of duties usually facing this job.

Writing. If you have information in your noodle, consider sharing it with others who could benefit from your advice. You can write training material, how-to articles and columns, even books about a wide range of music topics. Though writing can pay you some money, the real benefit to writing is the promotional advantages they provide. Being a published author makes you an instant expert in whatever area you write about. That's a credential you can take to the bank.

Pro/Files—Paul Biondi

Bang On Records, Bellmore, Long Island, NY
www.bangonrecords.com—paul@bangonrecords.com

What do you do in the music industry? Education and production services for songwriters, musicians and media content providers.

What promotions work the best and why? Internet promotion and placement in relevant databases and directories. Also word-of-mouth; networking; information workshops.

Where does the money come from? Most of the money comes from music education services such as songwriting workshops; demo production workshops; music instruction workshops; music therapy; individual music instruction. A smaller percentage comes from production services which includes arranging, producing and/or recording songwriter demos; BMI royalties from college radio and cable television broadcasts; gigs.

What were some of your past projects? We produced singer/songwriter Dominique Gizelle. Dominique's CD *Deep Down* was the first CD release from Bang On Records and we successfully promoted Dominique to college radio and cable television (specifically, Oprah's Oxygen Network). Also, we created and conducted a music education workshop series for SUNY at Stony Brook's Department of Social Work. The workshops helped social workers learn how to use music as an adjunct to counseling.

What has been your greatest achievement so far? Steady and methodical increase in income and exposure from our education and production services.

How did you do it? Four things continue to serve us: 1) We set specific and obtainable goals for Bang On Records. 2) We make sure our products and services exceed the expectations of our clients. 3) We take on projects that match, but never exceed, our expertise. 4) Although we can be perfectionists, which our clients appreciate, we're also very upbeat and easy to work with (we hear this a lot).

What lessons have you learned along the way? Do self-promotion every day even in the smallest, most informal ways. Promotion is often more important than any other activity. Three years ago I left behind a full-time job as a Music Therapist, and 20 additional part-time hours a week teaching guitar and gigging, to now doing music full-time. My business continues to thrive because I work my craft and expand my skills constantly. I also promote myself somehow, somewhere almost everyday. I think the people who don't constantly promote, haven't yet seen the rewards come back to them over and over again. When that begins to happen for them, as it did for me, self-promotion becomes the good friend you always want to spend time with each day. I plan to expand my successes in teaching, workshop presentations and producing songwriter demos, to producing music for film and television.

What is your current project or next goal? To reach our next goal for production revenue, we have the upcoming CD release of our second artist, Hurricane Jar. We plan to place this band's upbeat instrumental acoustic music on cable and network television and in quality independent films. Before we started production on the Hurricane Jar CD we also explored local merchant interest and found many who were interested in playing and selling the acoustic instrumental CD in their stores and restaurants. To reach our next goal for education services revenue, we plan on writing and self-publishing several lesson booklets with accompanying audio CDs. This will enable us to increase the number of products each client can purchase.

PART THREE:
MASTER RUTHLESS SELF-PROMOTION

"The shortest and best way to make your fortune is to let people see clearly that it is in their interests to promote yours."—Jean de La Bruyère

What did you do to make money today? Ask yourself this question fifteen minutes before you stop working. Your first inclination may be to check off the items you finished from your to-do list. Before you pick up the pen, make sure these accomplishments really contributed to your income. Probably most of them were busy work that did little, if anything, to bring in more business. While these tasks are important, they never replace the one thing you should do everyday:

Promote.

Every working day you should do something to promote your music business career. Pick up the phone and call a past client or new prospect. Send a promotional kit to a prospect via mail or e-mail. Answer telephone calls and e-mail from prospects and encourage them to purchase what you sell. Write a news release and deliver it to the media. Connect with a member of your network. Or do whatever works for you. Do something productive that generates either immediate income or potential, future, income. This approach of day-in, day-out promotion will remind you what it takes to succeed: constant diligence in delivering your message, and also your music products and services, to the people who need and want them. Commit now to proactive promotion because it will increase your sales and move you closer to your ultimate goals.

CHAPTER 10

Seven Steps to Promotion Success

"Success is going from failure to failure without a loss of enthusiasm." —
Anonymous

You can't decide to create some music product or offer some service without first deciding how you are going to promote and sell. Finding people who want what you sell and convincing them to buy it from you is the essence of promotion—and the reason your are in business in the first place. That's simple advice, but virtually useless without specific how-to-do-it detail. You can break this concept down into seven steps and learn to successfully promote your music business.

- What do you sell?
- What gig do you want to land?
- What does it take to get the sale?
- Are there any obstacles or drawbacks?
- Who is responsible for buying?
- How do you make contact?
- What will your pitch or offer be?

Use your answers to these questions to land any and all the business you want. Repeat this process as you create new products and services and/or identify new markets for them. People unconsciously follow these steps when they set out. Instead, consider making this your formal approach to promoting what you sell.

First, summarize these questions for each and every music product and service that you offer. This exercise helps you define the broader aspects of your promotional strategy. Second, add specific details as you answer the questions. Here you narrow down buyers to smaller groups or market segments and even into single prospects. Last, follow the steps to get what you want.

For example, your new band decides to play club dates. Here's the summary:

• What do you sell? Our band covers popular songs.
• What gig do you want to land? Club gigs.
• What does it take to get the sale? Our band must appeal to the club's interests. To discover these needs, we must visit clubs to check out other acts and the general atmosphere and talk to other bands that play the clubs.
• Are there any obstacles or drawbacks? We are new with no track record.
• Who is responsible for buying? The person who books bands at the club.
• How do you make contact? Get the phone numbers and addresses of key people.
• What will your pitch or offer be? Put together a promotional package. Create offers that encourage a response. Make initial contact, deliver demo, follow-up.

Now, narrow down this down to a single gig (or market) that you want to promote to and answer the same questions in specific detail.

• What do you sell? Our cover band sells entertainment and a good time through playing mostly modern favorites sprinkled with a few popular oldies.
• What gig do you want to land? Bob's Big Bar downtown
• What does it take to get the sale? Researching the club shows that having an entertaining band with emphasis on covers, especially high-energy dance numbers was what worked. Some originals O.K.
• Are there any obstacles or drawbacks? Won't hire an unknown act. Doesn't pay very well.
• Who is responsible for buying? Bob, the club owner, books the bands.
• How do you make contact? Call the club number to reach him, (555) 555-5555.
• What will your pitch or offer be? Introduce the band by phone and setup time to drop off demo and promotional material. Make an irresistible offer: Our band will work for a reduced rate on an off night (Tuesday night) as a trial. Follow up.

This fictional band should then research all the possible venues available to them and answer the same questions about each. If they decide to release an independent CD, they should start again with the summary version and move into detail with all the possible outlets for their CD sales.

Pro/Files—Amanda Easton

Solo: Amanda Easton, Cover band: The Martinis, Sydney, NSW, Australia
www.amandaeaston.com—amanda@amandaeaston.com

What do you do in the music industry? Self-managed recording artist (singer/songwriter) and corporate band owner/performer

What promotions work the best and why? To get corporate work, I put together high-quality bios, photos, demos and a corporate-style business letter and I approach large corporations in my city. It only takes one successful gig to lead to many more, thanks to recommendations. I think it is important to present the kind of business-like image that corporations are used to dealing with. They are often wary of bands and musicians because we are perceived as playing by different rules, but I've found if you gain their trust in the first instance by always promptly returning calls etc., they are more willing to let you get on with what your being hired for without interference. I think this level of professionalism is just as important in an original recording career.

Where does the money come from? 45% corporate functions; 30% freelance singing with various cover bands or as backing vocalist to established artists; 20% singing on harbor cruises; 5% acting work. Recording career just begun so not yet in profit mode!

What were some of your past projects? Current release of my self-penned debut single, "Celebrity," with national distribution; Performed with Powderfinger at Australian Record Industry Awards (ARIA). Backing vocalist for Wendy Matthews's tour, one of Australia's most successful vocalists, including national TV appearances. Corporate work for American Express, Noumea Casino (yes, three lovely well-paid days in Noumea), Taiwanese Consulate, Hewlett-Packard, KFC, etc.

What has been your greatest achievement so far? Getting a single out into the marketplace and on the airwaves.

How did you do it? With a hell of a lot of trial and error and extreme persistence.

What lessons have you learned along the way? Never assume other people will do their job properly! Always dot every *i* and cross every *t*. The most expensive service or service provider isn't necessarily the best one. The relationship you strike up with the people you hire and their level of enthusiasm is very important. Have a great team of trustworthy people around you, but still double check everything yourself! Never give up.

What is your current project or next goal? About to release the second single using the lessons I have learned from the first time around. Have more stringent project management in place and strict budgeting. Remember that although I do what I do for love, not money, having money will ensure I can continue do what I love!

WORKING THROUGH THESE PROMOTIONAL STEPS

Let's examine the seven questions in greater detail and how you can apply them to your situation. Again, you ask and answer these questions for *every* music product and service that you sell.

What do you sell? The previous chapters addressed this issue in depth. However, that discussion centered on features (start a band, run a record label, build a project studio, etc.). When it comes to promotion, features don't sell. You must think about all the benefits a buyer gets from what you sell. Benefits come in two varieties: immediate benefits and fundamental benefits. Immediate benefits are simple advantages people get when they buy your music products and services. For example, they buy your CD because the music entertains them. Fundamental benefits move beyond simple instant gratification. They are the *real* benefits people buy. And people want to have:

- Better relationships with family and friends

• More time (and/or the freedom) to devote to hobbies and leisure pursuits
• Their unique dreams and visions fulfilled
• Happiness and contentment
• Good health and a longer life
• More money or greater wealth
• Prestige, status, and fame
• More and better sex
• Acceptance of who they are by other people

You need to promote both the immediate benefits of what you offer and the fundamental ones. You may be selling an entertaining CD, but you are really selling happiness and contentment. You may be selling a book about making money in the music industry, but what you're really selling is a way to fulfill a unique dream and secure the status and recognition he or she so desperately desires.

Now, complete this sentence for every music product and service that you offer: _________ is what people (be specific) get when they buy my/our __________.

• Happiness and contentment is what dance music fans get when they buy my CD
• More money is what club owners get when they hire our band.

What gig do you want to land? With this question you uncover who will buy from you. Identify this market in two steps. First, determine the broadest sense of possible buyers. For example, you might answer "dance music fans" or "films needing soundtracks." Those categories get you started, but you need to refine them a bit: "dance music fans in the Chicago area" or "independent films needing soundtrack music."

Second, find the specific places or markets for your music. Where do Chicago area dance music fans congregate? Who makes indie films? Start searching to uncover possible places to promote what you sell. If you are already part of the Chicago dance music scene or indie film world, you may already know the answers. Otherwise, you'll have to start hunting. You want to look for venues, associations or clubs, retail stores, newsletters, magazines, Web sites, e-zines, and so forth. In short, where can you reach this market? Get specific.

Now, complete this sentence for every music product and service that you offer: _________ is a possible market for my/our __________.

• Chi-town Scene magazine is a possible market for our band's live act and CD publicity.

What does it take to get the sale? Once you find the people who are candidates for your music products and services, take the time to find out what appeals to them the most. What do they want from a music product or service like yours and how can you show them you meet their needs? You need to clearly identify the hot buttons that motivate your prospects to become clients and that further motivate existing clients to buy something from you again. These hot buttons, or selling appeals, must be in the promotional and sales materials you send out. It is likely that you will have multiple markets and must take a different, appropriate approach to each. Here you'll need to uncover the *specific benefits* that appeal to a given market. Keep in mind the pain/gain idea from earlier in this book: You want to help prospects get something more or get rid of something they don't want anymore.

Now, complete this sentence for every music product and service that you offer: To close sales, I/we need to clearly show people (be specific) how my/our ________________ helps them to get/get rid of ____________________.

• To close sales, I need to clearly show independent filmmakers how my original music composition services help to support their imagery and get people to remember their film's message.

CHART PARTS

Three music trades compile music "charts." The College Music Journal ***(www.cmj.com)*** *is used by college radio stations.* Gavin ***(www.gavin.com)*** *is used by radio programmers.* Billboard ***(www.billboard.com)*** *is the big time/big deal of the music industry. Billboard's charts are based on both Broadcast Data Services radio airplay tracking and SoundScan retail sales figures. Gavin's charts are compiled from a sampling of radio stations in the United States. The CMJ chart is based on a sampling of college radio stations. You can use these charts to research genres you plan to address. Find out who is on top and why. Use this information when planning your promotions.*

Are there any obstacles or drawbacks? Consider the downside to bringing your music products and services to the people you identified in the previous steps. Is the market crowded with competitors? Do you live in a rural area far away from the independent film producers? Look for ways to overcome these possible setbacks, too.

Now, complete this sentence for every music product and service that you offer: I/we could have trouble making sales because ______________. To overcome this I/we must ______________.

• We could have trouble making sales because there is only one club that hires original live acts. To overcome this we must look beyond our local scene and approach other venues out of town.

Who is responsible for buying? Get into research mode and find the *specific contact information* of the people you identified as prospects for hiring you or buying from you. How do you find this contact information? Start with the media. Several companies publish directories to the music industry. While some of these directories are available at good libraries and on-line, others you have to buy. These directories provide contact information for producers, publishers, record labels, distributors, music media (mags and newspapers), recording studios, production companies, and more. Spend some time flipping through the pages and you'll get the basic contact information you need.

• The *Recording Industry Sourcebook* ***(www.artistpro.com)*** online and in print is the definitive guide. Start here first.
• Music Registry ***(www.musicregistry.com)*** has directories to various parts of the music industry including the *A&R Registry*, the *Film/TV Music Guide*, and the *Music Publisher Registry*.
• *Musician's Atlas* ***(www.musiciansatlas.com)*** directory shows up on newsstands regularly.
• *The International Buyer's Guide* from Billboard ***(www.billboard.com)*** details labels, publishers, wholesalers, distributors, suppliers, associations and more. They also publish *The International Talent and Touring Directory*.
• *The Independent Musician's Contact Bible* is available from Indie Music ***(www.indie-music.com)***
• Mix Master Directory ***(www.mixonline.com)*** is another newsstand regular.
• I-Music Production Guide ***(www.1212.com)***

• Film Music Magazine *(www.filmmusicmag.com)* provides directories, books, annual rate survey, and so much more.
• Chicago Screen Production Bible *(www.screenmag.com)* Chicago production community guide.
• LA411 and NY411 *(www.cahners.com)* also publishes the Agents and Managers 411 and the 411 Digital (guide to game, software, and multimedia developers).
• Association for Independent Music *(www.afim.org)* publishes another resource directory specifically suited to independents
• You can also try directories put out by local Chambers of Commerce
• The Yellow Pages
• Any music magazines or newspapers published in your area, and
• Search online by going to the popular search engine Web sites.

For example, if a band needs to dig up possible clubs to play, consulting the entertainment directory in their local paper will yield calendar listings for upcoming performances. Visit the clubs and check out the other bands that play there. Get the contact information when you visit. Now you have the information you need to start promoting your live act in this example. What you end up doing is compiling a database of contacts that become the targets of your promotional efforts. For example, in your selling area (local, regional) an act's contact list might include :

• People who book musical acts including clubs, venues, festivals, colleges, etc.
• Stores that sell CDs.
• Media sources with a music focus including newspapers, magazines, Web sites, e-zines, etc.
• Any music organizations that support acts.
• Other acts, even individual musicians, to share information and otherwise cooperate
• Clients and prospects (your fans!)

Now, complete this sentence for every music product and service that you offer: To sell __________ to __________ I/we need to contact __________ .

• To sell my music composition services to Indie-Films-R-Us, Inc. I need to contact Joe Film, the production coordinator at (555) 555-5555.

SELLING THE MEDIA

Though at first glance you may think a buyer is only someone who actually purchases what you sell. Don't look at it this way. When a media source reviews your indie CD, they become a "buyer" and should be treated the same way you'd treat any other client. Stay in touch regularly and get them to "buy" from you again.

How do you make contact? The many promotional strategies that you can use preclude them from being discussed here. After you work through other parts of this process, come back and answer the final question.

Now, complete this sentence for every music product and service that you offer: To sell ________ to _________ , I/we need to use the following promotional ideas: _________ .

• To sell my music composition services to Indie-Films-R-Us, Inc., I need to use the following promotional ideas: send demo reel, follow up by phone regularly, put on newsletter list, send newsletter, advertising, and publicity reprints regularly.

• To sell our original band to Joe's Club, we need to use the following promotional ideas: send a promo kit with CD demo, include recommendation from other club owners who hired us, send postcards announcing upcoming gigs (and available dates), call regularly. When we get hired, book the next date after the first set is over.

What will our pitch be? To answer this last question, you need to devise an offer, something that you feel will motivate an immediate, positive response from the prospect. Your research should help you decide. Offers take many forms. To make sure people buy you must:

• Include both logical and emotional appeals (Logical: save $1000 when you buy now. Emotional: use the money you save to take that vacation you always dreamed about.).

• Push the gain of possessing what you sell (MusicGizmo makes your CDs louder. Radio stations sit up and take notice of your music!).

• Remove the pain the prospect already has (Stop sending out wimpy mixes that DJs just toss out. Get the MusicGizmo and make your music sizzle!).

• Appeal to procrastinators (Hurry! This offer expires today!!).

• Give discounts for the bargain hunters (Order This and That together and save $5 or *free* shipping.).

• Offer bonuses or premiums for those looking for something for nothing (Buy this, get that free).

• Place time limits on what you offer (Act now or you will lose out).

•Reverse the risks by including a money back guarantee.

Now, complete this sentence for every music product and service that you offer: The best offer to sell my/our _________ is to __________ .

• The best offer to sell our new band is to agree to work the first gig for only 40 percent of the door. When the club owner sees how we can fill the room, we can negotiate a better fee for future gigs.

THE COST OF PROMOTION

When it comes to promotion you can spend your time or your money. Most low-cost promotions, such as networking or publicity, force you to spend more time to get them to work effectively. Most high-priced promotions, ads for instance, require little investment of time.

As you plan your promotions, indicate how much money you plan to spend. You can choose either a set dollar amount or a percentage of your overall sales income. In either case, set a yearly figure and stick to it. The dollar amount is good at the start, and if you have relatively limited funds. However, quickly move to the percentage idea, say 5-10 percent of sales. This will vary as your income rises. As you get more successful, you'll make more money. Subsequently, you'll have more money available for additional promotion, which will increase your success exponentially.

CHAPTER 11

Developing Promotions

"'Be yourself' is about the worst advice you can give to some people."—
Tom Masson

Before promoting your work actively, you need to take care of two additional items: choosing your image and putting together your promotional material.

CRAFTING THE APPROPRIATE IMAGE(S)

The best way to illustrate the image concept is to think of a brand name. When somebody mentions Coke, you understand all about it. When somebody mentions the Beatles, a flood of information comes with those two words. You know what Coca-Cola and the Beatles are all about. You must find an image that tells the world what you are about, too.

You want your image to appeal to prospects and create instant rapport, so you must mirror their wants and lifestyle. Your personality must reflect *their* personality. Your message must be what they want to hear and your physical representation of your image must be what they want to see. Consider all the music genres. Each genre appeals to a select group with very specific attributes. The essence of rap music is wildly different from country. Now consider the top musical acts in these music genres. Aren't they the quintessential essence of what their music is all about? Country acts don't look or act like rap stars and vice versa.

Examine your core values. What are you all about? What are you trying to say and where are you trying to go with your music career? Second, examine the benefits your music products and services bring. What kind of music do you do? What do people get when they buy from you? Third, what are the specific lifestyle attributes of the people who would buy your products and services? Your answers to these three questions can help you formulate your message and image.

Choose your image. You can be an expert, sympathetic friend, rebel, victim, clown or fool, everyman or everywoman, sex symbol, bad boy/girl, whatever you decide is right for selling you and your stuff. Walk the walk; talk the talk. Make sure that everything you do supports, reinforces, and augments the image you choose. Your personality must fit this image and manifest itself in it. Dress the part, too. Part of your image includes the clothing you wear.

Crafting the package. After you establish your image and message, think about how you will package it, too. People invariably recall the package before they remember the product/service. Think of Coke again. What color jumps into your mind? Is it the brown color of the popular liquid? Or is it the bright red of its package? I'm sure your answer was red. It is this impression, and how it stays in the minds of people, that is so important. Carefully and consistently packaging your image is crucial to success in today's music industry.

Common packaging elements include how you dress, how you act, and how you express yourself. Your stage presence and at-work attitude are image attributes. The kind of music you play, the subject matter of your songs, your instrumentation—all these must complement your image, too. Specific design elements such as photography, color, name (band and company name, CD titles, etc.), logo, typestyle, and so forth also reinforce your image. Take the time to meticulously develop these elements and then use them consistently to represent you, your message, and your music products and services.

Multiple personalities. If your music business has separate entities, pursuits, and personalities, you should consider keeping them separate and promoting and managing them accordingly. For example, you may face a difficult challenge trying to promote your party cover band and jingle business in the same way, to the same people. It makes more sense to keep them discrete with different company names, letterhead, promotional material, and so forth. This may seem contrary to advice about letting people know about all that you do (to get more paying business), but in some circumstances you may be forced to keep the different aspects of your music business distinct.

ACTING YOUR ROLE

If you are a performer, you need to master your stage presence. You must learn to act on stage and in videos. The best musicians are solid performers with great stage and screen presence. They have charisma that connects with their audience. What sold George Martin on the Beatles? It wasn't their music—it was the Beatles themselves, their personalities, humor, and charm.

Changing your image. One band asked me about how to change their name and image. They had built quite a following, but felt a name change might help them shake their bar band image and become more professional. The band will spend a lot of time and energy telling people they are the same band, different name. If they have clear channels of contact (mailing list, web site, etc.) then they can easily inform their most devoted fans, but it will take time. I suggested two courses. One: keep the old name and make the image change by going to different clubs, changing the stage presence, whatever they want to do to appear more professional. Two: Change the name and image and land some new gigs. Don't tell anyone about the change, just do it and see what happens. Make sure they keep the old name/image and continue to play as before. Now compare the two incarnations of the band to see what works. Of course, I find nothing wrong with having two bands. One that plays the bar scene and another that lands weddings and corporate gigs. They can have two different names and two different images and still be comprised of the same band members.

CAN COLOR MAKE A SALE?

Choosing a color or color scheme to represent your music products and services can have great impact on your promotions. While color alone will rarely help you make sales, sticking to a color can help make your music business more memorable. Color works psychologically as most people have certain emotions and memories tied to colors. In a way, color works on similar terms as music to evoke a mood or feeling, inspire or motivate, and more. What do you think and feel when you see the color red? How about blue? What color(s) should you choose? Pick colors that fit your image and appeal to your segment of the music industry. You can follow these typical guidelines. Blue is masculine and pink is feminine. Green evokes natural things. And while red is often associated with low prices, burgundy is not. Dark blue is calm and easygoing. Blue to green is steadfast and dependable. Violet is elegant. Orange to red bursts with excitement and even sexuality. Yellow is stimulating. And black, gray, and brown are often seen as negatives. Let the color you choose represent what you are about and what benefits you bring to those who buy your music products and services.

DEVELOP PROMOTIONAL MATERIAL

You need specific promotional material that convinces prospects and clients of what you can do for them, when, where, how, and for what fee. Every promotional piece should:

• Talk directly to a person. Get personal and use a warm, sympathetic tone. Write/talk as a friend would write/talk to another friend. Use their name or "you" throughout the promotion.

• Push benefits. Buyers are skeptical. Carefully and completely answer their questions and objections. Make sure what you write persuades people to buy because you clearly show that what you sell is what they really want anyway.

• Diminish the fear factor. Buyers are justifiably scared of making a bad choice or getting ripped off. You need to carefully show them there are no risks when they buy from you. Offer a money back guarantee. Let them try before they buy, such as a free MP3 sample before buying the whole CD. Also, provide secure credit card processing for your online orders.

• Create action and urgency. Write in the active voice and use action verbs. Push, prod, motivate, captivate, and ultimately, sell what you offer.

• Include a compelling offer. Offers can be hard offers such as "buy this now" or they can be soft offers such as "call for more information" or "visit our Web site". Mix *both* hard and soft offers in every promotion you do.

• Have a deadline with consequences. The best offers have deadlines such as "Hurry! This offer expires May 1!!" The deadline motivates people to take action fast. Remind them of what happens when they don't act right away, too. "Order by Midnight tonight and save $10. After that you pay full price for our CD."

• Ask for immediate action. "To get all these benefits, click the link below to order your copy now!" As the salespeople of the world often say: ask for the order.

PROMOTIONAL PARTS

Every promotion (letter, flyer, Web page, postcard, and phone call) should follow this basic format.

- *Headline. Don't waste time. Put your strongest benefit right at the top of the page or in the subject line of your e-mail. If you're telephoning, your headline is your opening line.*

- *State the problem. After the headline, indicate that you understand the problems your clients or prospects face. These problems can be both the gain they want to acquire and/or the pain they want to do away with.*

- *Sell the solution. Indicate the solution to the problems you've outlined: the music products and services you sell!*

- *Pile on the benefits. Explain all the benefits of the solution you provide.*

- *At this point, you can discuss some of your product's or service's features.*

- *If necessary, take a moment to introduce the people behind what you are selling.*

- *Reviews from the media and testimonials from other satisfied clients can reassure people that you deliver what you promise. Include them liberally.*

- *Make your best offer and ask for the sale.*

- *Don't forget to include any necessary follow-up procedures, such as how to place an order.*

- *Use a post script or P. S. that restates your most compelling benefit and offers one more sales push.*

Pro/Files—Bill Watson

Play It Again Demos, Pittsburgh, PA, USA
http://www.billwatson.net

What do you do in the music industry? I produce music both for myself and for clients; write music, articles and books; and play live gigs.

What promotions work the best and why? Premium offers are my first choice because once you discount your price, be it for your band, a book, whatever, it trains the customer to expect bargains. Often that 15 percent discount is the only true profit (above the value of your labor, overhead, materials, etc.) you would have made. Give a discount and you're essentially trapping yourself into working for no profit. Instead, offer the club owner an extra half-hour of playing rather than a lower price to get your foot in the door, for example.

Where does the money come from? Music production; then guitar/bass playing (on recordings and from live playing situations); writing music, books, and articles.

What were some of your past projects? Putting together my own band springs to mind. We ended up being quite successful with bookings far into the future but it was a success because of what I'd learned in previous failed attempts.

What has been your greatest achievement so far? Writing "Guitar Shop: A Beginner's Guide to Lead and Rhythm Guitar." When I started I had no idea how to incorporate text and graphics in a manuscript so it was a challenge.

How did you do it? Learned as much as possible from books and Internet sources. Asked people who had more knowledge for help.

What lessons have you learned along the way? As Deming says, "Identify your true customer then don't just satisfy the customer, delight the customer." It's a good motto to run a business by. If you follow it and your pricing is right, it's hard to fail.

What is your current project or next goal? Streamlining some of the more mundane details of my business life by delegating them to allow more time for the bigger, more exciting activities.

CREATE BASIC PROMO MATERIAL

No matter what music products and services you plan to promote and sell, you need to have some basic promotional material to use. Though many of these promotional pieces can and should stand on their own, sometimes you'll put all the pieces together into one complete promotional kit. This is especially useful when approaching the media and some bigger prospects who know little, if anything, about you. Package your promotional kit in a folder imprinted with your band or company name. This way you can include or exclude pieces to custom-tailor what you send to your prospects. Additionally, this promotional material should be adapted to for delivery online (via e-mail and on your Web site).

Business cards. The lowly business card is a handy promotional item. While you obviously should include your contact information, also consider listing your primary music products and services along with a strong benefit about each. This way your card is a mini-brochure of your music business. Your e-mail signature is the on-line equivalent of your business card.

Sales letter. You need this basic sales material for *every* music product and service you sell. Take the time to draft a simple letter that you can print and mail, e-mail, put on a Web page, turn into a brochure, and more. Follow the tips on page 120 as you prepare this material. These letters should be easy to update and customize. For example, when selling your band to clubs, design a generic letter first and then slant each subsequent version slightly so that it targets each *specific* club you send it to.

Another sales letter is the cover letter. Never just send a brochure or CD through the mail without some kind of introductory note. I get demos regularly from people who just slip a CD in an envelope, scribble out my address, and drop it on me. I just drop them in the trash. The cover letter is your chance to make your pitch before the CD gets played, brochure gets read, and so forth. Don't blow your opportunity to increase the success of your contact.

Third-party credentials. Make sure you record and share all the good things your clients and the media say about you. Use reviews and testimonials in all your promotional material. These endorsements really work to decrease the fearful doubt a prospect may have before spending their cash with you. You can include snippets of reviews and client letters in smaller promotional pieces. Use a copy of the entire review clipping or client letter of recommendation when you send a more extensive promotional kit.

Basic FAQ. Using this format lets you present the most common questions people ask about what you sell and then answer each inquiry with the details you need to persuade. The approach both reminds your buyers of the challenges they face and helps you show them how you can solve their problems when they buy from you. Within the Q&A structure, you dispatch their sales objections, make an offer, and close the sale, too. This format can work in several versatile ways: as a letter, brochure, and even a Web page. It is particularly useful for higher-priced products and almost all services. Personally, I use this format to explain and promote my *Melomania* music library ***(www.jeffreypfisher.com/melo.html)***. Check out this example before you plan your version.

Brochure. Preparing a brochure about what you sell can help you combine many promotional elements into one neat sales package. A sales letter, brochure, and CD is probably all you'll ever need to promote just about anything musical. The simplest brochure is a single page of paper, folded twice to yield six-panels. Put a solid headline and picture on the cover and follow the FAQ format mentioned above. Include several third-party credentials, ordering information, prices, and, of course, your complete contact information in the brochure. A mini-catalog of all that you sell is another good idea for a brochure. List your products and services along with brief descriptions, costs, and how to order (book your act, buy your products, etc.).

Product or service sample. Since you will be promoting the music products and services that you sell, it make sense to include samples of what you offer. This can take many forms: an MP3 or two on your Web site to get fans to buy your full CD, a free copy of your indie CD for a media source to review, a music video to sell your live act to clubs, festivals, colleges, and so forth, a demo of your best scoring work when approaching a new soundtrack or jingle client, a list of your recent band bookings if you are a manager or booking agent. The possibilities go on and on.

If your sample is a demo, consider putting three to five complete musical examples on the CD. Choose your best songs that represent your style. Soundtrack and jingle composers can use a 3-5 minute montage of their best music woven together into a mini-commercial for their services. Place a few longer cuts after this powerful opening.

Biography. If *you* are primarily what you sell, write your bio as a journalist would tell your story. Include the key facts that provide credibility to your image and make sure you inject your personality and message into the story. Your biography should be a résumé that you write in narrative form. Write two versions: One, a short paragraph blurb of under 200 words that provides a general overview. Two, draft a two-page version that has greater detail. Remember this is a promotional document and should also include plugs for your music products and services skillfully embedded in the text.

Photographs. Tell your story with a few photos. Make sure the style of the photo and its content captures your personality and complements your image and what you are trying to say. Hire a professional photographer and get the right picture(s) you need to promote yourself effectively. Every musical act needs pictures to use when promoting their gigs. A professionally produced 8 x 10 is standard fare. You should include pictures of your CD covers if that applies, too. Some music professionals can get by without a picture—namely production oriented people or composers and songwriters, but you might throw a picture on the cover of your brochure anyway.

Photos also make securing publicity for easier. Print and Web media are always looking for quality visual materials to support their words. Include an action picture with your news release and you may improve your chances of your story being picked up.

Sell sheets. You may need simple flyers with all the features about your music products and services. For instance, a flyer about your indie CD would detail its name, songs, musical genre, price, retail and wholesale discounts, ordering information, and more. A party or cover band may include sets lists. A project studio might include an equipment list. A composer might list credits.

Other flyers, newsletters, postcards, and such. Create flyers that promote single, specific items such as an upcoming gig, a new CD, and so forth. Prepare a newsletter to share your most important news. Postcards are an inexpensive method to contact people. They can function as a mini-newsletter, gig calendar, CD release profile, new projects announcement, and/or make special offers. Make posters to promote your act and CD, if that applies, and include a copies when you mail to certain prospects. If you mail a promotional kit, include copies of this material, too.

Extras. Any other items you feel can assist your promotional cause are worth considering. You could include some of the swag you sell (sticker, cap, T-shirt, etc.) or other stuff. Voice-over artist Harlan Hogan sends clients and prospects a mouse pad imprinted with his contact information. The mouse pad, demo CD packaging, and other printed materials he uses all share a similar look to keep him in the minds of people who need his services.

YOUR ACT'S PROMO KIT

Here is what the typical promotional package should contain to promote your musical act:

- *Cover letter directed specifically to the prospect of this promotion*

- *Band biography*

- *Pictures posed and "on-the-job" action shots*

- *Media clippings (articles, reviews, other publicity, etc.)*

- *Other reviews and testimonials (a satisfied club owner who booked you, for instance).*

- *Flyers that announce your news (upcoming gigs, CD release, and so forth)*

- *Your latest CD. Don't be stingy. Though it may be the single most expensive piece in your package, it is the whole reason you are doing this. When it comes to radio stations, media reviewers, and other industry heavy hitters, hand out your independent music release like candy on Halloween!*

CHAPTER 12

Ocean of Promotion

"A celebrity is a person who works hard all his life to become well known, and then wears dark glasses to avoid being recognized." — Fred Allen

The previous chapters helped you refine your approach to promoting your music products and services. Working through the steps will tell you what you need to know about what people want to buy and generally how you will bring what you sell to their attention. Now you can consider the specific ways you can reach prospects and turn them into paying clients.

There is no great mystery to promoting successfully. You either reach prospects directly or you motivate prospects to get in touch with you. Picking up the telephone and pitching a gig to someone is an example of a direct promotion. Back-of-room CD sales and answering a fan's e-mail or telephone inquiry personally are other forms of direct promotion. Stapling a flyer about your next gig to a bulletin board is an example of an indirect promotion.

As you may guess, direct promotions take time and energy. You must make the calls and/or meet the prospect to close the sales. The upside is this: direct promotions are always more successful than indirect ones. It's the personal touch that makes the difference. The key is finding the right people. You can't just randomly call anyone, you must use the aforementioned approach to find suitable prospects and then work them hard.

Indirect promotions are all the things you do to get people to take action themselves. Basically, you throw your promotional message out there and hope it sticks. Indirect promotions include sales letters sent via postal or e-mail, ads of any kind, postcards, flyers mailed or posted, brochures, and your Web site. These promotions often take less time, but are not easy to make a success. You need to discover the "place" where people who want what you sell hang out and put your best promotional message right in front of them where they'll see it and take action! This "place" may be a Web site, a magazine, a club, an association, or something/somewhere else.

What you want all your promotions to do is generate leads and sales. Some people will either buy right away while others will indicate to you that they are solid candidates to buy from you in the near future. Buyers are your clients and you should keep in contact with them, encouraging them to buy from you again. The remaining prospects usually need additional prodding to get them to become clients. And you must continue to promote to them until they either become clients or lose interest.

VIRAL SPIRAL

Promotions can spread like a virus. (A good virus, not one of those destructive ones.) Your promotional virus can be much like a joke that gets forwarded to e-mail inboxes around the world. Your promotional message can spread similarly as more people pass it on. First, give something valuable away—a tip sheet, helpful article, free music, etc. Make sure your full contact information (such as a link to your Web site) goes with the free item. There should be no strings attached to this free thing, but it must be good enough to get people to want to see what else you have to offer. Essentially you want these people to BUY more from you right away after hearing, seeing, and/or reading the free stuff. Encourage everyone to pass on the free thing to spread the promotional virus further.

Does this work? Yes. I send articles to many online resources (Web sites, e-zines, and newsletters). They publish these pieces and people grab them and send them to their friends, family, and often re-publish the same articles on their own Web sites, in their newsletters, etc. These free things spread out across the world generating more and more traffic to my Web site, and increasing sales, too. One obvious drawback is that you don't get any money from the free thing. Its purpose is to generate sales of other music products and services you offer. You must be willing to give up this free thing forever to make this concept work.

WAYS TO PROMOTE

There are dozens of ways to promote your music products and services, most of which I detail in my *Ruthless Self-Promotion in the Music Industry* book. Here are the highlights of the most successful methods.

Pick up the phone. Calling past clients and reminding them of what you have is the single most effective way to generate new sales. When you have something new to sell (or you sell a service that people buy regularly), use your phone to make contact. I generate 90 percent of my repeat business through phone calls.

Making cold calls is another necessity. It can be a daunting task to pick up the handset and punch a stranger's number, but you must break through your fear. Look at it this way. You don't have the job yet, right? If you don't call, you definitely won't have the work. But when you *do* call, there's a chance you might get hired. Take the chance! Worse case, you get rejected. Don't despair. Find out why you were turned down and use that information to try again (here or elsewhere). Not so worse case: you get told about another possible gig. Try to land that gig instead.

How do you handle incoming calls, too? Answer the phone confidently and clearly with your company, act, or personal name. Immediately inquire about how you can help the caller. Also, set up a professional-sounding voice mail to catch missed calls. An act can benefit from a hotline that fans can call for their latest information. Plug the hotline at gigs and feature it prominently on all your promotional material.

Respond to inquiries. Some of your promotions will have people coming to you first. Act fast on these contacts. When you get an e-mail or phone call, drop everything and respond personally. Call the person back, e-mail a reply, or send them whatever information they request. Inquiries are hot prospects who often need only a little convincing to buy from you.

Join and participate in online forums, newsgroups, and other discussion groups. You can ask and answer questions that relate to your music products and services. You may even generate some good buzz and establish some beneficial relationships. Don't just rely on people coming to you, do what you can to stimulate their action by going to them first.

Some people think it is nuts to give out your telephone number and e-mail address to the general public. They fear they will be swamped with calls and messages from cranks. In reality, your fans, clients, and prospects make the majority of these contacts. You wouldn't turn down potential business, would you?

Encouraging people to contact you with comments and questions is a way to add the personal touch to your business transactions. You start selling one-to-one, and believe me, this is the way to really increase sales. People will be impressed and grateful that you took the time to personally address their issues. They will reward you with sales, loyalty, and good word of mouth as they spread the news of their experience with you. I practice this everyday; here's my number, (630) 378-4109, and e-mail address, jpf@jeffreypfisher.com. Feel free to get in touch with questions, problems, and, most importantly, your success stories.

Set up in-person sales situations. No letter, e-mail, or flyer is ever going to take the place of standing face-to-face with someone and making the sale. You can build rapport, address every objection, and win people over fast when you are in the flesh. When you finish work for a happy client, that's the perfect time to ask for another project or gig. If you have a prospect that's wavering on your proposal, often meeting this person on their turf will close the sale. Of course, back-of-room sales are always helped when the members of the musical act participate and interact with buying fans. Again, the personal touch really works in today's often sterile, anonymous world.

There are six main personalities you'll encounter with your music business dealings: leaders, supporters, optimists, bean counters, adversaries, and MORs. Leaders are control freaks. Supporters value relationships over other issues. Optimists usually possess the gift of gab and prefer socializing over mundane matters. The complete opposite of this type are the bean counters who meticulously look at everything presented to them. You may also encounter adversaries who never agree or like what you do and you'll meet a few middle of the roadies who never make decisions on their own. Recognizing these personality types is usually quite easy. Make sure you tailor your sales presentation to appeal to the tendencies of the person you're facing.

Making a sale, whether is takes six seconds or six months, follows this basic cycle:

• Meet. A prospect connects with you in some way, by phone, in person, on your Web site.

• Study. You find out what the person needs either through an interview or through your research.

• Work together. You and your prospect hammer out the details in a way that clearly shows the buyer that you can do or provide what she wants. You rely on your painstakingly crafted promotional material to do this for you when this isn't an in-person sales situation.

• Ask for the order. Once mutually beneficial arrangements have been made, close the sale.

• Deliver. Now is the time to hand over the products or services you sold. It is also the ideal time to remind your new client that she made a good choice.

• Stay in touch. Don't let the sale or the client get away. Regularly remind her of how you can help her again.

LIVE GIG CHECKLIST

• *Send a nice handwritten thank you note to the person who hired you.*

• *Make sure your gear is working well. Also, stop by the venue before the gig to see what the sound people need (or you need to bring).*

• *Make sure all the people in the band and crew have business cards and/or other promotional material. Plus, make sure everybody can talk intelligently about the band (where you are playing next, how to book you, where to get the CD, etc.).*

• *Create flyers/postcards profiling upcoming gigs, CD release, and Web site. Place these promotions on every table when you arrive and refresh them during the gig. Strategically place them around the room where you play: on stage, on tables and chairs, the bar, on bulletin boards, in the bathroom, and anywhere else that people will find them, too. Alternately, create a program for your show that includes your act's name and picture, contact information, set list, upcoming gigs, bio, details about your CDs (and how to buy them), a way to sign up for the mailing list, and more. Add some value to the piece that makes people want to hold on to it. You could include a story about the band, song lyrics, an inexpensive give-away (sticker, temp tattoo), and perhaps a sample CD.*

• *Provide the club with a rubber stamp with*

www.yourdomainnamehere.com to use when stamping hands at the front door (of course you need a Web site to make this work effectively).

• Give something free away—sticker, magnet, sample CD—when people sign up for your mailing list (get postal and e-mail addresses at the same time to promote in the future).

• Set up a display on stage that promotes your CD, swag, and upcoming gigs.

• Set up and staff a sales area to sell your CDs and swag.

• Sell your stuff in $10 and $20 increments (easy to make change). Try to upgrade every buyer to the next monetary level.

• Have a contest where the winner gets a free CD or T-shirt. Choose the winner just before the break. Escort the winner to the sales area taking everybody else with you at break time.

GOOD PRESENTATION = GREAT SALES

Major retailers spend gobs of cash creating packaging and displays that stimulate sales. Make your products look more attractive and professional, and you will generate more sales. Also, you should make your sales area look enticing and inviting, too.

• Set up in a visible area with good traffic flow.

• Use a table that's big enough for displaying your products with room for you to work (autograph, make change, fill out receipts, and bag)

• Height rules. Get those products up to eye level where people can see them better. A couple of plastic crates slipped under the table cloth can provide the necessary lift.

• Buy a large tablecloth to cover the table, including any hidden display racks. Use your image colors and/or print your logo on it so it can be seen when the cloth is draped.

• Use small, collapsible easels to display price lists where everybody can see them.

• Use photos and posters on a wall behind the table to attract attention. CD covers and price lists work well on the wall, too.

• Use little receipt books (two-ply, carbon-less) to record transactions. Otherwise, just record the product quantities before you begin and total them up when you close down. Reconcile those numbers with the cash you brought in. If you accept credit cards, you'll need supplies to handle those transactions, too.

• Meet and greet everybody who stops by. Answer questions, field the praise. Also, make sure you stand behind or next to the table, don't sit. Take along some Sharpies for autographing CDs and photos, and other products.

• Have a mailing list sign up area with blank address forms and a box for people to drop them into.

• Be sure to have extra programs, sample CDs, newsletters, postcards, business cards, catalogs, and order forms for those who aren't buying now. Don't wait for people to pick them up. Grab a stack and start handing them out.

Send a letter/postcard/e-mail. Dropping a reminder in the mail or e-mail is a terrific promotional strategy when approaching your fans and other previous buyers another time. Do you have people who inquired about you, but never became clients? Did you give up on them? Instead, contact them again and see if you can help them now. Often, people who originally inquired have left their position and there is a new person in place who has never heard of you.

Conversely, sending a promotion to a cold list is the least effective way to promote. However, if you carefully refine your possible prospects, dropping a sales letter in the mail can make a good initial contact that you follow up with a cold call. Don't rely solely on mail though. It's great for first contact, but *really* needs follow up — phone and in person — to work effectively. Mail is too passive to work entirely on its own. You need to get active and promote harder. Try small ads, publicity, and cold calls along with your mailings. In short, use all the promotional techniques you can think of ... ruthlessly!

A newsletter is one way to approach both past clients and prospects. As you build your contact list, keep them informed about what you have going on. At gigs, you can encourage people to sign up and then stay in contact with them regularly. This newsletter can be a simple affair, even just a postcard or e-mail. Employ a consistent look and feel to your newsletter and send it to your contacts regularly (one a month is good). Topics for this promotion include recently completed projects, upcoming gigs, other news, biographies, profiles of your music products and services, and, of course, how and where to buy them. Fill in these departments with your latest news and share it with your clients and prospects. Also, consider including special offers (discounts, premiums, and so forth) with your newsletter.

E-MAIL SUCCESS SECRETS

When you use e-mail to promote your music products and services, follow these tips.

• *Don't send spam, but do send promotions to people who have already identified themselves as wanting to hear from you.*

• *Be careful what you write in the subject line. If it looks like advertising or other junk e-mail, your message might get deleted before being read.*

• *Try to personalize your message. Either write to a person one-to-one or use a generic description: "Greetings to all yourbandname fans!"*

• *Make sure the e-mail is easy to read. Use short, simple words and short paragraphs. It's OK to include some hard-sell, just make sure you liberally sprinkle in plenty of benefits for your readers, too.*

• *Try to include testimonials or other endorsements that support whatever music products and services you are selling.*

• *Make it easy for people to respond by providing a clickable link or two in your message. To make that work, be sure to write the entire address e. g. http://www.artistpro.com.*

• *Use a signature at the end of all your e-mail messages that provides a brief promotional message (including links) about what you offer.*

Deliver a promo kit. Rarely is it a good idea to ship your entire promotional kit out the door to some unsuspecting prospect. Promo kits are best used as a follow up to some other contact that you make (by phone, letter, e-mail, networking, even in person). When a prospect asks for more specific information, that's when your promo kit can do the job. It's ideal for providing full background material to the media (or other prospects) before they come to a gig, interview you, or review your CD.

Network. Building a network of contacts requires that you firmly establish and entrench yourself in your little corner of the music world. How can you approach a possible prospect without knowing what's going on around you? You need to get out to see what others are doing and where your opportunities lie. Networking allows you to gather useful information (and share what you know) and make valuable contacts with people who can help you. For example, to be a successful soundtrack composer, you must associate with people who need music for their audio-visual presentations. Joining and participating with the people who are already good candidates for what you sell will help you make sales in the long run.

Get out and meet people. Get personal with club owners, distributors, retail stores, online avenues, A/V producers—whoever is a critical component to your success. Don't wait for them to come to you, go to them and pursue what you need. You also need to get out to be seen and stay in circulation. People have short memories; make sure they don't forget you and what you have to benefit them.

BECOME A JOINER

As the saying goes: "A wise man knows everything; a shrewd one, everybody." Your best opportunity for getting information and news, networking within the industry, and securing general support for your efforts is to join the many associations that permeate the music industry. Some of these groups offer specific benefits such as unions with their wage scales, group medical insurance, and other perks. You can also look outside the music industry and join local organizations such as your chamber of commerce and Rotary. Your alumni association can be a source for contacts and business, too. You can also start your own group in your area. Many songwriter and performer associations are started by people like you looking for a way to connect and support one another.

- *National Academy of Recording Arts and Sciences (NARAS), The Grammy™ people. Contact* ***memservices@grammy.com*** *for details.*

- *The International Music Products Association* ***(www.namm.com)*** *is another possibility.*

• *The South by Southwest* **(www.sxsw.com)** *music expo is also worth considering.*

At its simplest, networking means letting as many people know what you can do, and that you'd appreciate their spreading the word for you. Simultaneously, you listen to what other people have to offer and work to tell the people *you know* about them. Networks are everywhere—your friends and family make up one. Industry contacts make up another as does the media people you know. If you associate with other bands and musicians, you form another network to support one another. Building these networks, helping other people, and getting help for yourself is vital to making your music business viable and long-lasting.

Networking is both give and take. You want to help the other person as much as they want to help you. You try to find them leads or work and they try to find new gigs for you, too. Perhaps you are familiar with the concept of "Six Degrees of Separation" that states that you are only six people away from anybody else on the planet. Through a network of contacts you can reach the people you need. Of course, today there aren't even six degrees separating many people. Thanks to the Internet, you are no more than a search engine away from finding, contacting, and building a relationship with just about anyone.

Building your industry contacts goes beyond simple schmoozing. You can expand and perpetuate your word of mouth. You can network to diversify your products and services. You can network to expand your business without actually adding to your payroll. Networking—in all these examples and on all levels—means you must create reciprocal and mutually beneficial agreements between all parties. You sell my CD, I'll sell yours. You help me get in touch with a potential new client, I'll help you get access to another. You can set up these networks quite easily. They work like ever expanding pyramids, you tell two friends, they tell two friends, and so on. Networks grow when you feed and nurture them.

TESTING YOUR RESULTS

Always test your promotional ideas when you can by trying them out in low risk situations. Not sure if the price is right for your CD? Try approaching similar people with different prices and gauge the results. Planning a new promotion? Try it on a sample of people to see if it works first before committing additional resources. Also, always ask people about how and where they heard of you. What they tell you provides insight as to where you promotional resources are best spent. Never forget that success is the real test. If something is working right, don't meddle. If not, figure out what's wrong and fix it fast.

Use word of mouth. If you asked 100 people in the music industry what the best promotion is, 90% would say word of mouth. If you asked that 90% what that meant, only a handful could tell you. The elusive word-of-mouth promotional strategy implies that you do nothing and people just naturally seek you out. This is, of course, ludicrous. Successful word of mouth requires your constant influence.

• Deliver quality music products and services. Nothing creates repeat and new business better than good work in the first place. Getting good reviews, charting, winning awards, and other credentials all reinforce your standing in the industry. People discover your abilities and want to have them for themselves—they seek you out and hire you!

• Spread the word. Success breeds more success, so make sure you tell everybody about what you've accomplished. Send a newsletter, use publicity, share copies of reviews and testimonials with clients and new prospects. In other words, never rely solely on people finding you by accident. Work hard to generate word-of-mouth buzz.

• Ask people to tell others. Remind your clients, fans, relatives, network(s), and other business peers of all that you have available and encourage them to pass on your information to *their* friends, relatives, colleagues, and more. Provide some promotional material that they can distribute, too.

• Get referrals from satisfied clients. Don't wait for people to offer names. Ask for contact information of other acquaintances that are candidates for your music products and services. Alternately, offer incentives (cash!) for referrals. A band could offer $50 to whoever gets them their next gig.

• Make your clients look good in front of *their* clients and competition. This way you either will get more work from the same client or get inroads to other prospects. Publicly recognizing and thanking a client can pay rich dividends for you as well.

• Display your contact information prominently. Put it on your CDs, swag, and on everything that you use to promote and to handle your daily business matters. Make it easy for people to find and get in touch with you.

• Cross-promote. Make sure you mention all the other music products and services you offer within all your promotions. For example, plug your first CD in the booklet for your second disc. You never know what people may see or buy first. You don't want to lose out on additional sales just because people don't know all that you have to offer. S-p-e-l-l it out for them!

• Always have promotional material ready to go and always with you. Carry business cards, brochures, sample CDs, and have a few complete promotional packages in the trunk of your car. You never know when an opportunity might arise, be prepared to drop everything and work to make a sale at any time!

Pro/Files—Ol'Kutty

Ninetrigger, St. Louis, MO USA
http://www.ninetrigger.com - dirtyninetrigger@aol.com

What do you do in the music industry? We're a four piece rapcore/ new school metal band

What promotions work the best and why? Free stuff (ex: CDs, stickers, toilet paper with your band name on it)

Where does the money come from? We have actually gotten a P/T band job, where three out of the four of us are able to work, from shows, and we use the money out of our own pocket.

What were some of your past projects? We found cheap 6 minute blank tapes, bought tape labels from the same place, and made copies all day of 2 songs off of our demo CD "Observe to

Follow." Then, took some art work our guitar player whipped up on his PC, went to Kinko's and had mass quantities made, and folded them to make cassette sleeves for our tapes.

What has been your greatest achievement so far? Hitting a national show with 200 cassettes, of the same genre that we knew would come see us.

How did you do it? Got to the show a little early, and waited. Good luck also if there's a big crowd. They will maul you for something free. You will leave wishing you had 1000 more tapes and/or CDs, to hand out.

What lessons have you learned along the way? Handing out flyers only, is the long, and frustrating way of making a career of your music!

What is your current project or next goal? To fill the club every time we play out.

Get some publicity. A media review or article is a tacit endorsement of your music products and services. More people will believe what the media says about you over anything you or your promotional material says. That means working to get media coverage is crucial to the on-going success of your music business.

Publicity can be simple such as when you send in a calendar notice about your gig at a specific venue. Getting reviews and feature articles written about you is somewhat more complicated. Fortunately, when you understand "the plug," your publicity efforts will be rewarded. Basically, you want some media source to either let you promote your latest project or plug it for you. What is the essence of the plug? Follow this simple equation: *Provide value=earn a plug.* The amount of plug you get is directly proportional or equal to the value you provide. For example, celebrities appears on the Letterman show wanting to promote their latest films. They provide value (entertainment) to the talk show and in exchange for that, the TV show let's them show a clip and plug the movie. Here's how this concept can work for you. Let's say you want a newsletter to plug your CD. How do you cultivate this plug? You could write a short how-to article for the newsletter about how you produced your CD or the lessons you learned. This article provides value—information and knowledge—that the newsletter can use to help its readers. In exchange for that valuable item, the newsletter lets you promote (plug) your CD. It's that simple. Start brainstorming ideas that let you provide something of real value to media sources and earn the promotional plugs you need.

REVIEWS

When you send your musical creation into the world, there will be other people who will comment on it. Media and other reviews are necessary to making sales. They do not come without their disappointments. Some will like everything you do; others will find fault in everything. When a review is positive, celebrate. When a review is negative, learn from it. If those same bad reviews get you down, follow these words of wisdom:

- *"To escape criticism—do nothing, say nothing, be nothing."*—Elbert Hubbard
- *"Problems are messages."*—Shakti Gawain
- *"No one can make you feel inferior without your consent."*—Eleanor Roosevelt
- *"The man who can't dance thinks the band is no good."*—Proverb

Publicity usually starts by contacting a media source, either by phone or through a news release. Most prefer a release either mailed, faxed, or e-mailed. Scour your local media for possible places to send your publicity. Next, look to the Web for more opportunities. Here are a few possible places to start.

- The All-In-One Media Directory ***(www.gebbieinc.com)***

- Music Industry News Network ***(www.mi2n.com)***

- U.S. Newspaper Links ***(www.usnewspaperlinks.com)*** From here you can find links to newspapers, radio stations, and TV stations in the United States.

- News Directory ***(www.newsdirectory.com)*** Here you can find information about newspapers, magazines, and other general music media, including college press (especially useful for acts targeting that market).

• Find music journalists, including reviewers, on-line *(www.musicjournalist.com)*, too.

Once you get the contact information you need, follow these publicity steps.

• Print your contact information on every promotional piece you use so the media can find you easily.

• Get your music business listed in the many free directories available on-line and in print.

• If in a band, get your upcoming gigs listed in calendar listings by sending a brief news release.

• Locate the general media and music media that serves your particular areas including radio and TV, newspapers, magazines, newsletters, Web sites, e-zines, even specific writers and editors.

• Ask for the editorial calendars for the media to see if any upcoming articles are opportunities for you to promote your music business.

• Send news releases, article ideas, and promotional material, including CDs for review, to the right media contacts.

• Follow-up the contact you make with the media and send thank you notes when they cover you.

• Use copies of your publicity to both get more plugs from different media and in other promotional ways (mail a reprint to new prospects, for example).

GETTING ON RADIO AND TV

Although radio airplay is important to major success for a musical act, don't ignore other radio and TV shows that can provide other publicity opportunities. Some radio stations and local TV shows feature indie acts. Here's how to get on those programs and plug your wares.

• *Find the radio and TV stations and/or shows that appeal to your audience*

• *Listen or watch the station*

• *Find the right program fit*

• *Develop an angle that fits both the target program and audience*

• *Find the show's producer (call the station and ask: "who produces the blank show?")*

• *Contact this producer by phone*

• *Follow up with your promotional material*

• *Follow up again to get booked*

• *Get on and use your time to promote well. Remember: provide value and earn a plug.*

• *Send thank you notes to everybody!*

BEATLES EATS

A long running staple in Chicago radio is the "Breakfast with the Beatles" show. A couple of hours of the Fab Four each and every Sunday morning. The area tribute bands appear on the show regularly playing and plugging their gigs and Web sites. They generate a lot of buzz and fans in and around the Chicagoland area by connecting through this radio show. Is there a similar opportunity in your neck of the woods?

Take out ads. Advertising to promote your music business can be effective, but costly. Ads are expensive because the only way to make them work for you is to repeat them. Constantly. Far too many ingenue promoters blow the wad on a single, high-priced ad and then wonder why nothing happens. We all get bombarded by ad messages everyday and that makes standing out from the cacophony a formidable task. First, find the right publications that appeal to the people you want to reach. The more narrow the focus, the better chance you have of succeeding. Second, take out several smaller ads instead of one big ad. Repetition of your ad's message will work its magic on prospects. Third, follow the promotional preparation tips earlier in this chapter. Fourth, include both hard and soft offers in the ad. You either want people to buy now or contact you in some way so you can keep in touch with them and make additional offers. Fifth, consider splitting costs of ads by pooling resources. For instance, offer to split the cost of an ad for a gig between your act and the venue. The club plays half and you pay the rest.

LANDING LUCRATIVE COLLEGE GIGS

To better illustrate these moneymaking music components, let's see what it takes to get your band a paying gig at a college or university. Schools have student or campus activities departments responsible for hosting events that appeal to the student body. These departments usually have budgets for entertainment. Fees range from $750 to $1500 for a couple of sets. Some colleges may throw in meals and basic lodging, too. Research will show that colleges like acts with a well-balanced set and therefore, good cover bands will always sell better than an all original act. Contrarily, college students are usually very receptive to new acts and, with the proper promotion, a mostly original act can still land a gig.

Consider staying local or within a few hundred miles to make your travel easy and free (you can return on the same day). If you have family in more distant areas, and can get free lodging, consider those areas for your promotions. Now find the contact information you need by visiting college and university Web sites, consulting the Musician's Atlas, and other resources. You should be aware that these departments book bands months (even years!) in advance. Also, since colleges need entertainment during the fall, winter, and early spring, your band can keep its summers free to land some outdoor festival shows and other warm-weather parties.

Put together your promotional kit. Don't depend on a single mailing. Instead, keep contacting your leads. For example, send a teaser sales letter and flyer, follow that up with a phone call, send your full promotion kit next, and follow that up, too. Have a contract ready to go in case you get offered the gig. Also, call other area schools (and other clubs and venues) to let them know you're in town. You might be able to set up multiple gigs in one area. One band I knew used to create a mini-tour and hit several colleges and clubs in a regional tour. They'd be away for a couple of weeks working steadily and repeat a similar tour once or twice each year.

YOUR MONEYMAKING WEB SITE

Today, virtually everyone in the music industry can benefit from a Web site. With most music bought online, the Web is the place to be. Set up your Web site as your personal Web community and storefront where everybody comes to get information and to buy from you. Your site should carry all the information prospects need to make buying decisions. There should be information specifically for the media, too. If it applies, there should be a section devoted to your vendor and other supplier needs. Your net presence should also appeal to your clients and provide value-added products and services just for them.

ON THE NET AGAIN...

Willie Nelson ***(www.willienelson.com)*** *talked with Yahoo! Internet Life (May 2001): "The best thing about the Internet is the connection with people. An artist always used to be forced to go through the label. The Net means that I can talk direct to people. The Web site is just an extension of who we are. We run it the way we do our music—it's pretty much a family thing. My daughters and grand-daughters do a lot of the work on the site, and we use it to talk to people who are interested in what we do."*

Follow these basic steps when getting your music business online:

Sign up for Internet access. You usually pay a flat rate and get a certain number of hours or unlimited access to the Net. You can get a dial-up account, cable modem, or other high-speed account. I used to suggest going local, but after having my ISP go belly up, instead choose a major player for your Internet connection. You can count on the likes of AOL and AT&T being around for a long time to come. Their service is typically more reliable, too.

Find some space. When you sign up for Internet access, chances are your Internet Service Provider (ISP) gives you space to host your Web pages as part of that regular Internet connection fee. If not, you can buy separate hosting space. Audio and video files are large and can quickly consume your allotted space. Make sure you have adequate resources for your site. The downside to an ISP site is it's bound to have a weird Internet address (URL). So, instead...

Register your own domain. With your space set, go to Network Solutions and register your own domain. They cost $35 a year, but for an additional $35 you can have your "virtual domain" routed to any weird address you have. This way people type in http://www.yournamehere.com and are automatically sent to your *real* URL. After that, use navigation links on your site. Once people arrive at a site, they usually don't care or notice what the actual URL is.

Get e-mail at that domain. Make sure you sign up for e-mail when you register your domain so that you can get yourname@yournamehere.com. Again, signing up with Network Solutions means your e-mail address will be around for a long time. I lost my e-mail address, one I'd promoted for nearly ten years, when my ISP went bankrupt. Don't let this happen to you.

TURNKEY WEB SITE PACKAGE

*Addr.com **(www.addr.com)** sells a great package that includes lots of server space, e-mail accounts, lots of traffic bandwidth, domain name hosting, and more for under ten bucks a month (as of this writing).*

Plan your basic site on paper before you start designing it. Visit sites put out by other people who promote music products and services similar to yours. What is both good and bad about their approach? How can you improve on their ideas? Think about your content. What is the best way to present it? Make your site a store that includes detailed product sheets, articles, reviews, newsletters, audio and video samples, pictures, and more. Keep it simple, easy to navigate, and content-rich! Start with this:

- Home page to introduce your site. Include navigation to all the other content on your site from here.

- Page(s) that describe your music products and services with links to order them. Include your online samples and demos here (such as an MP3 music file).

- Page(s) that contain your recommendations for *other* products and services with ordering links.

- Page(s) with biographical and/or other background information.

- Page(s) containing whatever you feel is important to your music business (upcoming tour dates or other events, breaking news, links to other sites, lyrics, music and video files, and more.)

Killermontstreet.com started as a fan-run site for Aztec Camera and Roddy Frame. The site was so well done that it became the official site, backed by the artist and label.

Program the pages. There are several good tools for designing, programming, and maintaining your Web site. I use HoTMetaLPro ***(www.softquad.com)***. Alternately, hire someone to create and maintain your Web site. Be sure to match the look of your Web presence to your image. Develop a theme for the site's presentation and carry that theme throughout. Keep important information at the top of your pages. Put contact information on every page (e-mail, mailing address, and telephone numbers). Also, watch your download times. Keep graphics small (have thumbnails link to larger files). Tell people the file sizes for MP3s and other large files, too. Use navigation links to make it easy to move around your site. Make sure the writing works, free of grammatical and spelling errors, too.

Go live. Once you have everything in place, carefully go through your site to make sure the links work and that everything looks and feels right. Test your site with different browsers and software platforms, at different screen resolutions, and using varied connection speeds. Adjust the site so that it looks its best for the majority of users. When you are satisfied that you are ready, post the pages.

Get people to your site. Obviously, you need to generate traffic to your Web site to reap the most benefits. Promote your site on-line and off-line. Register with the main search engines. Send news releases, post to applicable newsgroups and mailing lists, send direct mail and e-mail to clients and prospects, swap links, and more. Also, display your Web address on business cards, letterhead, brochures, ads, T-shirts, stickers, temp tattoos, CDs—indeed all promotions that you use.

Capture contact information. Encourage people who visit your site to contact you in some way. This way you get their e-mail (or postal) address and can send them future promotions. Offer a free newsletter, provide a free product or service (in exchange for their information), or use another creative way to identify visitors.

MUSIC WEB SITES

In addition to your own Web site for your music promotion, also take advantage of the other Web sites that exist to help promote and sell your music. The services and charges vary from site-to-site, so make sure you read and understand what you get before you sign up (and start paying). Consider joining as many of these sites as you can afford to pay and maintain.

*Broadjam **(www.broadjam.com)** Helps get your music on other sites, too.*

EarBuzz ***(www.earbuzz.com)*** *Takes orders and handles fulfillment.*

Internet Underground Music Archive ***(www.iuma.com)*** *The original indie music site.*

Live365 ***(www.live365.com)*** *Run your own radio station with your (and/or other's) music.*

MP3.com ***(www.mp3.com)*** *The name everybody knows and where everybody goes.*

Vitaminic ***(www.vitaminic.com)*** *Europe's popular download site.*

OTHER PROMOTION NOTIONS

Here are a few other promotional ideas to consider as you pursue your moneymaking music career.

Get wacky. *Offbeat promotions can sometimes work, depending on the image you convey with your career. Unusual promotions run the gamut from delivering demos dressed in gorilla suits to publicity stunts. Voice artist Harlan Hogan* ***(www.harlanhogan.com)*** *produced a radio-style parody of the advertising scene and includes the soundtrack at the end of his demo CD. He promotes this radio play, and people who order it get his demo at the same time.*

Do an in-store appearance. *Set up a display area where you can play unplugged sets, play your CD, hand out flyers, sign autographs, and generally meet, greet, and sell CDs. You may not sell a lot of copies, but probably far more than you would with your CD in the bins next to more famous acts. Alternately, be a street performer and play acoustic sets wherever you legally can. Again, set up a display and play your CD during breaks (through a portable boombox). Hopefully, you'll sell some CDs and earn a little scratch performing, too.*

One solo artist shared this tip in my Moneymaking Music Tip of the Week *newsletter. "There are always folks at concerts who don't have money for CDs, or have friends who'd want a copy, and so forth. On the way out, I stop at record stores (getting information from the clubs) and leave CDs on consignment. I plug the stores at concerts and on flyers I print before the tour. On the way back, I collect my money, any unsold CDs, and fill any back orders."*

Look for special sales. *Does your music tie in with a particular store, product, or business? Approach them and ask about putting together a deal. One pharmaceutical company bought an independent jazz CD and delivered it to doctors along with samples of their latest medical wonder. The jazz music was a good fit between the product and the professional market (and music tastes) of whom they were trying to reach.*

PART FOUR: MANAGE YOUR MUSIC CAREER

"Never mistake knowledge for wisdom. One helps you make a living; the other helps you make a life."—Sandra Carey

The business of music is *your* business. You need to understand the intricacies of starting, managing, and sustaining your moneymaking music career. Knowing how to manage your affairs effectively puts you in the enviable position of being a successful music entrepreneur.

CHAPTER 13

Get Your Music Business Together

"The way to get things done is not to mind who gets the credit for doing them." — Benjamin Jowett

Why do you need to be in business for yourself? There are several advantages to running a real business that you need to understand.

• Mental and emotional. Being in business isn't something you do while you wait around for something better to come along. Your business and career are related, synergistic, and one and the same. Making this mental shift to "I am in business for myself" or "I run my own music business" will go a long way toward maintaining your emotional and psychological well being. Handling your own business takes courage and conviction, and those qualities help you navigate the storms making your successes all that much sweeter. Plus, you'll be able to say that you did it all yourself.

• Professionalism and legitimacy. Having a real, tangible business is one credential that people take seriously. You don't freelance; you operate a small business. You are perceived as a pro, not as someone looking for the easy way out. This professional attitude should permeate your contact with people to make closing sales easier. People in the music industry fight the stigma that it's all one big party. It's not. The vast majority of people with whom you have contact would prefer to deal with a professional rather than some rowdy, disorganized wannabe.

• Legal. There are certain legal advantages to running your own legitimate business including liability protection, money-raising strategies, and more.

• Financial. There are a bevy of financial advantages to owning your own business. For example, your current lifestyle can be converted into your business lifestyle having your business now pay some of your personal expenses. More specifics later in this book.

• Promotion. It's just plain easier to promote the image of a carefully crafted small business than its individual parts. You could say "Hi I'm Joe Pro, a freelance music producer." Better still, you should take this approach: "Hi, I'm Joe Pro, my independent music production company, MusicPro, finds, cultivates, packages, and promotes new musical talent."

GET LEGAL

If you've diligently followed the steps leading up to this point, you've laid the groundwork required for planning, starting, and promoting your music business. Now turn your attention toward creating the legitimate, legal structure to support it. This section is in the order you need to follow. In some cases, you can't move forward to the next step unless you complete the previous.

Choose a name. Naming your music business is an important step. Your band name is the most obvious choice, if that applies. Other music business professionals should choose a name that complements your image and message and that gives an indication of the music products and services you provide. You can simply use your own name or create a fictitious title. Come up with a few alternative names before you decide. Run a trademark search to make sure the name you choose is available. Consider registering your trademark to your name if you feel that is important. Information about Trademarks is in the next chapter. Use Bandname.com ***(www.bandname.com)*** as a resource for both checking to see if a name is unavailable and/or to register your unique name. They offer some other tools, too. Don't take the chance that someone may already have the rights to the name you want. You'll save yourself a lot of problems if you check first.

Locate your office. Everybody needs a central place to house a music business. It can be as simple as a desk in the corner of your bedroom to a basement project studio, even up to a storefront on a busy street. Even if you are on the road most of the time, establish a main address anyway. For many, the home office is the ideal choice. The cost is minimal and can even save you money on your taxes if you meet the requirements. Your town may have specific rules that govern your home-based business (see Zoning below), so be sure to meet them. The location of your office doesn't need to be your address, though. If you'd prefer a separate address or if plan on moving in the near future, consider buying an address (either a P.O. Box or one at those mailbox places). Otherwise, you'll waste precious time and money telling the world that you moved.

Install a telephone. Get a separate line just for your business. It can be a land line or wireless. Put voice-mail on this phone that picks up even when you're using the line. That way people who call never get a busy signal. Record a simple, professional-sounding outgoing message on the voice mail for callers to hear. If you choose a dial-up Internet account, get another line dedicated for that purpose. It can double as a fax line, if you need that. If you haven't already, establish your e-mail address and Web URL at this time, too.

Select the business form. You must establish a legal structure for your business. After reviewing the basic information here, consult with your tax preparer and perhaps a lawyer before choosing. The tax expert should explain the financial advantages of these business organizational forms and how they apply to your particular financial situation. Your lawyer should explain the liability issues and how they may affect you now or in the future.

• Sole proprietor. This is the simplest legal form to choose, and is picked over 90 percent of the time. This legal form is pure self-employment with all business assets and liabilities the full responsibility of its single owner. You report your business income and expenses as part of your personal income tax return using Schedule C. Also, you are personally responsible for any problems that arise including legal liability. In other words, should someone sue you and win, they collect from your *personal* assets.

• Partnership. There is very little difference between partnerships and a sole-proprietor. The partnership itself files a separate report of its income and deductions from business activities, but the partners themselves record the *actual* business transactions on their personal income tax returns using the percentages agreed upon during their initial partnership agreement, 50-50 for instance. All partners are once again personally liable for any claims made against the business. If one partner skips, the other partner(s) can be liable for 100 percent of the damages. Because of these problems, and the fact that partnership lines of authority can get cloudy, have a lawyer draft a comprehensive partnership agreement.

• Corporation. The corporate form makes the business its own "person," so to speak. The business files its own taxes and pays taxes on its profits. Profits then go to the owners or shareholders who then report that income as a dividend. The great advantage to corporations is their limit on personal liability. The corporation itself is responsible for the assets and liabilities incurred on its behalf. The people who run it or own it are insulated from those judgments. However, this liability issue is not black and white, and depending on the case, employees and owners can be held accountable. One additional benefit to setting up a corporation is that it can issue stocks and bonds as a way to raise money. Because setting up a corporation is more intricate than the previous forms, consider retaining an attorney to get started.

• Subchapter S Corporation. This is an offshoot of the corporate form. Instead of the corporation paying taxes on its profits, the money goes directly to the business owners, who report these gains as dividends on their personal tax returns.

• Limited Liability Company. This new business form is a hybrid of the corporate and partnership legal forms. Governed by individual state law, its biggest advantage is that the company principals are not personally liable for its debts.

PARTNERSHIP AGREEMENT

Should you choose the partnership form for your music business, have an attorney draft the formal agreement. These are some of the questions you should ask and answer with your agreement.

• *What is the name of the partnership?*

• *Who are the partners? Include their names, addresses, and Tax IDs.*

• *What are the duties for each partner? Be very specific in this section. Effective partnerships have individual members with distinct skills, clearly-defined roles, and divisions of labor. With different skills, personalities, and jobs (one sells; the other creates) your partnership stands a better chance at sustaining the business.*

• What is the percentage of ownership in the partnership? Even if only two parties are involved, it is probably best to let one partner be in the majority, say 51 percent to the other's 49 percent. Don't forget to address who would own subsequent property (and in what percentages) including copyrights, trademarks, etc. Note that melody and lyrics are given copyright protection as is the recording as a whole (sound recording), but the individual parts are only marginally protected. If you write the whole song, but the drummer contributes a killer drum track, you may or may not want to give any ownership percentage. Also, if this applies, indicate who owns the band name trademark (including logo and other images).

• What does each partner bring to the business? This would include startup money, equipment, intellectual property (e. g. songs), and so forth. It may be better for individuals to own their own equipment rather than have the partnership buy and own it.

• How are expenses and income divided up? This should be at the same percentage of ownership. Make sure you include a formal approval process for all purchases otherwise you run the risk of one partner spending too much without the other partner's consent.

• How do you hire and fire employees, contractors, and advisors?

• How does the partnership dissolve and/or how can one partner buy-out the other? Don't forget to include a way to end the partnership.

Tax ID. Your music business needs a tax identification number for income tax purposes. Sole proprietors use their personal Social Security numbers. Partnerships and corporations must get their own unique Employer Identification Number (EIN) to identify the business to the IRS. Sole proprietors also need an EIN if you hire employees. Contact the IRS ***(www.irs.gov)*** for details on filling out their Form SS-4, *Application for Employer Identification Number.*

Register your DBA(s). Now that you've chosen your name, trademarked it if necessary, selected your business form, and secured the proper tax ID, you need to file your fictitious name statement or "doing business as" (dba) in the county where your business is located. Contact your county clerk's office for details about registering your dba. Typically, you fill out a form, pay a registration fee, and must meet their publication requirements. That simply means you must take out a legal notice in an approved newspaper that explains who you are and what your fictitious name will be.

These ads are standard fare and usually affordable. Once you meet all these requirements, you can begin using your business name legally.

Get necessary permits and licenses. Most municipalities have strict guidelines for operating your business in your hometown. Contact your local clerk's office and explain that you are starting a business (home-based or otherwise) in your town. They will provide you with the specific procedures for you to follow. This can include filling out a detailed form about your intended business and paying any required fees. For example, my home-based company must buy a business license each year ($60) and meet certain zoning requirements (see below).

Comply with zoning in your municipality. When home studios started popping up around the country, and as more and more people began working from their homes, the issue of zoning regulations reared its ugly head. In short, residential areas are not intended for business purposes. If you operate your music business from your own home, you risk breaking the law in your area. Thankfully, most municipalities understand the need for home based businesses and have procedures to cover them. When you inquire about your business license, ask about the zoning issue, too. If your music business doesn't meet the zoning regulations, you can ask for a variance from your municipality. For example, while I can operate my business from my basement project studio, I can't have clients visiting all the time. If I were running a small commercial recording studio, this zoning regulation would be a big problem. In my case, I rarely have clients visit, choosing instead to either go to their offices or use my phone, e-mail, and the Web to communicate. If you choose to locate your music business in an area zoned for business, you should not have any zoning difficulties. Ask to be sure before you take any major steps (i.e. spend any money).

Apply for sales tax permit. Some states require you to collect and subsequently pay sales tax on all sales you make within your state. As of this writing, interstate commerce is still exempt from sales taxes. The specific requirements vary from state to state. The only way to get the right information is to contact your state's department of revenue or equivalent. Explain that you will be selling products in the state and need to know the procedures for dealing with sales tax collection and payment. Using a third-party credit card processing service that it based in a state with no sales tax effectively makes all your transactions sales tax free. However, this issue is regularly under scrutiny and the rules of Internet commerce can change overnight. Keep yourself informed.

Print business forms. With your name, address, and other legal matters behind you, now is the time to establish one physical representation of your music business. Go to a print shop and pick out letterhead, matching envelopes, shipping labels, and business cards. Envelopes hold letters, shipping labels cover the products you mail, and the business card is ready for many situations. These forms will serve you well for many years so take extra care to design and print them. Include your full contact information, including e-mail and Web address on the letterhead, labels, and cards. You don't necessarily need separate forms for most business functions. Use your letterhead for everything: general correspondence, promotional material, invoices, contracts, and more. This approach keeps your name, logo, and contact information on every piece of paper leaving your office.

FULL–OR PART-TIME?

The information in this and my other books applies whether you choose to pursue your musical endeavors full- or part-time. You are not a failure if you need a day job to supplement your music earnings. Sometimes your moneymaking music adventure is a series of steps that eventually leads to a full-time career. Other times, music may never occupy more than a few hours a month. The choice is yours. Moonlighting while you work at another job or work a part-time day job and the rest on your music are two strategies that you can employ. When your musical income surpasses your other earnings, then consider going full-time. Another possibility is to rely on a spouse's salary while you build your business. Alternately, build up a nest egg (either personally or through investors) and launch yourself full-time using these funds to cover your expenses until you begin rolling in some dough.

I started out moonlighting and then went to the single salary (my wife's) tactic while simultaneously turning my former employer into my first client. I essentially did much of the same work, albeit spending much less time, from my office, and at a considerable increase in pay. Working from my project studio, I made videos, doing the music and sound, scored soundtracks and wrote jingles, and put my stamp on several other creative projects. The first month was slow, but after that I started earning enough money to replace my lost income. Several years later, when my son Adam arrived, my wife and I swapped. She stopped working full-time and we relied on just my business income. She works part-time now and runs a little business on the side, too (I like to think she learned that from me).

Set up your financial record keeping. Now you can begin to address the specifics of your music financials. This includes bank accounts, income and expense procedures, bookkeeping, and more. If you take on employees, be sure you understand the regulations applying to them. There are specific forms that must be filed and procedures you must follow. Since these financial issues are so important, they are treated in detail in another chapter.

Understand your taxes. Hot on the heels of accomplishing proper financial management is knowing your particular tax situation. Depending on the legal form you choose, there will be specific tax filing procedures, forms to fill out, and estimated or quarterly taxes to be paid. Set up a meeting with your tax advisor to discuss and plan for your income tax requirements. Get more details in another chapter.

GET MONEY

You will need some seed money to start and run your music business. Shoot for enough cash on hand to run your business for three months without any income. Don't forget you need an *additional* amount yourself to cover your personal expenses during that same time period. How much you need really depends on what you have already and what you need to get before you can pursue your vision. A band may just need some cash to put together a demo and other promotional material while a project studio or soundtrack/jingle composer may need an extensive investment in equipment.

Unfortunately, too many people feel they must have it all ready before starting their business. They spend huge wads of cash to get everything from office furniture to professionally-designed stationery *before* a single dollar has walked through their door. It may be better to pare your start-up costs to the bone and instead create a detailed plan for future acquisitions, as income to justify them becomes a reality. For example, don't buy a copier when you can go to Kinko's instead. If the volume warrants it in the future, and the expenditure can save you both time and money, then, and only then, buy the copier. Here are some typical startup expenses:

• Employee wages. If you are hiring people, you'd better have enough change around to pay them for several weeks before you start earning.

• Rent. If you're grabbing office or retail space, you will need deposits and several months rent saved to see you through your initial lean times.

• Equipment (music and office). Decide the essentials you need to manage your business. Make getting a computer a priority. A powerful computer can be a prudent purchase enabling you to handle many music and business tasks simultaneously.

• Telephone. You need a dedicated business telephone line.

• Other utilities. You may need to make deposits and pay for electricity, gas, water, and more. If you operate at home, this shouldn't be an issue.

• Internet and e-mail. You need an Internet connection and e-mail address.

• Advertising and promotional costs. A new business usually must spend, spend, spend to get the word out initially. If you are starting from scratch, set aside a substantial amount to put together and launch your initial promotional blitz.

• Web site development and hosting. You will need funds to create and maintain your music business Internet presence, register your unique domain name, join other on-line sites, and more.

• Operating expenses. You need to have money available to pay for all those pesky little expenses that creep up regularly such as postage costs, paper for your printer, and other office trappings.

Once you arrive at your start-up figures, add a little contingent of *at least* 20 percent to cover you for unforeseen circumstances. Knowing your expenses shows you what you must earn to keep your business viable. Once you get the money, you better turn your attention toward generating some profit. While it is not unusual to take a loss for a year or two with your burgeoning music business, you'll want to get in the black fast.

Raising the cash you need. There are several places you can get the money you need to either start your music business or get an infusion of cash to cover special circumstances.

• Personal savings. Have you set aside some money for a rainy day? Perhaps your music business startup is the ideal use for that slush fund. If you have little in savings, now is the time to start setting aside 10-15 percent of your current earnings to build up the funds you need. If you are already running your music business, start plowing the same percentage back into your business to fund equipment purchases, promotions, and more.

• Family and friends. You can ask other people to invest in your business. This is really just a loan that you promise to pay back with interest. This can be a touchy issue for many, but you can lessen the problems by setting up formal loan agreements that include the amount borrowed and the specific payback terms (how much, how often, and at what interest rate). Just because you are friends or are related doesn't mean you can't approach this subject professionally.

• Clients. You can raise money from your clients in several ways. Concentrate on getting more clients and/or charging more for your music products and services. The money you make in either case can be used for your music business. On big projects, request a down payment or advance before starting work. This is common in the soundtrack and jingle world where you often get between 33 percent and 50 percent up front. Getting a 50 percent deposit to hold a gig date is common for in-demand performers, too.

• Pre-orders. Let your clients and supporters know in advance of an upcoming new product. Ask them to pay up front (even offer a slight discount) and promise to send them the finished product first before anybody else can get it. This technique is great for raising cash to pay off the final stages of a project, such as duplication and packaging. I paid the printing bill on a book project entirely from pre-orders. I'd broken even before the book was actually printed! One band discovered a unique way to both promote their act, sell some CDs, and raise cash at the same time. Ancient Future offered 500 signed and numbered limited edition preview CD-R copies for sale at $30 each through their Web site *(www.ancient-future.com)*. The money raised funded the release and promotion of the final CD to retail outlets.

• Suppliers. If you rely on other suppliers to either provide products or render services, ask for extended credit terms. For example, many companies will bill you net 30 (meaning you don't have to pay the bill for 30 days). In certain circumstances, you can negotiate for longer terms. A good tactic is to pay half-net 30 and the remaining half 30 days later. That gives you more time to raise the cash you need (or get paid for an upcoming project or gig). Alternately, some suppliers may give you a discount for paying right away, usually between 2-5 percent. It doesn't hurt to ask. If they say no, you are no worse off. If they say yes, you save some money provided you have the cash already, of course.

• Sponsorships and endorsements. If you have an established, strong customer or fan base, there may be some advertisers that want to reach the same people. You may convince them to sponsor your music business or band. In short, they pay some of your costs in exchange for promotional opportunities. The established band with a couple of dozen gigs lined up is in a better position than the novice band with nothing under their belt. Create a promotional piece that tells your band's (or music business) story including details about the people you reach. Next, setup some sponsorship opportunities and the dollar amount involved. You must explain the benefits to each sponsorship level (and you can have various levels: $100 Web banner, $1,000 sign, $10,000 summer tour sponsor, etc.). Sponsorships could include logos on the band's sign, posters, swag, and so forth, banner ads on the Web site, full-blown ads tucked in with CDs, prizes for contests, and other opportunities. With this in hand, approach possible sponsors and show the benefits of backing your band or music business. You can actively seek endorsement deals from music (and other) product sellers, too. In some cases, the equipment maker may come to you and ask you to lend your name to their product. You promote their gear in exchange for some consideration (money, free gear, etc.).

• Leasing and renting. You don't have to own everything. It may be more financially wise to rent some equipment. Your payments will be lower and only incurred as needed. Leasing is another alternative, but it can be difficult to lease small dollar amounts.

• Barter. Why use money when you can trade for what you need? Look for ways to offer your products and/or services to others who can pay you back through *their* products and services. To avoid tax time hassles, make these exchanges equal in value (called like/kind). What you give and get cancel each other out (the "income" = the "expense"). Another variation on this tactic is to trade your time for something, working part-time to earn money or help on a project.

• Credit cards. I hasten to mention this at all. I strongly feel that credit cards are never the way to fund your business or your life. They are a convenient way to purchase items you already plan on buying in the first place. And they can be a good short-term, stop-gap financial tool. They are *not* the path to building your business. Use your credit to pay for any necessary expenses when your cash is low, temporarily. However, pay the balance right away. Know and use your statement rollover and grace period to your advantage and get extra time to raise cash and pay off the debt without paying any finance charges, too. When you know you'll either be getting reimbursed from a client or that future income is coming due, this strategy can be very powerful.

• Loan. You can go down to your friendly bank and ask them to give you money. They will want a detailed business plan and/or some assets to secure the loan. If you own your home, you could use your home equity for business funds, but be careful. Lose the business; lose your house.

• Investors. There are people who invest in people and their ideas. What you must understand is these investors want something in return. That may be interest on their money or a share of future profits. Therefore, you should look at these investments as nothing more than a loan that must be repaid. One type of investment used frequently in the music industry is the speculative or spec deal.

SPECULATIVE DEALS

People in creative industries are often full of big ideas while being simultaneously plagued by a lack of money. They turn to several inventive solutions to overcome this condition, the most well-known being the spec deal. Speculative deals usually involve one party giving another party a service, either free or at considerably reduced cost, in exchange for more money in the future. In essence, one party invests in the other in the hopes of possible future gain. For example, a recording studio gives a band free recording time to produce their independent CD. The band promises to pay for the studio time when the record sells. I can hear you all shouting: "Yeah, right!"

The very nature of speculative deals make them sound as if somebody is going to get screwed. While that is often the case, it doesn't need to be that way. Doing projects on spec can be a reasonable proposition provided you take certain steps to ensure an equitable deal for all parties involved. Since a spec deal is essentially a contract, detail the deal's provisions in a formal letter of agreement. Be very clear about what exactly comprises the spec deal. What are the services being provided and how will they be used? Agree upon the total, final price and how the deal is to be paid off (e.g. one-third in advance, one-third after mastering, one-third 90 days later). Instead of putting the deal together completely free, include a small stipend up front or insist on regular progress payments. Don't forget to include the dates that apply for the deal's conditions. Also, include name, addresses, and phone numbers of the parties involved. Make two copies of this agreement, have each party sign both copies and keep one copy for their records. Here's an example:

"The Band will record, mix, and master their latest CD titled Fat Chance at NiceGuy Studios. The standard recording rate is $35 per hour. NiceGuy Studios will provide studio time at the reduced rate of $10 per hour payable upon completion of each session. The Band agrees to pay NiceGuy Studios a royalty of $1 for every Fat Chance CD sold."

Notice that making the band pay for their studio time COD means the studio gets some money at regular intervals. The band also realizes how much time they spent on the project, and having paid for the time, often perform better and use the time wisely. The royalty payment is the real speculative part of the deal. If the band sells well, the studio could receive substantial revenues, even in excess of the studio rate charges. In this case, the studio must have a strong belief in the band's potential. It would probably be prudent to find ways to help the band make additional sales as there is a vested interest in these sales for both parties.

GET EXTRA HELP WHERE YOU NEED IT

No matter how big or small your music business is or becomes, you may need a little help occasionally. Though I encourage you to handle many of your tasks yourself, especially at the beginning, your business may grow quickly, leaving you little time to manage all the details. That is the ideal time to get some help.

Here is a startup list of possible helpers: accountant, banker, booking agent, bookkeeper, computer and electronics technician, copywriter, equipment rental companies, graphic designer, insurance agent, investment adviser or financial planner, lawyer, manager, musicians and other talent, photographer, printer, pro audio and music stores, project and commercial recording studios, promotion consultant, travel agent, and more. These people can advise you on certain matters and/or pick up the slack when you get busy. What's especially attractive about getting help is you can hire and pay for these professionals as needed. There's no need to have permanent employees or partners when you can simply contract out some tasks. For example, you might have a bookkeeper come in twice a month, use an accountant at tax time, hire a lawyer to review a new contract, and use a photographer at your open house or CD release party.

Follow this simple advice when you add anyone to your team. Treat them fairly as you wish to be treated yourself. Remember everything that bugs you about being employed by someone else and vow not to repeat those errors. Train the people you hire by going through a task's steps once or twice. Then, give them the space and resources they need to do the job you've assigned in their own way. By all means give them guidelines, but then let them go to it. Don't micro or macro manage any person or project.

Hiring the best. Before you choose any helpers, examine your real needs. Don't hire a full-fledged accountant when a (less expensive) bookkeeper will suffice. Consider hiring independent contractors, other firms, and temps first *before* adding partners or full-fledged employees to your business. To locate professional services, ask for tips from friends, family, peers, and your business network. Once you get a possible name or two, contact the professional and interview them about their services, fees, and other matters. Base your final choice on the answers you get. Consider also trying any new firm or person on a trial basis. Give them a project and see how they perform. If the work is satisfactory, reward them with more projects. If they fail to deliver what you want, take your business elsewhere.

Employees. If you're hiring an employee, take out an ad (newspaper, flyer, Internet posting, etc.) and collect résumés. Carefully go through them and choose a few likely candidates. Interview these people by phone first to narrow your choices further. Set up in-person interviews with the most promising individuals. During the interview ask about skills, aspirations, salary needs, references, and so forth. Take good notes, review them carefully, and check references before you make your final choice.

HIRING A MANAGER

Before you hire someone to manage your career, manage it yourself first. You will learn a lot in the process. This valuable information and experience will serve you well for many years to come whether you continue to self-manage or hire outside help. You'll know what's involved in running a successful career and can then both ask the right questions of your manager and put in place proper oversight that protects your career and money. When choosing a manager follow the same tips for choosing help in this book. Also, be prepared to supply a manager with the following information:

- *Your experience playing and recording.*

- *The key facts about your image, credentials, and reputation.*

- *Whether you have a trademark to the band or business name.*

- *Who writes your material and who owns that copyright?*

- *What is the business form of your music business (sole-proprietor, partnership, corporation)?*

- *Provide the details about any existing contracts or agreements such as with a booking agent, publisher, record label, and so forth.*

- *Include your complete financial situation including assets, liabilities, income history, and tax returns.*

- *If you are member of any unions.*

- *Whether you have any insurance (medical, property, liability)*

Get a trusted adviser. Is there someone whose opinion you value? This may be a long-time friend, significant other, or business peer. You can also hire a consultant for assistance. Paying for advice from a knowledgeable professional may provide you with the extra push your music business needs to get to the next level. In any case, let the person(s) you choose contribute to your success. The key here is trust. There can't be baggage with this relationship and you can't worry about bruised egos and politeness. You want someone who will be candid, honest, and forthright. Use this ally as a sounding board for new ideas, a shoulder to cry on, and to help you make critical decisions.

Find a mentor. Is there somebody whom you admire already doing the music work you want to do? Perhaps you could learn from or even work directly with this person. You may be surprised at how receptive successful people can be when asked for advice or help from an up-and-comer. A mentor can fill in gaps in your knowledge with real-world experience. A mentor may even provide the emotional comfort and support you may need to weather your career's ups and downs. This kind soul can provide advice and direction, or just be an educated ear for your ideas. Your mentor can help you build the relationships with key people that are so important to success. A mentor can all at once be a teacher, confidant, and friend. Track down a mentor or two you feel might help. Write them a nice letter and see what happens. Take this person to lunch and learn what you can. Not every inquiry you make will be successful, but you might just find the help you need. You won't know unless you search and ask.

Alternately, interview the movers and shakers. Call or meet with people whom you feel have real insight into your particular part of the music industry. Ask to interview them at a time when it is convenient for their schedule. Prepare 8-10 questions and deliver them in advance of your scheduled time. When the interview begins, quickly and efficiently work through the questions to get the information you need. Also, don't be surprised when you initiate contact and the person is ready to talk right then. Have your questions ready to go in case you catch them in a particularly open and talkative mood.

Pro/Files—Dawn Maracle

Tiger Rose Productions, Austin, TX USA
www.dawnmaracle.com. - Tifhaljar@aol.com

What do you do in the music industry? Write lyrics and music/perform/vocalist/guitarist–lead–rhythm–bass/keys/sound tech/music director/teacher/management

What promotions work the best and why? Word of mouth is #1 and the best ways I have found to generate that is causing some sort of stir. It can be by way of personal appearances or by way of planting a verbal buzz, etc. Create something to talk about.

Where does the money come from? You! You must be willing to invest in yourself first. If you don't have money then you have to earn some and save some or go out in search of an investor who believes in you and your talents enough to go so far as to part with his or her own money and that is tough to do if you have nothing to show as a return on their money. So, again it is up to you to get enough together to produce your self to a level to at least have something to show a potential investor.

What were some of your past projects? Developing my logo. Staging events. Writing 22 songs for a musical. Creating material for slated CDs. Producing my groups and acts and taking them on the road. 5 different Studio projects. Acting in movies and musicals. My largest project was in 1993 when I wrote the music for a musical, The Boars Head. It was a dinner theater production in California. I not only wrote the material for the show but, I was the music director, sound stage manager and had the leading role. Talk about being wiped out at the end!

What has been your greatest achievement so far? My 4.0 in college. In the music industry it has been that I have met all of my earlier goals.

How did you do it? I never wavered or quit and I always took risks!

What lessons have you learned along the way? Listen, Listen, Listen!

Don't ever think you know it all because it will take you off track. You always need to be listening and gathering all you can from those who know the business. There is always something new to learn. This is an ever-changing industry. If you have a thin skin you better get out or toughen up! This is a very tough business and few are kind to you! YOU have to believe in yourself and your talents and don't be afraid to let others know you have what it takes!

What is your current project or next goal? I am working on trying to get a recording contract for myself, while I am currently building my Web site. I am trying to learn all that I can in order to build this site given that this is one of those ever changing technologies that I mentioned earlier that is vital to my business of music. I am also learning all that I can about my computer recording studio I have built in order to keep up with today's sound technology and produce a higher quality product.

GET ORGANIZED AND GET GOING

You need to put in place some structure for managing your daily business routine. When you learn to manage your time, business, and finances better, you will become more effective and ultimately, more successful. If you have employees or partners, you can divvy up the workload. First, of course, you need to figure out what that workload is. If you run your business by yourself, you need to prioritize tasks and set aside time to complete them.

Use a computer. We hate to admit it, but the computer is crucial to business today. You simply can't survive without its help. This is why I urge you to get a computer if you don't already have one and start using it to manage the details of your professional music industry career. Your computer can help you keep track of so many important pieces of information: To do lists, calendar, appointments, contact information, promotions, sales, general business letters, e-mail, Web site management, finances, and so much more. Here's what you need:

• A basic computer with a modem and Internet access. Buy the biggest, fastest computer you can afford. A laptop can be a good choice if you travel frequently or will work a day job while you run your music career on the side. The portable lets you take your office/business everywhere.

• Word processor. Use this for all your general correspondence and promotional material. You can also store ideas, lyrics, set lists, long-term plans, equipment inventory, invoices, and so much more.

• Contact manager. You need a way to organize all the clients, prospects, suppliers, media contacts, network members, and more. You can use a simple address book or a more sophisticated database system that offers more features, such as Act!

• Appointment calendar and to-do list. You will be busy with your career, so rely on your computer to remind you of important meetings, due dates, and tasks.

• Internet browser and e-mail program. The Internet is a tool for so much business from research and promotion to buying and selling. E-mail is *the way* to communicate so you'd better have a good program in place. If you need to manage large distribution lists (such as a newsletter mailing to your fans), consider using the freeware Pegasus Mail ***(www.pmail.com)***. This program lets you easily update the lists (adding and deleting subscribers) and suppress the "TO" field to make sure nobody sees your long list of subscribers. Neither Netscape nor Outlook give you the flexibility that Pegasus does. Alternately, Yahoo! Groups (groups.yahoo.com) is ideal for this purpose, too.

• Accounting and bookkeeping software. If you don't know your expenses or income, how can you possibly run your music business efficiently? Using a program such as Microsoft Money, Peachtree, or Quicken is a powerful financial tool. You can sort and see so much information that you'll always know where you stand.

• Anything else you consider essential. I use Softquad's HotMetal Pro for managing my Web site and several music software programs including Sonic Foundry's Acid Pro, Vegas Video, and Sound Forge, Propellerhead's Reason, T-Racks Mastering, and Easy CD creator.

I recently joined the ranks of the '"digerati" and now use a personal digital assistant (PDA). I'm not sure how I ever got along without it (a refrain I've heard from many digerati cohorts). My Palm *(www.palm.com)* and its parent program, Palm Desktop, let me manage contacts, appointments, and to-dos and synchronize these data between the Palm/Desktop. I also use a portable keyboard with the Palm, which makes taking notes and jotting down ideas a snap. The Palm and my wireless phone make the ultimate portable office. You can take your office anywhere and conduct business more efficiently. I feel this combination is simple, powerful, and more convenient than a laptop.

• You can actually manage your business information on-line from anywhere in the world through the unique service provided by Live Wire Contacts *(www.livewirecontacts.com)*. It is essentially an online contact manager, calendar, to-do, group e-mailer, and more suited to musicians.

Use a calendar. A to-do list and calendar should be your constant companions. Use them to record short- and long-term goals, projects, appointments, promotional timelines, and more. You can use a paper calendar or a computer-based equivalent. To get started, go back to your goals and grab your calendar. List the items you need to accomplish and establish specific deadlines for each. Break down larger tasks into smaller steps and assign interim deadlines for them, too. Put these to-dos in your calendar and consult it regularly, adjusting it as needed. Make sure you keep adding to the calendar, extending your new goals and deadlines into the future.

Set up a tickler system. Often you need reminders of deadlines, specific events, or actions you need to take in the future. For example, a band may need to book a festival gig six months from now when the festival planners start accepting applications. You don't want to miss that deadline. Record the information in advance on your calendar and use highlighters or Post-it flags to remind you. Or set up an alarm reminder if you use a computer scheduler or Palm, as I do.

Establish a daily routine. While I don't feel you need to be chained to your desk, it does help if you have some semblance of order to your business life. It starts first with recognizing your particular working style. Personally, I'm a slow starter who can't get into big projects until later in the day. I'm my most creative and most efficient in the afternoon and early evening. So, my mornings are ideal for mundane matters: paperwork, bookkeeping, making phone calls and responding to e-mail, processing Web and mail orders, and so on. I save the afternoon for client projects and nighttime, after my son goes to bed, for personal projects. If you are stronger in the morning and weary after three, your schedule might find you doing your best work before lunch and then attending to other matters later. A gigging band might work all weekend, take off Monday and Tuesday, and then take care of business during the remaining days. You need to discover what works for you and then stick with it.

Set up your fulfillment department. Whether product orders come through your Web site, over the phone, or through other means, you need a system for handling and shipping them. You need supplies including padded envelopes, labels, and packing tape. Depending on your volume, you may want a scale and postage meter or establish an account with another delivery service. A small three foot desk-height table coupled to a bookshelf is ideal for order processing. Store your product on the bookshelves and shipping supplies underneath the table. Process your orders the same time each day. Record the transaction, print an invoice (marked paid, if applicable), grab the products, an envelope, and pack the order. Make a trip to the post office at the end of the day or call the delivery service for pick-up.

A TYPICAL DAY AT JEFFREY'S OFFICE

9:00-12:00—Download e-mail, respond to inquiries, initiate some promotions, and check Web orders. Process orders (get product, print inserts and mailing labels, stuff envelopes). Make phone calls related to projects, promotions, or other business tasks. Begin and finish minor business tasks (research, supplier inquiry, client CD copies, update Web site, Tip of Week *newsletter, etc.)*

12:00-1:00—Handle bookkeeping and other record-keeping duties. Lunch, too.

1:00-4:30—Pursue main project for the day (composing, writing, recording or mixing, or whatever is needed).

4:30-5:00—Go through and process daily business mail (bills, checks, orders, inquiries). Visit post office to mail orders and bank to deposit checks. Check and respond to e-mail and make additional telephone calls, if needed

5:00-5:30—Wrap up project for the day. Plan the next work day's activities. File papers.

Other notes: I prefer to schedule meetings in the morning because I get more creative work done in the afternoon. Also, the workday frequently extends beyond 5:30 or picks up again after 9:00 in the evening when under tight deadlines or when I feel especially motivated or creative.

Manage your time wisely. Don't waste time on unimportant tasks. Prioritize everything. First, don't over schedule your time. Everything usually takes longer than you imagine so plan for unforeseen difficulties and interruptions. Set aside specific time for the most urgent projects, letting lesser needs go for later times. Bigger projects are best approached in steps. Work a little on them each day (that's how a CD gets finished ... or a book gets written!). Keep up with recordkeeping, bookkeeping, and filing. Twice a year, set aside an evening to clean out your office. When you are busy, stuff piles up. Ruthlessly weed out the keepers from the recyclers. Take a few minutes at the end of the day to tidy up, file, and organize and you'll be better off generally.

When you're overwhelmed with your workload, as prudent moneymaking music followers usually are, don't lose sight of what's really important. You can't bury your nose in your latest music creation at the risk of letting everything else go away. News flash: it won't go away. It will only get worse. Experience shows that trying to accomplish specific things each and every day can keep you on track and support you emotionally in times of strife. What is the single most important thing you need to do today? What's the next most important? Now, arrange your day to complete those two items *before* moving on to other business matters. This diligence will serve you well. Here are some additional tips:

• Deadlines work. Set them and meet them.

• Set aside uninterrupted time each day to take care of your most crucial work. Let your voice mail grab any calls and reply to those e-mails later.

• Keep it simple. Establish routines for processing orders, recording information, tracking your financials, returning phone calls and e-mail, and more. Tweak your approach until it works well for you.

• Set up a filing system that lets you easily store and retrieve important information such as client correspondence and contact details, project and gig notes, promotional material, contracts, and other material. Use your computer for much of this by creating folders and files and arranging them in ways that make sense to you. I suggest placing specific key words in your computer files to make searching for "lost" information fast. Of course, you need standard paper files for material you can't keep on the computer.

• Use generic responses. Chances are you'll be asked the same questions over and over. Create general e-mail and letter responses to cover your most frequent situations. Prepare these answers in advance and use them when pressed and to save time.

• Group similar tasks into blocks of time. For instance, make all your phone calls sequentially during one marathon session during the day.

• Download your e-mail several times during the day. Respond to urgent needs immediately, but let the other less pressing issues go until the time of your day that you deal with them. I find it easier to reply promptly to people because it shows that I care about their needs and it keeps the e-mail from piling up, too. Generic responses help here, too.

• Having trouble connecting with someone by phone? Either try e-mail, fax, or agree on a specific, scheduled telephone meeting. That way you can pick a time that is convenient for both of you.

• Go through your mail quickly. Shred the junk. Take care of important matters fast and deal with the remaining at their scheduled time.

• It is O.K. to say no. Don't feel guilty about declining. Heed the advice of Josh Billings: "One-half of the troubles of this life can be traced to saying yes too quickly and not saying no soon enough." If it's a client, work to help them solve their need some other way (recommend another solution for them). If the query is from someone else, tactfully explain that you are busy and then schedule a rain check.

• Take a break. You need periodic rest periods throughout your day to recharge and re-energize. Stretching and brief interludes of moderate to intense physical activity are useful, too. They clear your head and in the case of certain exercises, protect your body from repetitive stress injuries, too. Also, take more extended breaks from your music business including long weekends and regular full vacations.

VACATION SCHEDULE

Many self-employed people complain that it can be difficult, if not impossible, to get away at all. You hate to lose any work, and the mountain that usually piles up while you are away makes leaving and returning no fun at all. The best suggestion is to schedule a regular vacation time and stick to it. Don't let anything interfere with these dates and make sure you tell your best clients well in advance of this scheduled time. Mid-summer can work for some or around the winter holidays for others. Pick your two weeks and keep them sacrosanct.

Treat your clients well. Repeat business is what sustains your music career. Make client care a top priority! Your approach to daily business should be this: Make the ordinary extraordinary; put on a smile and go the extra mile. It's a simple concept that will serve you well as you deal with prospects and buyers alike. Add a personal touch to all your client contact. People prefer talking to a real person, not some impersonal "business." Your positive, enthusiastic attitude goes a long was toward making your clients feel comfortable and satisfied. Treat your clients as you expect to be treated when *you* are the buyer. When you enjoy helping people, you will be more successful. To take care of your clients, be empathetic and show you understand and care about them. Even the biggest problem can sometimes become an opportunity for future sales. But don't ignore the small complaints either. Your clients will tell you what's wrong with what you're doing. Are you listening? Finally, the more you know about the people who buy your music products and services, the better your position will be to help them, anticipate and overcome problems, and generally nurture your ongoing success.

CHAPTER 14

Cover Your Ass(ets)

"There are moments when everything goes well. Don't be frightened. It won't last."—Jules Renard

Assets are the tangible property that you own (either through your business or personally). Assets include your music gear, office equipment, real estate, savings, and so forth. These are what most people think of. Additionally, there are other assets you should be aware of and need to protect.

• Talent. How do you protect your talent? By using it and by augmenting it. Honing your craft and improving your skills regularly makes you a better music professional.

• Reputation. You will work hard to earn your reputation. Don't let it be tarnished through abuse, sloth, or other reasons. You want to protect it, grow it, keep it, and benefit from it. A reputation can be ruined in minutes and take several years to earn back. Work hard to build your reputation through maintaining your image and acquiring the credentials that support it.

• Relationships. Your network of clients, suppliers, media, mentors, and other people forms the foundation of your business. You must actively engage in feeding your contact network. As the axiom says: "It's not what you know, but rather *who* you know." You don't want to loose clients in droves, destroy profitable deals with other vendors, or forget to support the people who support you. Spend time and money to keep your business relationships amiable. Don't just take, give first, and earn what you need in return.

• Intellectual property. The songs, music and lyrics, that you create and have full or partial ownership to is another sort of property. A popular song is a revenue source for you, and you want to protect that future money as well as you possibly can. All creative works are considered property and the way to protect them is through enforcing the laws designed to secure them: copyrights, trademarks, and even patents. Copyright protects creative works including songs, books, movies, etc. Trademarks protect names, slogans, and logos. Patents protect inventions and formulas such as pharmaceuticals. Ideas are free to all. You can't prevent someone from stealing your original idea. If that were true, we wouldn't have all those sound-alike/look-alike bands today. While trademarks and copyrights last for many years, patents expire relatively quickly.

• Health and wealth. Protecting your health serves two purposes. One, you protect your ability to earn. Without being able to earn money, you lose out on your life goals. Two, you protect your other savings—money that could easily be wiped out should you suffer some major illness. Living a more healthy lifestyle and grabbing a health insurance policy are the ways you protect your health. Also, life insurance gives you peace of mind to protect your family by cushioning the blow should they lose you and you ability to support them. Disability and liability insurance are other such ways to protect your financial assets. Many people have a greater chance of becoming permanently disabled than being killed prematurely. And in this litigious society, protecting your assets through an umbrella liability policy can be a prudent move for many.

• Music products and services. While these are usually the manifestations of your talent and intellectual property, make sure that they continue to provide money to you. Protect any specialized, proprietary technology that you create. Don't let 5000 CDs and other merchandise get destroyed by a flood or fire. If you have a partner who provides a specific skill, you don't want that valuable asset to walk and become your competitor. Take the necessary steps to protect yourself in all these situations, too.

COPYRIGHT

Nothing sends a shiver of fear down a musician's spine faster than the mention of that loathsome nine-letter word. Part of the problem stems from the sheer bulk of misinformation that surrounds the magical, mystical world of copyright. Forget what you've heard or read. This is the definitive word, right here, right now. Are you ready?

Copyright protection is automatic.

It's true. Aside from recording your creative work in some way—write it down (chords, melody, and lyrics) or record it in some form (tape, CD, digital computer file, etc.)—you need do nothing else to get copyright protection for your musical works. You don't have to mail it to yourself, give it to a lawyer, or put the © on it. I repeat: copyright protection is automatic.

Who gets the copyright protection? The author of the original work is the copyright owner; the creator owns. An exception to the is rule is a "work for hire" (see below). This owner has, under Section 106 of the US Copyright Law, "the exclusive rights to do and to authorize any of the following: (1) to reproduce the copyrighted work in copies; (2) to prepare derivative works based upon the copyrighted work; (3) to distribute copies ... to the public by sale or other transfer of ownership, or by rental, lease, or lending; (4) in the case of literary, musical, dramatic ... and motion pictures and other audiovisual works, to perform the copyrighted work publicly; and (5) in the case of literary ... pictorial, graphic, or sculptural works, including the individual images of a motion picture or other audiovisual work, to display the copyrighted work publicly." These five rights are exclusive and can be enforced at the owner's discretion. It is, of course, illegal for anyone to violate any of the rights provided to the owner of the copyright. The copyright lasts for the author's life plus 70 additional years.

A work that is prepared "by an employee within the scope of his or her employment" is considered a work made for hire. The copyright ownership belongs to the employer. Work that is "commissioned for use as a contribution to a collective work" is a work made for hire only if the parties expressly agree in a written instrument signed by them. For example, if you hire a guitarist to play on your CD, you might want to have their musical contribution fall under this "work for hire" provision. They get paid for the session, but have no further claims on the composition. A talent release is all that you need in this situation.

TALENT RELEASE

Here's a sample talent release you can use. Print it on your letterhead and fill in the missing pieces. Have the person print and sign their name and write the date at the bottom of the release. Give a copy to them with their wages and file the original yourself.

For value received in the amount of $ (indicate dollar amount), *I,* (print their name here), *the undersigned, give and grant* (your company name here), *its affiliates, successors, and assigns the unqualified right, privilege, and permission to reproduce in every manner or form, publish and circulate video, sound recordings, or films of recordings of my* (indicate what they did here e. g. voice and/or musical contribution) *arising from* (indicate project title here) *and I hereby grant, assign, and transfer all my rights and interest therein. I specifically authorize and empower* (your company name here) *to cause any such videos, films, or sound recordings of my* (indicate what they did here e. g. voice and/or musical contribution), *to be copyrighted or in any other manner to be legally registered in the name of* (your company name here). *My contribution to this work shall be considered a "work made for hire," and as such, I, my heirs, executors, administrators, and assigns, hereby remise, release and discharge* (your company name here) *for and from any and all claims of any kind whatsoever on account of the use of such recordings, including, but not limited to any and all claims for damages for libel, slander, and invasion of the right of privacy. I am of lawful age and sound mind, and have read and understand this Authorization of Release.*

What about the poor man's copyright where you mail yourself a copy via registered mail? Since you are given copyright protection the instant you record your song in some way, there is absolutely no need to mail a copy by registered mail. As evidence in an infringement suit this step might help your case, but you would be much better off registering with the copyright office or giving your music to an attorney along with a dated and notarized statement of your claim to authorship.

It is not required to use the copyright symbol. If you do, either © 2003 Jeffrey P. Fisher or Copyright 2003 Jeffrey P. Fisher is the correct format. Also, you do not need to register your copyright to get the five rights mentioned above. However, there are advantages to registering your creative work with the U.S. Copyright Office. First, you establish a public record of your claim to the creative work and second, you must register before filing any infringement suit.

Contact the U.S. Copyright Office ***(www.loc.gov/copyright/)*** for more information. To register your music and lyrics, send these three elements in the same envelope: (1) A properly completed application form; (2) A nonrefundable filing fee (check for the latest dollar amount) for each application; and (3) Two copies of a non-returnable deposit of the work being registered. Mail this to: Register of Copyrights, Copyright Office, Library of Congress, Washington, DC 20559. Use form PA: to register your copyright to music (melody) and lyrics only. Use form SR: to register the actual sound recordings—the specific way the music and lyrics are conveyed.

STEALING BENEFITS NOBODY

Let me offer an editorial comment on copyright infringement and the MP3 controversies. What we really need is better education about what intellectual property rights really mean. A parent would quickly admonish a child for stealing a CD from a record store. However, that same parent may go home, rip a few tracks from the same CD, and e-mail the MP3s to a friend. This, too, is stealing. People who would never steal often unknowingly, but sometimes willfully, infringe on copyrights because they just don't understand. Buying this book gives you the right to read it; it does not give you the right to makes copies and give them away (or sell them for that matter). If these same people knew that copyright infringement is stealing, the landscape just might change. I've never downloaded copyrighted material that was pirated. The thought never crosses my mind because I know it's wrong. I don't steal from stores either for the same reason. Since there will always be pirates. Why not offer incentives for people to turn them in? Whistleblowers who report misuse and abuse by offending parties should be encouraged and rewarded in some way.

TRADEMARKS, SERVICE MARKS, AND PATENTS

You can trademark your music business name and its logo and service mark your slogan. According to the U.S. Patent and Trademark Office a trademark is "any word, name, symbol, or device, or any combination, used, or intended to be used, in commerce to identify and distinguish the goods of one manufacturer or seller from goods manufactured or sold by others." They define a service mark, as "any word, name, symbol, device, or any combination, used, or intended to be used, in commerce, to identify and distinguish the services of one provider from services provided by others."

Trademark rights last indefinitely as long as the owner continues to use the mark. Before you can stake your claim to the trademark, you must search to see if it is available. You can search at one of over seventy Patent and Trademark Depository Libraries (PTDLs) located throughout the United States or simply go on-line *(www.uspto.gov/web/menu/tm.html)*. Once you determine that a trademark is available, you can start using your trademark/service mark immediately. You can even use the ™ designation to indicate that your brand name/slogan belongs to you.

Registering your trademark gives you several advantages including notice to the public of your claim of ownership of the mark, a legal presumption of ownership nationwide, and the exclusive right to use the mark on or in connection with the goods or services set forth in the registration. Trademark registration lasts for 10 years and is renewable in 10-year increments. Once registering your trademark, you can use the circle R designation: ®. You may access the trademark forms, plus information about applying for a trademark, at the U.S. Patent and Trademark Office Web site *(www.uspto.gov)*.

Patents. If you invent something, you may want to protect it with a patent. Since this is rare in the music industry, we'll save valuable space and just direct you to the U.S. Patent and Trademark Office Web site *(www.uspto.gov)* for further study.

MEDICAL INSURANCE

Since *you* are your business, protecting the health of your most valuable asset is crucial. A health insurance policy can be expensive, but don't neglect your need for one. It's a bit of a game, really. You're hoping that you'll use your insurance while the insurance carrier is hoping you won't. Play the game! Here in the US, we must find our own health care coverage (other countries, such as Canada, provide health care for their citizens). Before purchasing your own policy, look for alternatives. Can you join a group policy in some way such as through a trade association, union, or other group with whom you belong? For example, NAMM *(www.namm.com)*, the International Music Products Association, offers access to a group policy to its members. Can you get on a working spouse's policy? If you've exhausted all those possibilities, you'll need to consider grabbing your own health insurance coverage.

The Internet makes researching this issue a snap. You can wade through the myriad of options, compare policies, and more. Try *www.ehealthinsurance.com* for starters. Another source for insurance—property, liability, and health—specifically for musicians is *www.musicproinsurance.com.*

Typically, you can choose among a major medical policy that covers most medical expenses once you meet certain criteria, HMO and PPO choices, or a basic catastrophic policy that may only cover emergencies and surgery. With only basic coverage you will have to pay for routine care out of your own pocket, but a major illness should be covered. You must weigh the potential savings with the downside of having routine care or several mild illnesses eating up your savings. Here are the key questions you need answered when you consider a health care plan.

What is the policy type? Choices include major medical, catastrophic, HMO, PPO, or other hybrids. Major medical policies let you choose your doctors and hospitals (and are therefore the most costly policies). HMO and PPO policies use networks of doctors and hospitals, and you must choose from approved practitioners to get coverage. You will pay more from your own pocket for any out-of-network doctors you use. Make sure you are comfortable with the choices given to you before choosing an HMO or PPO policy. For example, your PPO coverage may be limited to your local health care providers. If you travel frequently, you risk having to use out of network services that may cost you significantly more.

Also note, joining some HMOs and PPOs can lower the costs you are still required to pay. These policies usually have negotiated rates with in-network providers that save you money even when you are still under your deductible. For instance, the fees for a family member's routine care were reduced significantly by staying in the network. After these savings, the remaining amount was applied to our deductible, and subsequently paid by me. Without the policy, I would have paid 85 percent more for the *same* routine medical care. That's a good deal.

What is the premium? This is the money you pay to get the coverage described in your policy. The premium is based on the type of policy, the deductible, the co-pay amounts, and what the policy includes. You generally have to pay extra for certain coverage, such as maternity. Self-employed business owners do not get 100 percent of their medical insurance premiums deducted on their 1040 tax form until the 2003 tax year. They are 100 percent deductible on Schedule A—Itemized Deductions, if you exceed the restrictions.

What is the deductible? You must pay for all your initial medical costs from your own pocket before your insurance carrier contributes. This amount is called the deductible and is usually a yearly fee. Higher deductibles can translate to lower premiums. You may find that the premium difference between a $500 deductible and a $1000 one is negligible. While you may save on your premium with the higher deductible, you risk paying more should you incur substantial expenses. Do the math to be sure. If you insure more than one person under the policy, each person must meet their *own* deductible with a family deductible limit usually equal to three times an individual's amount.

Co-pay percentage or amount? Even after you meet the deductible, you are still responsible for sharing some of your medical costs. Typically, insurance picks up 80 percent while you cover the remaining amount. HMOs and PPOs often have other co-pay requirements outside of your deductible and out-of-pocket contributions. For instance, I pay $30 for every doctor office visit both before *and* after my deductible gets met.

What is the total out-of-pocket limit? This is the maximum amount of money that you pay in any given policy term (including your deductible and your co-pay amounts). After you reach this limit, your insurance carrier then pays 100 percent of your additional medical expenses. Also, most policies enforce a lifetime limit on the total amount they'll pay for you, usually in the millions.

What is covered in the policy? Your insurance carrier will send you a detailed listing of all that your policy includes. Read this carefully. It will indicate any procedures that are excluded, too. You may also find limitations on certain aspects of your coverage as well. If you don't understand what you read, call the insurance provider and ask for an explanation. And if you don't like what you discover, consider another policy.

Are prescription drugs covered? Pharmaceuticals can be costly. A single bout of bronchitis cost me nearly $200 for medicine (not to mention the doctor visit). If your policy costs just a little more to get drug coverage, it might be prudent to pay the extra fee. You'll probably save money in the long run.

Keep good records and monitor your bills carefully. Because medical expenses, including the premiums you pay for insurance, are tax deductible, it's prudent to keep track of them. Set up a three-ring binder to hold the paperwork and track your expenses on a few sheets of paper you keep in the binder. Alternately, use a computer software program to track your medical expenses. Most importantly, keep an eagle eye on your medical bills. Compare the statements you get from doctors, hospitals, and labs and compare them to the statements from your insurance carrier. Look for errors and get them corrected when you find them. I'd say 1 in every 5 of my medical bills has an error of some kind. These errors work out in your favor in the majority. Take the time to make sure you pay only the correct amounts. It's worth it, believe me.

LEAD A HEALTHY LIFESTYLE

Protecting your health is made simpler when you take steps to stay healthy in the first place. One significant concept in Taoist thought is the concept of Chi, *or life energy. Taoists believe that* Chi *is the basic energy source in nature. Cultivating* Chi *keeps a person healthy. Whether you subscribe to this belief or not, you can still benefit from its basic tenets. According to author Laurence Boldt in his groundbreaking book,* The Tao of Abundance, *there are ten simple ways to cultivate* Chi:

• *Be cheerful. Happiness is the best contagion. Do your part to spread some sunshine around. Happy people live longer and enjoy life more, too.*

• *Breathe. Shallow breathing is not nearly as effective as regular, good deep breathing. Practice inhaling deeply and less often and experience the calming effect it has on you. Deep breathing improves circulation, reduces stress, and better nourishes your blood and vital organs.*

• *Move your body. You must exercise regularly. Stretch every day and/or practice Yoga or Tai Chi. Also, get your heart rate up an least three times a week for 20 minutes through vigorous activities such as aerobics, walking, running, cycling, etc.*

• *Rest your body. We all need to replenish our bodies and our minds. The right amount of restful sleep will make you more energetic and creative. Short power naps work for some people, too.*

• *Master your emotions. Don't let your anger, disappointment, or fears fester inside you. Find ways to diminish these harmful feelings. Talking them out either informally with good friends or through professional therapy are sure-fire ways to get a grip.*

• *Meditate. You don't have to practice this art formally because you can just set aside some quiet time to contemplate. Find a comfortable place to sit, empty your mind of nagging interruptions, and just focus on a single thought or idea. I'm reminded of a quote: "Some times I sits and think and some times I just sits."*

• *Simplify. Clutter is a nuisance that has a way of physically building up in our lives as we acquire more possessions and mentally overtaking our lives when we take on more responsibilities. Too many distractions and complications create stress you can do without. If you have too many demands on your life, consider sacrificing the non-essentials. Take time to clear out the junk that fills your home and office, too. Focus on only what's most important to you and trust yourself to let the other stuff go.*

• *Spend time in nature. There is an adventure in nearly every nook and cranny of our physical world. Go outside and soak up your surroundings while you marvel at the wonders. Our Earth is paradoxically complex and elegantly simple. For example, animals breathe in oxygen and give off carbon dioxide while plants take in the carbon dioxide and give off oxygen. Beautiful.*

• *Eat well. The food pyramid makes sense. If you follow it 80-90 percent of your days, you'll have more energy and be healthier. The other 10 percent-20 percent can satisfy your cravings when you deviate from the right eating road.*

• *Cultivate an awareness of your surroundings. This is your wake-up call to, well, wake up! Pay attention to what is happening around you and be part of it. Put your energy in the moment and don't dwell in the past or worry about the future. In the poignant words of* Caddyshack*: "Be the ball, Danny."*

PROPERTY INSURANCE

You need to protect the physical property that you own, too. If you consider your gear personal property, your homeowner's or renter's insurance policy should protect it. Ask your insurance carrier to be sure. Equipment you use strictly for your music business may not be protected by that same personal property insurance policy. Your insurance carrier may require you to take out a special rider with that policy, and pay an additional premium. You may have to buy a separate policy to protect your business assets instead. Consider liability insurance to protect you in the event someone suffers an accident at your workplace (even if that's your home office), too. To make sure these issues meet your needs, make an appointment with your insurance carrier to go over the specifics of your situation in detail. Ask and get answers to these questions:

What perils are excluded? You need to be sure that you aren't taking any unnecessary risks. Make sure that the perils you may face (fire, water, theft, and natural disaster) are covered. Acts of war are never covered. Of course, the chances of a war wiping out your equipment are rare. And even if it did happen, you'd probably have a lot more to worry about besides the loss of your gear.

When and where is the coverage effective? What happens if you cover only home use and something gets stolen from your car on the way to a gig?

What is the premium? This is the amount you pay for a certain level of coverage in dollars. Make sure the coverage dollar amount you choose accurately reflects the gear you have or will replace. Don't pay for coverage you don't need, but don't risk coming up short either.

What is the deductible? This is the minimum loss you must have before the insurance kicks in. For example, if you have a $250 deductible and suffer a $1000 loss, upon approval of the claim, the insurance company will send you a check for $750. You are responsible for the first $250. This next point is really important: Unlike medical deductibles which accrue during the year, loss policies are *per incident.* You will pay the deductible for *each* claim that you make. If gear keeps disappearing, and you send in multiple claims during the year, it could end up costing you more than you planned.

What are the policy limits? This is usually a total dollar amount per occurrence. Is this enough to cover you in the event of total disaster? Also, does the policy pay replacement cost or cash value? Replacement cost pays you the amount to fully replace the item lost while the cash value pays only the item's current market value. If your synth gets ripped, and you choose to replace it, you will get the amount needed to buy a new, comparable synth that is "like kind and value" (even if it costs more than the original purchase). Make sure you have a clear understanding of what your policy provides. At cash value you'd probably receive only 10-20 percent of the original price you paid. Some policies say that if you choose not to replace the item you will only get the cash value. One of my clients suffered a theft loss and after spending countless hours totaling up the replacement value of the stolen items, they decided not to replace them. They were surprised when the insurance settlement came, as it had the far, far lower cash value figures instead of the anticipated replacement numbers.

How are claims settled? You want details about what you must do to expedite approval. For example, if an item gets stolen, does the insurance carrier require a police report?

What documentation do you need? Do what the insurance carrier suggests. This will include keeping a record of your property. Take an inventory of all that you own and use for your music business. During the inventory, document the name, model number, serial number, original purchase price, and purchase date of every piece of gear (computer software, too). Store this document off-site and give a copy to your insurance agent for your file. This inventory document helps you better file a claim should you suffer a loss. For gear that appreciates in value, such as vintage musical equipment, have regular appraisals and share the values with your insurance company. Along with the written inventory record, take photographs or videotape your gear, too. Store this additional evidence off-site (at a relative or in a safety deposit box).

OTHER INSURANCE

Consider these other insurance options to further protect your music industry career.

Auto insurance. If you use a vehicle for your music business, make sure you insure it adequately. If you use your car or van both for business and personal use, check with your insurance carrier to make sure you have the correct coverage, too. The same issues for property insurance (as discussed above) generally apply for vehicle insurance. Make sure you read and understand your policy fully.

Disability insurance. What would you do if you lost your ability to work either for a short-time or permanently? A disability insurance policy pays some of your lost income. However, it can take six months or more to start paying after your disability claim gets approved. This means you will need savings to hold you over during the interim. Typical policies pay 60-70 percent of the income you had at the time you were disabled. Because it is more likely that you may suffer a disability over any other type of peril, this insurance is worth checking into, though it can be expensive. Also note that Social Security will kick in if you are declared permanently disabled before you reach retirement age, but the money paid to you will be small.

Umbrella liability insurance. If you have substantial assets (home, other property, savings, and so forth) you should consider protecting them from lawsuits arising out of your work. Your assets can be liquidated to satisfy a settlement should you lose in court. A liability policy can pay that settlement for you. The umbrella designation simply means it can cover a variety of liability issues which will be detailed in the policy underwritten by the insurance carrier you chose. The premium is based on the amount of coverage you purchase, a million dollars, for instance.

Life insurance. This policy pays your beneficiaries a lump sum settlement when you die. The premium you pay for coverage is based on the amount of the death benefit, your age, and a few other factors. If you have other people who depend on your income, such as children, then you should consider a policy to provide for their future.

CONTRACTS

A contract protects the parties involved in business transactions. The music business is filled with contracts, and you'd better become adept at understanding them. Contracts can vary in the extremes, ranging from a verbal agreement, with or without a handshake, to simple client purchase orders, up to full blown forays into the land of legal mumbo-jumbo. No matter what the eventual form, all contracts share these essentials.

• Who the contract is for (you and your client, you and the record label, etc.)

• What you must do to satisfy the terms of the contract (this details the specific product(s) and/or service(s) that will be delivered).

• When you must do it by (the deadline).

• How much you get paid when you do it.

• What will happen if you don't do it.

• Who owns the rights (copyright, trademark, etc.) to the work you do.

• Any other standard bits such amendment procedures, dispute settlements, and so forth.

Don't be intimidated by the lofty wording in most contracts. The intent is to write the terms with precision and avoid misinterpretations. This can make contracts difficult to read, but easy to comprehend. The best advice: if you don't understand something, get it explained until you do. Hire an attorney to review major contracts and perhaps a trusted business advisor to look over simple terms. Never be afraid to make changes to a contract or request different terms. I've asked, and been granted, clauses to be changed or deleted, for more money, and for other terms to be adjusted. These negotiations need not be contentious. Most are amiable with both parties getting satisfactory win-win terms.

Keep any contracts that you personally use simple and to the point. Follow the basic format above and draft a simple letter to cover most of your contractual situations. People who hire you may have their own contracts, most of which are standard fare that you can be relatively confident are equitable (or the best deal you can reasonably expect). Get them reviewed before you sign, though.

EXAMPLE CONTRACT FOR PLAYING

If your act lands a gig, it may be prudent to have the venue sign a contract that you prepare. Print this on your letterhead and include these parts.

• *Venue name and contact information*

• Performance date and length (how many sets of what duration)

• The fee for the performance and its terms. Possible terms might be a single flat fee, a flat fee plus the door (all or percentage), the door only, or other terms. If the fee is based on the door, mention the ticket price or cover charge and the venue's capacity to further clarify the band's fee. Some venues may request a cut of merchandise sales, say 10 percent. Be sure to include these terms in this section.

• Amount of a deposit and when it is due (upon signing the agreement).

• Remaining amount and when it is due (at the end of the second set, for instance).

• Cancellation terms. Include a part that releases the band and the venue from the contract should some "act of nature" interfere with the planned performance. Indicate other cancellation terms, by the band and the venue and any fees involved. For example, if the venue cancels the gig less than 48 hours in advance, the band keeps the deposit.

• Promotion. Detail the responsibilities of both the band and the venue for promoting and advertising including methods and dollar amounts.

• Make two copies of such an agreement and have both the band and the venue sign each copy. They keep one and you keep the other. If you will be gigging a lot, consider having an attorney draft a suitable contract for you.

EXAMPLE BOOKING AGENT AGREEMENT

In such an agreement include the following:

• Contact information
• Duties of the booking agent
• Term of the agreement (one year)
• Territory (e. g. northern Illinois, southern Wisconsin, and northwestern Indiana)
• Fee (10 percent-15 percent of bookings)
• Termination guidelines to dissolve the contract

TYPICAL RECORDING CONTRACT

Whether you choose to run your own label or sign with one, these are the customary parts included in the recording contract.

- *Contact information of all parties involved, artist and label.*

- *Details of the contracted project, e.g. a recording. What is required by the artist and what the label must do to release it. If the label fails to release the recording by a certain date, certain rights should revert back to the artist.*

- *Royalty information. Typical royalties fall between 10-15 percent of the retail price. The contract will mention the amount of the advance and detail deductions against those royalties. Labels hold back 10 percent for breakage and returns. The artist must also pay for packaging costs which is another 10-25 percent deducted from their royalties. The artists generally pay all recording costs. The artist also may pay up to 75 percent of music video costs. Contracts also mention the payment terms (quarterly, for instance) and the accounting practices used by the label. Artists get certain rights to examine the label's books, too.*

- *Contract term. The contract may last for a specific time frame or number of recordings. There is usually an option clause for the label to renew this term under similar provisions.*

- *Details about the promotional commitment from the label. What the label will provide for tour support is often included, too.*

- *Controlled compositions clause. Labels prefer to pay only 75 percent of statutory mechanical fees for compositions written by the artist themselves. The label keeps the other 25 percent and the remaining 75 percent gets split between writer(s) and publisher(s).*

- *Other standard legal clauses such as indemnification, dissolution, dispute policies, and so forth.*

SET YOUR PRICE AND GET IT

How much should you charge for your music products and services? "When the well's dry, we know the worth of water," said Benjamin Franklin. In the real world, discover what other people are charging for similar circumstances. Call your competition and ask. Visit Web sites and dig up fees. Find out what the clubs are paying from bands that are playing there. Also, find out what the bands are charging for indie CDs and swag. Use industry surveys to know how much to charge for your next TV soundtrack or jingle. In short, you need to research carefully to get an idea of what any given product or service is worth. The best advice is this: You must charge the most you can and keep your costs at a minimum to make the most money from your music products and services!

Watch the specific expenses as they relate to a project and price accordingly. Typical expense based pricing ranges from 2 to 8 times your cost. If it costs you $2 to make a CD, you should charge from $4 to $16 for it. Alternately, use your costs to simply project your break-even level. If you spend $4500 to make a CD, and your research says that $15 is the right price, then you must sell 300 CDs to break-even. Sales beyond this level puts profit on your pocket.

Knowing your costs also helps you offer discounts and other special deals when circumstances arise. You don't want to risk selling at an unprofitable level. Make sure you know what you paid before you decide what to charge.

Services. These are by far the most difficult to price. The only way to effectively choose the right price is through experience. The more work you do, the better idea you'll get about what other people are willing to pay. You have to test your pricing, and you may lose a few gigs because your price is either too high (expensive) or too low (lack of experience). Do the detective work and set your fees. Try it out on a few clients and make adjustments. People also have a specific budgets and you must decide if you can do the work involved for the amount of money being offered. Sometimes the cash is insulting. Other times it's adequate. Rarely is it generous.

Service providers should bid by the project, but base that fee on your hourly or daily rate that you determine you want to make. Also, add in any additional expenses you expect to incur. How do you determine your hourly rate? First, decide on an annual income that you feel will support your chosen lifestyle. Refer back to your goals to come up with the figure. Let's say your number is $50,000. There are about 2000 hours available each year to work. However, you will spend time promoting your business, managing it, and so forth. Plan on billing only about half your time, say 1000 hours. Your hourly rate would be $50 an hour, and your daily rate, $400 (50,000 / 1000 = 50 x 8 = 400).

If it takes you two days to complete a client project, you'd charge $800. This fee would only cover your time. Any other expenses (people, places, and material) that you incurred would be added to your bill with a markup between 15-40 percent. For example, if a studio charges you $100 to master a client's mix, charge your client between $115-140 on top of your $800 fee. This is a simplified approach to pricing services, but nevertheless a good starting point. If you are a booking agent, for example, and the average booking brings you $200. You need to make 250 bookings to meet your $50,000 goal (about 5 a week).

It is also a good practice to set a minimum fee for the service work you do. Don't agree to work unless this minimum is met. Performers should check the minimum wage established by the musician's union in your area as a guideline. Two hours might be a minimum booking at your project studio while a composer might charge at least a half-day's work for any soundtrack or jingle work. Small projects and clients-who-cry-poor-house can really tax your resources without any real remuneration. You spend a lot of time and get very little money. Instead use your minimum fee as a way to weed out the nickel and dime clients and instead get more lucrative business.

WORK FOR FREE

You deserve to be paid for the work you do. Never work for free. That said, there is an exception. If you are young and green, consider working for free (or charge a minuscule, token fee) to establish your track record and generate some credentials. Make sure you can leverage the free work into bigger and better things. Get a testimonial and letter of recommendation from the client. Demand the client be a positive business reference when other prospects ask for one. Secure a big credit (on the CD, on-screen, etc.). Promote your success ruthlessly (news releases, Web, newsletter, ads, and other promotions). In other words, instead of getting cash for your work, barter for other goodies that will help you be more successful in the future. Also note, one or two free gigs should be all it takes to get up and running. After that, start charging!

Products. Several elements go into pricing products. Unless you have something unique to sell, chances are you'll be selling similar items typical of the music industry (CDs, T-shirts, instruments, etc.). The prices for these items are generally the same. You're not going to get $20 for your indie CD when the average cost is under $15. What goes into pricing a product? You must do this analysis for every product you produce.

• Costs. These costs include your direct costs of making the product such as recording, mixing, mastering, duplicating, packaging, promoting, and distributing a CD. The indirect costs of managing a product is your business overhead.

• Wholesale price. This is the price you charge wholesalers and distributors. This price is usually between 50-65 percent of the retail price.

• Short discount price. You may sell your product to retailers or other dealers using simple short discounts, say 15 percent off the retail price. They keep this as their commission on the sale.

• Commission price. I break this out because you may have associations with on-line retailers who take unusual amounts when selling. Amazon.com takes 55 percent while a credit card processing service may take 9 percent of the sales you generate.

• Retail price. This is the price charged by retailers, including you when you sell direct. Stores that buy will usually pay 40-50 percent of this price.

• On a $15 CD. Wholesaler pays $6-7.50; Short discount pays $12; Commission price $13.65; Retail $7.50 to 9.00.

You can clearly see that the wholesaler makes money by buying at a steep discount before selling to the retailer. If the wholesaler buys from you for 50 percent off and sells to the retailer for 40 percent off, they make 10 percent (or $1.50 in our example). The retailer makes $6 and you make $7.50. However, you must pay all your direct costs out of the $7.50. If the CD costs you $4 each, you only make $3.50 per sale in this example. It would take 1000 units to make $3500. Not bad money, but when you consider how hard it is to move 1000 units for most independent bands, well, you can see that this is a losing proposition. Lowering your costs and raising your price are ways to overcome this.

MELOMANIA VS. ATMOSPHERICS

I produce my music library in-house. Although there were some costs to produce the thing, these were mostly general overhead costs—computer and software used for other business purposes. So, making the library was essentially free. The direct cost is what I pay to burn the CDs, package, and mail them, about $5.00. All are sold by me, so the only fee is what I get charged to process on-line orders (9 percent). I sell the CDs for $99 and net $85.09. Now sales of only 50 CDs brings in over $4254. Even with a smaller market that buys production library music, you can clearly see how small numbers can create a profitable venture. Granted, this is a high fee, low cost example ... but that fits the Moneymaking Music philosophy snugly. Now, contrast this example to my Atmospherics *CD which I sell for $14.95. It costs me roughly $3.95 to make and mail them, and I net $11. Selling 50 copies of this regular music release brings in just $550.*

CHAPTER 15

Manage Your Music Money

"Money is like a sixth sense without which you cannot make a complete use of the other five." — Sumerset Maugham

When it comes to managing your music money, you have essentially three duties:

• Collect income from the music products and services that you sell.

• Pay expenses related to the music products and services that you sell.

• Keep records of the income you get and expenses you pay. These records both keep you informed of your true financial picture and are necessary for income tax purposes.

INCOME – EXPENSES = PROFIT

This deceptively simple equation is at the base of the moneymaking music philosophy. You must know and understand the two key parts: make more *and* spend less. These two work best in tandem. If you want to make more money, you need to sell more music products and services. Additionally, you will keep more money when you cut your expenses. Making more and spending less creates a substantial difference—your profit! Saving and investing your profits can also generate additional income for you now and in the future. Saving means preserving cash for other things—investing in your business, saving for rainy day goals, and even for your eventual retirement. Most importantly, having money in reserve gives you the freedom to make less and spend more when the mood, opportunity, or necessity demands it.

While the vast majority of this book centers on making more

money with your musical endeavors, now is the time to focus on *keeping* more of what you do make. It's no good to make $1000 doing something if it costs you $999 to get there. However, reducing the $999 expense to just $900 gives you an 11 percent return, that's better than the stock market's historical average. What this clearly shows is that it is often far, far easier to reduce expenses rather than increase your income projections, especially in an unknown area. Anything you can do to control costs can significantly affect the money you do make and your ultimate return on investment.

ROI WHO?

It costs money to make money. You earn your income by spending money to operate your music business. Look at these expenses as your investment in your business and carefully monitor them. To calculate your return on that investment, subtract your expenses from your income to get your profit. Divide your profit by those same expenses. Multiply the result by 100 to get your ROI percentage.

$100–90 = 10/90 = .11 x 100 = 11.11 percent. Every dollar you spend brings in $1.11.

$100–10 = 90/10 = 9 x 100 = 900 percent! Every dollar you spend brings in $10.

What these two extremes clearly show is that even without increasing revenues, you can still significantly alter your return by carefully controlling your expenses.

Another useful number is your average order size. How much money does a client typically spend? To calculate the average order size, divide your sales dollars by the number of transactions.

2000/100 = $20.

In this example, the average sale is $20. If you need $400, you need to find 20 new clients or get less clients to spend more money when they do buy.

TAKE CARE OF THE MONEY ISSUE

Just as you had to legally setup your business, you need to put in place some basic financial strategies to maintain your legitimacy.

Start a business checking account. A business account is somewhat different from a personal checking account. Checks you receive must be deposited in full (you can't get cash back). Banks usually impose a monthly service fee and charge for each transaction (checks you write or deposit), too. These fees can add up substantially, so it pays to shop around. Go to the banks in your area and inquire about business accounts. Look for advertised or new account specials. For example, recently a new bank opened down the street with a free-for-life new business account promotion. I switched from an account where I was paying nearly $10 a month to the totally free account. The 15 minutes it took to set-up the new account saves me $120 or more per year. Plus, this bank is closer than the last.

You'll need your business papers (DBA, tax ID, etc.) when you open the account. The bank will try to sell you business checks and a rubber stamp (for endorsing the backs of checks for deposit). Their fees are usually way too high. Instead, tactfully decline and order your checks and stamp online ***(www.designerchecks.com*** and ***www.stampman.com)***.

Deposit all your business income into that account. Though your account statement will reflect your total deposits, you'll probably want to track your income a little more meticulously (more below). Deposit any cash you receive from sales into your account, too. For checks that you receive, endorse them with your rubber stamp and deposit them into the account. You can also accept direct deposit money transfers (called ACH transactions) in the account. For example, many credit card processing services send online earnings direct to your business checking account.

Pay all your music-business related expenses using checks drawn on that same account. This simplifies your bookkeeping by giving you a documented paper trail of all your business purchases. Note what the expense was in the memo section of every check you write.

Additionally, apply for a new or designate an existing credit card for business purposes. You'll need it for online purchases and when traveling. Treat this card as a charge card and pay the balance on time and in full each month.

Set up a basic bookkeeping system. You need accurate records of both your income and expenses. Keep your receipts, business checking account statements, credit card statements, and canceled checks as evidence of these business transactions. You also need to document your income and expenses in some way (on paper or with software). You will need this documentation to support your tax records. Therefore, the best method for tracking your money is by setting up categories for both income sources and expenses.

You will earn income through a variety of methods, including performing, product sales, royalties, composition services, production services, teaching, and others ways that apply to your situation. While it is tempting to lump all your income into a single category, it is better to split your income among your primary activities. This way you can plainly see where your money comes from and therefore, where to best spend your resources. You can concentrate on profitable ventures and let the unprofitable ones slide. For example, a solo artist may have three main categories: playing, CD sales, and royalties. If the artist has more than one CD, she might choose to subdivide the CD revenue to better track which CDs sell better. She may also decide to break her royalties down to mechanical, performance, and sheet music groups.

For your expenses, use the categories found on the Schedule C tax form. As with your income sources, you may want to split these rather broad categories into smaller sub-categories. You may even wish to attribute certain expenses to specific income. For example, the solo artist from above might want to track her expenses by performance because some gigs may be more profitable than others. You may not need all these categories; pick only those that apply to your situation.

• Cost of goods sold (see next chapter)

• Advertising. This is the money you spend promoting your music business. You could include gifts you give to clients here, limited to $25 each.

• Car and truck expenses (see next chapter)

• Commissions, fees. Record what you pay independent contractors and other suppliers to deliver services to your music business. If you pay an independent contractor more than $600 in a year, you must file a 1099 with the IRS (and give a copy to the contractor) that indicates the amount you paid. The independent contractor is responsible for reporting the income and paying any taxes on that income. Union dues or fees for any associations you belong to could also be recorded here.

• Depreciation and section 179 expense deduction (see next chapter)

• Insurance (other than health). This would include separate business property and liability insurance. If you take the home-office deduction, property insurance may be reported there instead.

• Interest mortgage, other. Any interest you pay strictly on business loans. For the home-office deduction, your mortgage interest would be reported on that form, *not* here.

• Legal and professional. Fees paid to attorneys, accountants, tax advisors, managers, and so forth.

• Office expense. Expenses incurred to operate your office, such as your postage/shipping, telephone.

• Rent/lease (vehicles, other business property). Two separate lines for recording and deducting these payments should they apply to you. Recording studio rental charges could go under rent other business property (or it could be a cost of goods sold if used for CD production)

• Repairs and maintenance. Fix your gear used for business and deduct that expense here.

• Supplies. Strings, sheet music, paper, pens, blank CDs, etc.

• Taxes and licenses. Sales tax, business license, and other fees, but *not* income or self-employment taxes (they are computed and reported elsewhere). You should track them, though.

• Travel expenses. Airfare, lodging, car/van rental, and so forth.

• Meals and Entertainment. Only half the dollar amount of these expenses can be deducted.

• Utilities. If you use the home-office deduction, your utilities would be reported with that, *not* here.

• Wages, salaries. What you pay to employees. You wouldn't really record your own wages here unless you were a corporation. As a partnership or sole-proprietor, any profit that's left over *after* you pay your expenses become your wages.

• Other. Education expenses, for instance.

• Expenses for business use of your home (see next chapter)

PAY YOURSELF

Should sole proprietors and partnerships take a regular draw from the business as wages? You can choose to siphon a set amount from your business account as your salary, leaving the rest to pay regular bills. Any money that's left over at the end of the year would also be your wages because any business profit is income in this situation. The problem with taking a regular wage is it will probably be your largest expense, and you might not have the money each month. Conversely, your wage draw may be too small. You will then accrue a substantial non-interest bearing balance (business checking accounts do not earn interest). My suggestion is this: instead of a regular wage, keep enough money in the business checking account to cover upcoming expenses, plus a small contingency to cover unexpected bills, and then withdraw the remaining amount as your pay. Move this money to your personal account(s) where you can invest and/or earn interest on the money. Your salary may fluctuate wildly, which is another reason to plan carefully and monitor your finances regularly.

EZ WAY

If your humble music business has less than $2,500 in expenses, you can use the IRS Schedule C-EZ. It has essentially three lines: gross receipts, total expenses, net profit. For part-time, small ventures, and start-ups this is the way to go. Just because the form is short doesn't mean you can't track your income and expenses in greater detail, though. You'll want to get in the habit of following the regular Schedule C categories because you'll use them as your business grows.

Because documentation is so important, adapt this method to your situation. Go to the store and pick up the following basic supplies:

• 9" x 12" clasp envelopes. You will need one envelope for each income and expense category. You can use file folders, but envelopes work better and keep papers from falling out.

- Large three-ring binder with dividers
- Ledger paper or regular college ruled paper
- 3-hole punch, stapler, and pen

With these supplies, you can set up and run your bookkeeping and filing system. First, write your income and expense categories on the envelopes, one category each. Designate an abbreviation for each category. Use single letter abbreviations for expenses and two-letter abbreviations for income to make coding your receipts easier ('A' for advertising and 'PL' for playing gigs, for example). Put this abbreviation on the envelope, too. Also, write the tax year on each envelope (e.g. 2003) to keep your documentation separate from subsequent years. Create two more envelopes, one to hold your business account bank statements and another for your credit card statements. When you're done, you should have a stack of empty envelopes that correspond to the income and expense categories you determined that applied to you.

ACCOUNT ACCOUNTING

Here are the accounts or category codes I use to manage my company's finances.

Income account categories: Live and session performances (LS), composing and arranging scores and jingles (SJ), studio audio production (SA), on-hold production (OH), multimedia production (SM), consulting services (CS), music library sales (ML), record sales (CD), writing (WB), equipment sales or rental (ES), and lessons and teaching (LT).

Expense categories: Auto expenses (A), business meals and entertainment (B), postage and shipping (S), advertising (V), printing (P), musical equipment and supplies (M), office supplies (O), travel expenses (T), phone (H), equipment or studio rental (E), fees paid to talent (F), legal and accounting fees (X), and cost of equipment over $200 (D).

Next, create a ledger to record your transactions. Punch a dozen sheets of paper and put them in the binder. Write the tax year on the top of each page and number them sequentially. Create columns across the page including date, description, category, amount, check or invoice number, and mileage. You can divide the amount column into two separate columns, one for income and the other for expenses, if you want. Alternately, keep the single amount column and put parenthesis around expenses—($50)—to further help differentiate them from income. When you are finished, your ledger should look something like this:

Date	Description	Category	Amount	Invoice/Check #	Mileage

Punch a few more sheets and place them after a divider in the binder. Create columns across this page including date, client name, invoice number, amount, and due date. This section is your Accounts Receivable (A/R). It helps you keep track of money that is owed to you by clients to whom you extend credit. When you see a due date approaching, call the client and remind her the bill is due. When clients miss a due date, contact them and demand payment. Don't let these uncollected amounts go. Get tough. Also, use your A/R to remind you of money due to you in the future, such as royalties.

Set up two more sections in the binder using dividers. Punch some paper and use a separate sheet for each expense and income category, coding them accordingly. Use these pages to keep running totals of all your transactions by category. The best time to do this is monthly, transferring the amounts from the main ledger to the corresponding totals. This way you can monitor your income and expenses regularly.

Keep your books. When you incur an expense, write the information in the ledger. Be sure to include the date, a description of the expense, its category, the amount, the check number you used, and any mileage you incurred to pay the expense (more on car/truck expenses in the next chapter). Write the category code in the memo section of the check you write and also on the receipt you get from the purchase. File this receipt in the corresponding envelope (advertising expense in the 'A' envelope, for instance). If you pay an expense by credit card, put 'CC' in the check number ledger column. Code and file the receipt in the proper envelope.

When you make a sale, print an invoice or receipt. Invoices are ideal when you perform a service while receipts are better for product sales. Print invoices on your letterhead. You can pick up receipt books at any office supply store. Get the carbonless two-ply kind so you can give your buyer a copy and keep the other one for yourself. Code the invoice or receipt with the income category to which it belongs. Record the transaction details in the ledger. If this is a cash sale, file the receipt copy in the proper envelope, and deposit the money in your business account. If the buyer pays by check, either make a copy of the check and staple it to your receipt copy or write the check number on the receipt and file this in the proper envelope. Deposit the checks into your account. If you accept credit cards with your own merchant account, staple your CC transaction copy to your copy of the receipt and file them. Obviously, you may have several transactions a day, so you need to work out a system that makes sense for your particular situation.

When you extend credit to a client, produce an invoice. Make two copies, keep one, and send the other to the client. Record the transaction in your A/R section of the binder. File your invoice copy in a divided section after the A/R section. When you get paid for a specific invoice, record the transaction in the regular ledger. Make a copy of the check, or keep the stub. Staple the check copy or stub to your invoice copy after removing it from the binder and then file it in the proper income envelope. Deposit the check in your business account. Delete the transaction from your A/R by simply drawing a line through it.

Here's how your paper ledger might look:

Date	Description	Category	Amount	Invoice/Check #	Mileage
1/21	Ad in "Entertainment" newspaper	A	(50)	#1234	
1/22	Meeting with Big Club owner, landed Feb 11 gig!				44
1/22	January 1 "Great Venue" gig	PL	500	#999	
1/23	Office supply store: envelopes, paper, and stapler for bookkeeping	S	(22.31)	CC	8
1/24	CCNow: payment for Web orders, 1/1-1/15	CD	270.49	Direct deposit	
1/24	Guitar shop: new strings and picks	S	(8.73)	#1235	12

INVOICES

Follow these tips when you cut invoices for clients.

- *Print invoices on your regular letterhead. Put the word "invoice" at the top in big, bold letters.*

- *Include the date of the invoice*

- *Indicate the buyer's contact information*

- *Number your invoices. Start at 1001 and move up from there. Also, include the client's purchase order number(s) if that applies.*

- *List the services provided and the unit cost*

- *List the products sold and the unit cost*

- *List any expenses you incurred that you are charging back and the cost*

- *Be very specific and break larger costs into several tiny chunks so clients clearly see and understand what they received from you.*

- *Total the amounts and indicate the Total Amount Due at the bottom in big, bold letters.*

- *Indicate your payment terms, such as net 30.*

- *Tell the client who to make the check payable to and where they should send their check. If you accept credit cards or PayPal, provide the instructions for those payment methods.*

PAYMENT TERMS

You can either insist on being paid upon delivery (COD) or you can extend credit. When you make direct product or service sales, either in person or through the Web, the buyer pays you up front and you then deliver the goods. When you extend credit, you deliver the goods or perform the service first and invoice the buyer with payment terms. They pay you later depending on the invoice terms. A typical term for invoices is net 30, meaning the client pays the bill in full within 30 days. Be careful when you extend credit as you may waste valuable time and energy tracking down the money. For new clients, either insist on COD terms or ½ up front and the remaining ½ either COD or net 30. This deposit protects you somewhat. The deposit also makes sense for large projects that may take a long time to finish as does a series of progress payments (¼ up front, ¼net 30, ¼ net 60, and the remaining ¼ net 90).

Computer to the rescue. Now obviously this looks like a lot of work. At first, the demand on your time will be minimal. The bigger you grow, the more difficult and time-consuming this becomes. At that point it is best to switch to a computer software accounting program. You still need the envelopes for filing invoices and receipts and you still use the categories, but you rely on the software for your ledger. You can even setup an A/R account in the software, too. There are several products from which to choose, with Quicken and MS Money being the most popular. These programs let you meticulously keep track of your music income and expenses. What's especially useful about computerized bookkeeping is the level of detail you can keep on each transaction. You can setup categories and break them down into several sub-categories. You can create reports about your business finances, including the information you need to prepare your taxes. You can even print checks and/or use electronic bill paying through the software.

For instance, I keep track of the money earned and expenses incurred from the writing I do separately from other business revenues. I use a main category called "Revenue" that has several sub-accounts including "Writing." I further divide the writing into "Books" and "Other," and divide the books into individual titles. This lets me check specific income and expenses for each book project. For example, let's say I get a $500 royalty for this book. I would record that as income under the **Revenue >> Writing>> Books>> MMM** category. At the same time, I mail a promotional review copy to a magazine which costs $15 to overnight. I would record this expense as **Office Expenses>> Postage>> Books>> MMM** to show that this was a general office expense that should be applied to this book. The net profits from this example would show $485 (500 - 15). For tax record keeping, the $500 would show up under the umbrella Revenue (gross receipts) while the postage expense would be lumped together with other similar expenses as an "office expense." This kind of detail is powerful. For instance, you may want to further detail your royalties to synchronization, mechanical, and sheet music and record them by song or CD.

PUT YOUR FINANCES ON AUTO-PILOT

One helpful strategy for reducing the time you take managing your finances is to automate your routine. Using software goes a long way toward making bookkeeping a snap. Additionally, take advantage of direct deposits and direct debits from your business account. Many regular bills can be set-up to be automatically deducted when due. Payments from credit cards orders can be direct deposited to your account. You can also sign up for an automatic investment program and have a sum transferred to your investment account regularly. This automation can be painless, however, make sure you keep an eye on your statements to make sure everything is correct.

Monitor your financial situation regularly. You need to see if you are really making money. With monthly totals for all your categories, review them for problems. Are you bringing in enough money? If not, what areas are lacking and why? What can you do to stimulate sales in those areas? Are you spending too much for certain things? Why? What can you do to reduce those expenses? When you examine your expenses, first look at fixed costs. These are those expenses that change little from month to month (rent, telephone charges, etc.). Are there ways to reduce these (cheaper rent, new telephone plan, etc.)? Next, check those variable costs. These are those expenses that change regularly. They are the easiest categories to get out of control. Reel them in if the figures show you are spending unwisely. Also, compare your financial situation year to year and look for steady growth. You may also see seasonal trends and can plan accordingly (promote harder to overcome downturns, for instance).

Always shop around for the best prices on those expenses you can't cut out (insurance, bank accounts, travel, telephone services, Internet fees and web hosting, etc.). There are two ways to look at cutting expenses: the money you save and the return on investment. For example, if something that usually costs $2 is on sale for $1 you save $1 or 50 percent. That's the standard way of looking at it. However, you can look at it another way. You can see that $1 now buys what $2 used to buy, or a 100 percent return on investment. That's hard to earn on Wall Street. It's easy on-line and at the store.

Your bookkeeping makes income tax preparation a snap. Believe me, taking the time to work on your business finances regularly will save you time and headaches in the long run. Also, you alone are responsible for the documentation that supports the figures on your income tax return. It is in your best interest to be accurate and keep *every* receipt. Also, if you hire someone to handle your finances, you should still carefully check their work regularly, especially tax related issues. Even if someone else prepares your forms, it is YOUR NAME on the 1040. You sign it and therefore you are liable for any mistakes. If you don't think this is important just ask someone who has either been audited unfavorably or experienced other IRS problems. Ask Willie Nelson what he thinks about this issue. I'm sure he can provide some good advice for you.

WINDFALLS

What do you do if you suddenly come into a substantial amount of money (as in record label advance)? Do you blow the wad on frivolous frills and tawdry doo-dads? I hope not. Carefully and wisely managing the money can really make such an unexpected windfall that much sweeter.

• *First, make sure you understand the tax ramifications of your windfall. Do you need to pay income taxes on the amount? You would if this was regular music business income, but probably wouldn't if this was a gift or an inheritance. If you do owe income taxes, skim that amount right off the top and put it in a safe, interest bearing account until the tax bill comes due.*

• *Second, use the remaining amount to pay off your consumer debt, the biggest offender being personal credit cards. If you're paying the minimum amount at the usually huge interest rates, you are wise to get rid of that debt fast.*

• *Third, look at your goals and earmark some of this money toward building your business.*

• *Fourth, invest some money in yourself, specifically improving your skills and therefore your marketability.*

• *Fifth, do you need some new resources? Use some of the cash to acquire what you need, such as new gear.*

• *Sixth, set aside the usual 10-15 percent you normally sock away for a rainy day or in your retirement plan.*

• *Last, use a small token amount of your gain for fun and recreation. Take a simple vacation, go out to dinner, buy those CDs you've been meaning to add to your collection.*

KEEP YOUR CASH FLOWING

Controlling your cash flow is vital. You may experience great fluctuations in both income and expenses along with other unexpected twists and turns. Proper planning combined with meticulous oversight of your finances is the real way to survive this ride. The balance you must strike is never having too much cash sitting in a business account or coming up short at a critical time. Keep track of upcoming bills including fixed costs such as rent, estimated tax payments, and retirement plan contributions so you don't face a cash crunch. One technique I use repeatedly is to project expenses, both personal and business, a few months ahead, adding in a 10—20 percent margin of error. Next, subtract any income that's due during the same period, and then divide that final total by my hourly rate to see how much I need to bill during the next three months to meet my obligations.

One time I had over $12,000 in my A/R and a meager $41 in my checking account. While I did have emergency cash elsewhere, I didn't want to tap it until matters got really bad. The emergency fund was also invested in the stock market, and the market was down, meaning I wouldn't get the best return if I cashed in shares, not to mention the capital gains tax if I did cash them in. Through a little bit of polite prodding of clients with unpaid invoices, the money started trickling in and my bills got paid in time. Use these cash flow strategies to help should you experience similar foibles:

• Invoice clients quickly, but don't offer liberal credit terms. If you've been giving them net 30, shorten it to net 15 or even 10.

• Extend your credit terms with your suppliers, such as net 60 or more. This way you can put off some bills until your income catches up.

• Get deposits on future work. Asking for one-third to one-half in advance of work to be delivered is both prudent and great for the cash flow. Acts should insist on a down payment to hold a future date. Other music professionals should definitely require deposits, and even a series of progress payments, for long, custom projects.

• Collect money owed to you. Don't let delinquent clients get away. Demand payment.

• Use a credit card to float costs temporarily that you know you will recoup in the near future. For example, I've had to buy products and services that I turn around and sell to my clients. Make the purchase on credit, invoice the client, and collect the cash before the CC bill comes due.

• Take advantage of interest-free payment plans such as no payments or interest for six months or three payments of $19.95 that are offered by some companies.

• Set up sources for emergency cash such as a credit line at the bank or other savings.

CREDIT CARD PAYMENTS

Accepting credit cards makes it easy for people to buy your music products and services. If you sell on-line, you definitely need to take plastic. While you can apply for merchant status and process CC transactions in-house, it might be wiser for you join with one of the popular Web-based services.

CCNow ***(www.ccnow.com)*** can process credit cards for you, keeping their 9 percent commission on the sales you generate. Their order system includes a shopping cart and secure processing. People buy direct from your Web site, adding items to their shopping cart. When they are ready to check out, they click a link from your site and are taken to the CCNow site to finish. CCNow even helps you create all the links you need to use their services from your Web site. Your buyers finish their transaction using the CCNow system by entering their contact information and CC number. Once the order is approved, the buyer gets a confirmation via e-mail. CCNow also e-mails you the order details so you can then pack up the products and ship them direct to your buyer. Before you sign up, read CCNow's agreement. For example, you can only sell products that you ship to buyers. You can't sell services or deliver products either in person or via the Web (such as having people pay for an MP3 download). Another similar service, but with different rules and rate structure is Kagi ***(www.kagi.com)***.

PayPal ***(www.paypal.com)*** is another service that can process credit cards. Their Premier account is ideal for your music business. You can send money to anybody with an e-mail address and their fees for your receiving payment (2.2 percent plus $0.30 per transaction as of this writing) are unbeatable. Best of all you can sell products *and* services. You can invoice people via e-mail and they pay you with their credit card. For product sales, you can sell individual items via e-mail or from your Web site and/or set up a shopping cart system for your Web pages. PayPal even helps provide the HTML code you need to make their system work with your Web pages. The order processing steps are similar to that explained above.

CHAPTER 16

The Taxing Side of Your Music Money

"The big print giveth and the fine print taketh away."—J. Fulton Sheen

Business expenses serve two purposes: they allow you to pursue your business income and they help you save money on your taxes. You are taxed on your income *after* you subtract your expenses. In other words, your business *profits* get taxed. Therefore, keep track of expenses and you save money on tax day. What kind of expenses can you deduct? According to the IRS, "to be deductible a business expense must be both ordinary and necessary." Ordinary expenses are those typically accepted in the music industry while necessary implies that the expense helps you run your business and generate income. That broad definition means that many expenses related to your pursuit of business qualifies as a legitimate deduction: ads you take out, gear you buy, fee for the designer who created your CD cover, postage for promotional kits, and so on. Many of these items may have been personal expenses in the past. Not anymore. Now that you are *in* business, these personal expenses transform into business deductions.

Understand the tax impact of every business purchase you make. Let's say you buy a *Musician's Atlas* magazine, a CD by a new band, and a set of guitar strings. The total bill comes to $25. You spend the money, get the stuff, and that's it. There's little need to keep track of this purchase because it doesn't affect your financial situation beyond your wallet. These personal expenses don't impact your taxes at all.

However, if your are in business for yourself, you can convert these same expenses to business expenses and realize some tax savings. Why are these legitimate business deductions? The magazine helps you find new gigs and promotional opportunities, the

CD is for you to learn a song so your cover band can play it at your next gig, the strings you need for the guitar you use when you play. Pay the $25 and keep the receipt (record the transaction following the earlier bookkeeping advice). You can then take $25 off on your Schedule C. This expense offsets any income you receive. That essentially reduces your overall income and the tax you have to pay on it. If you are in the 27 percent tax bracket (moving to 25 percent by 2006), pay the 15.3 percent self-employment tax, and have a 3 percent state tax, for every $25 you earn, you pay roughly $11.33 in taxes. The inverse is also true. For every $25 you spend, you *save* $11.33 in taxes. Although you still spend the $25, you deduct this expense against business income ($25 in income–$25 expense = 0 profit). You subsequently save $11.33 come April 15. You would have had to pay that in taxes on the $25 income you made. Now do you see why tracking your expenses is so vital?

Another way to look at this is how the tax savings translate into a real discount on the business items you buy. In other words, you saved 45.3 percent on your $25 purchase; you paid only $13.67 when you factor in the tax savings. The best part of business deductions is you lower your income on paper *without affecting your lifestyle* (you were going to spend the money anyway)! You still get the magazine you need to read, music to listen to, and strings to keep you sounding good. This conversion of personal expenses to business expenses is the main financial advantage to being in business for yourself. The formula is: Business expense x tax rate = your savings.

The tax rate is the effective tax rate on the last dollar you earn (federal bracket, self-employment tax, state, and local taxes). There are other issues that affect your business and taxes, too.

SELF-EMPLOYMENT TAX

When you work for yourself you not only have to pay the tax on your income, you must also contribute to Social Security and Medicare just like any other worker. Unfortunately, you must contribute both the employee *and* employer portion, which totals 15.3 percent. Yes, that's right. Fifteen point three percent of *every* dollar you make goes to support Social Security and Medicare. This is *in addition* to your income taxes. You do get half of that amount as a first-page deduction on your regular 1040, but that's not a dollar-for-dollar deduction, though. You figure your self-employment tax when you prepare your taxes and may have to pay them quarterly (see *Tax timetable* below).

TAX TIMETABLE

Everybody knows that April 15 is tax day, which is when your returns are due. As a self-employed small music business owner, there are a few other dates you need to know. Typically, you'll need to pay quarterly estimated taxes. This payment includes both the tax on your income and your self-employment tax (your contribution to Social Security and Medicare). The amount you pay to avoid penalties must be either 100 percent of the previous year's tax bill or 90 percent of the current year payable in four equal installments due April 15, June 15, September 15, and January 15 of the next year. If you substantially underpay your estimated taxes, you will owe a penalty in addition to making up any shortfall.

If you have a particularly good year you may end up with a sizable bill come April 15 because you'll be paying back taxes on the previous year and *paying your estimated taxes for the current year at the same time. If you contribute to a retirement plan, those deposits must be made by April 15, too. This is yet another reason to watch your finances carefully. You need to make sure you have enough money to meet your tax obligations when they are due.*

PRESUMPTION OF PROFIT

Your business must be motivated by profit. And you must show a profit from your music business three out of every five years or the IRS may declare your business to be a hobby. You will forfeit your business deductions and owe any back taxes. This is called the hobby loss rule. While its not uncommon to be in the red the first year or two, you'd better get into the black ASAP. Showing one dollar in profit every year will not make you popular among the tax agents either. What will probably happen is you will start to make money—really good money—and you won't need to worry about this rulc.

COST OF GOODS SOLD

When you sell products, you can keep the costs incurred to produce those products separate from other typical expenses. These figures include the costs of making the product (material, supplies, and labor) and storing it. You will also need to keep track of the inventory value both at the beginning and end of the year. You must use the accrual method of accounting when you have inventories. Seek the help of a qualified tax advisor when this inventory issue applies to you. One way around the inventory issue is to make sure you have no inventory: create products on demand and carefully control your purchases of other products you sell.

ACCOUNTING METHODS

The IRS requires you to choose an accounting method for your business. Your decision is best discussed with a tax preparer. You have two choices:

• *Cash. You record business income and expenses for the year in which you get the money or actually pay the expense. For example, you may invoice a client in late December 2002 and not get the check until January 2003. The income belongs on your 2003 taxes even though you did the work in 2002.*

• *Accrual. You report income and deduct expenses when you record or are liable for them. If the same example from above used accrual accounting, the income would be reported in 2002, when the invoice was sent.*

CAPITAL EXPENSES

These include business start-up costs, business assets (large purchases), and improvements (building renovation). Capital expenses must be amortized or depreciated. That means you deduct a portion of the total cost over several years. Business start-up costs would be any expenses you incur before you actually start your business. You deduct them in equal amounts for five years. For example, say your start-up expenses are $1000. You deduct $200 each year for the next five tax years. Business assets would include equipment you buy for your business including music gear, office furniture, computer, and similar items. If what you buy has a useful life beyond one year, you must spread its cost over several years.

However, you *can* deduct the full amount of depreciable property in the year you buy it using the Section 179 deduction, up to the limit allowed ($25,000 in 2003). Taking the deduction on a major equipment purchase all at once can save you from paying additional income taxes that year. However, it may be more advantageous to spread the costs over time. The right decision depends on your situation. Remember to calculate the true cost of a high-priced purchase by referring back to the discussion on business expenses earlier in this chapter.

How do you determine whether a purchase is a capital expense or just a regular one? First, use the useful life rule: Does what you purchase last for more than a year? A copy machine does but the paper you use in it doesn't. Record the copy machine as a capital expense and the paper as an office expense. What about a three-hole punch that lasts for more than a year? Use the second rule: What does the purchase cost? The small charge for the three-hole punch means it can be an ordinary office expense, not a capital purchase. Set a dollar limit of $100-200 to make sure you don't record small equipment purchases as capital expenses when they should simply be classified as supplies.

BUSINESS USE OF YOUR HOME

If you run your music business from your home, you may be able to deduct a portion of your home expenses as business expenses. There are specific rules that govern whether your home office qualifies: it must be exclusive for your business, used regularly, and be your principal place of business. If you dedicate a room in your home and only use it for business (keep all personal items out of the space), that room can qualify for the home-office deduction. However, make sure you use the space regularly and that it is your main (or only) place of business. If you run a project studio in your home, you probably meet all the requirements. If you are a touring band and you occasionally use your home to manage your affairs, you might not qualify or your deduction may be limited because you do most of your real work outside the office (on stage).

If you qualify for the deduction, first determine how much of your home your office comprises as a percentage. Dividing the square footage of the office by the total square footage of your home is the simplest method. If your home is 1850 ft^2 and office 225 ft^2, your business percentage is 12 percent. You can then take 12 percent of your personal housing expenses as business deductions including rent or mortgage interest, property taxes, utilities (gas, electricity, water/sewer), insurance, repairs, and depreciation (tax form 8829). If you apply a portion of your mortgage interest toward the home office the *remaining* amount is still deductible if you itemize your personal deductions, too.

Now the IRS is happy to give you this tax break if you meet their rules as explained above. There is one more rule that they require of homeowners (it doesn't apply to renters). If you sell your home while claiming the home office deduction, any profits from the sale become business income at the *same* percentage you used to figure your deductions. Following the above example, if you make $10,000 on your house sale, $1200 becomes ordinary business income. You must weigh the amount you can deduct against the possible tax consequences of a house sale. Alternately, if you stop taking the home office deduction for two tax years prior to the sale of your home, this rule doesn't apply.

VEHICLE EXPENSES

If you use your vehicle for your music business, you have another source for business deductions. You have two choices: actual expenses or standard mileage rate. You can either choose to deduct all the actual expenses related to your vehicle's business use, including gas, repairs, and depreciation, or you can just take a standard amount for every business mile you drive. This rate (currently around $0.34/mile) is set by the IRS each year. You must carefully document expenses and/or record your business mileage in a diary. This documentation must include the purpose of the vehicle use and the mileage. Now you know the real purpose of the mileage ledger column in the earlier chapter.

If your vehicle is for both business and personal use, you need to also determine the business use percentage. If your vehicle is only for business, this doesn't apply. You must write down the odometer reading at the start of each year to determine your total mileage and use a diary to track your business mileage for the year. To determine the business use percentage, divide your business mileage by the total miles driven (2500 / 10,000 = .25 or 25 percent business use). Now use this percentage when calculating the portion of your actual expenses that you can deduct. Alternately, multiply the business mileage by the standard rate to arrive at your standard mileage rate deduction amount.

Even if you take the standard mileage deduction, you can still deduct the full cost of any tolls or parking fees you incur when using your vehicle for business. Also, if you have a loan on your car, you can deduct the interest charges (at the business use percentage) when you take the standard mileage rate.

PERSONAL TAXES, TOO.

The IRS reports that 70 percent of all tax filers take only the standard deduction when preparing their personal taxes. Make sure you carefully scrutinize your personal deductions and take full advantage of every tax break due to you. Also, you shouldn't be getting large tax refunds either. Refunds are not gifts. This is your *money that you gave, interest free, to the state and federal governments. It is everybody's responsibility to pay exactly what you owe in taxes and not a cent more.*

RETIREMENT

There are specific tax advantages when you contribute to a qualified retirement plan. Saving for the future is part of running your own music career successfully. Thankfully, the U. S. of A. provides some incentives for creating, funding, and managing a retirement investment. The funds you contribute or the growth you accumulate can lower your tax burden. When you defer some of your earnings through a legitimate retirement plan, you reduce your taxable income and therefore the money you pay in taxes. Discuss these retirement plan options with your tax and/or financial adviser.

401(k). If you have a day job, and are eligible, contribute to the 401(k) or similar plan. Alternately, depending on your music business, you may be able to set up your own plan. The money you send to the plan reduces your taxable income. You'll pay taxes on that money, and its growth, when you withdraw funds upon retirement. Some employers offer to match the funds you set aside. A few even match dollar for dollar. That's a 100 percent return, instantly doubling your money. The maximum amount you can contribute to 401(k)s, 403(b)s, and 457 plans is moving steadily higher: $11,000 in 2002 and up to $15,000 by 2006.

IRAs. The money you contribute to a traditional IRA also reduces your taxable income. You realize the deduction on the first page of your 1040 tax form. As with the 401(k) example, you pay income taxes when you withdraw the money in the future. The idea is your tax bracket may be lower when you retire. The contribution amount to IRAs is moving up, too: $3000 each year for 2002-2004, $4000 for 2005-2007, and $5000 for 2008 and beyond.

The Roth IRA is the complete opposite of the regular IRA. Instead of giving you an immediate tax break on the money you contribute, you fund it with *after-tax* dollars. In the future, you can then withdraw the money plus any growth tax free. The contribution limits are the same as the regular IRA.

GET RICH WITH YOUR IRA

The new IRA contribution limits are a good deal for most Americans. If you contribute the maximum amount of $5000 (about $416 a month when that's allowed after 2008) and that money grows at 10 percent each year, a 25 year-old will have $2,630,817 at retirement, a 35 year-old, $940,363, and a 45 year-old, $315,897. Now five grand is a lot to put away if you only bring down 20K. The impact is lower if you can produce $50,000 or more from your music business.

SEPs. The Simplified Employee Pension plan is ideal for self-employed music professionals. It is a special form of the IRA, but can't be setup as a Roth. However, you can contribute up to 15 percent of your business income with a limit of $30,000. (Actually, the formula for calculating your deduction effectively limits your contribution to about 13 percent. According to the IRS, you must subtract the deductions for one-half of your self-employment tax and the contributions to your own SEP-IRA from your income and then multiply *that* sum by 15 percent.) If your income varies, your contribution amount varies accordingly, until you reach the maximum. You deduct the money you put in your SEP on the first page of your 1040. If you have employees, they too can join the SEP program. You setup the SEP by filing form 5305-SEP and funding it.

SIMPLE. These plans are another choice for small employers, somewhat similar to a 401(k). The contribution limits rise from $7,000 to $10,000 by 2005.

YEAR-END TAX SAVINGS

One effective method for saving on your taxes comes at the end of each year. If you reduce your income, you pay less on your taxes. I'm not suggesting stopping work in December, though. Instead, put off *collecting* money until the next year. In other words, bill those December clients later so the money comes in during January. You'll have to pay taxes on the money later, but not sooner. Also, look for ways to increase your business spending. Don't squander money. Instead, look at next year's plans to check if it wouldn't be more prudent to incur some future expenses this year. You'll get more deductions and save on your taxes accordingly. Typical ideas for year-end spending sprees include promotions, postage, office supplies, and their ilk.

IRS HELP

*There are several Internal Revenue Service publications and forms that you may need for your music business career. Download them from the IRS web site (**www.irs.gov**).*

- *#334, Tax guide for small business*
- *#463, Travel, entertainment, gift, and car expenses*
- *#533, Self-employment tax*
- *#535, Business expenses*
- *#541, Partnerships*
- *#542, Corporations*
- *#583, Starting a business and keeping records*
- *#587, Business use of your home.*

- *The IRS also publishes a CD-ROM that contains all these publications, related tax forms, and more that you need to research and understand all these issues. Go to the IRS web site and order the latest edition of their The Small Business Resource Guide 2003.*

- *Taxplanet (**www.taxplanet.com**) is another source for tax information.*

PART FIVE: GROW YOUR MUSIC-SUCCESS FORTUNE

““It does not matter how slowly you go so long as you do not stop.”—Confucius

I’m constantly amazed how many creative people ignore their need to invest for the future. Saving and investing are part of being successful. If you are forced to live from gig to gig, you are not truly running your music business career as effectively as you should. And unless you want to be dragged to your deathbed still working, you are going to want to slow down somewhat in your later years.

Having adequate savings gives you certain freedoms and choices you might not otherwise have. Running your own music business career demands planning for your financial future, and saving some money is a central precept. The profits you realize from your music industry activities need to be invested so that you accumulate a tidy nest egg that allows you to retire and live off the proceeds generated by today’s hard work. Eventually, all your money will come from your investments. Therefore, the decisions you make today will affect your future lifestyle. Choose wisely.

CHAPTER 17

Make the Most of Your Music Money

"Riches do not consist in the possession of treasures, but in the use made of them." — Napoleon I

Investing is just another way for you to make money.

Let's say you make a lousy dollar on your first musical gig, whatever that may be. If you are 18 and deposit that buck in an investment that returns 10 percent each year, at age 65 you will have $108. Forty-seven years of compounding interest will grow that meager dollar to over 100 times its original value. Earn and save $1,000, and that grows to $108,000, and $10,000 grows to over one million dollars. That's right. Put $10,000 in the bank on your eighteenth birthday and retire with a cool million without ever saving another dollar.

WHERE TO INVEST?

Investing goes way beyond merely saving money and depositing for growth in a bank, stock, bond, mutual fund, etc. While that form of investing is crucial to real monetary success, there are a few other forms of investment to consider as well. Make sure you make these investments a central part of your overall business plan.

• Invest in yourself. Make yourself a better person by mastering new skills and savoring new experiences. Get some education in areas where you currently lack and parlay your new skill into wealth. Take classes, buy books and CDs, go on trips, experience new things, and more.

• Invest is in your relationships, both business and personal. Today is the perfect day to start building those crucial connections.

The more people you know, the more opportunities will open up to you.

• Invest is in your business to sustain and grow it. That doesn't mean you should run to the music store and buy more gear. It really means adding music products and services and also spending resources to promote them. By carefully investing your professional resources (talent, time, energy, and yes, money) you will invariably generate more money than most conventional investments. For example. Sock $1,000 in an investment paying 7 percent and get $70 a year. Spend $1,000 promoting or developing a new music service or product that allows you to secure business totaling $1,700 in profit. Now you've made a wiser investment. It'll take nearly a decade for the former *investment* to equal the return on the latter *expenditure.*

Invest in tangible goods. Put some savings into things you can wrap your hands around. Real estate, gold, and collectibles are typical tangible investments.

Invest in the economy. Put your money to work for you through a variety of conventional investment choices: stocks and bonds.

INCOME COMES IN TWO FLAVORS

Active income is what you earn from your music business career. It's the profit from the sale of your music products and services—playing, recording, royalties, merchandising, etc. *Passive* income comes from the investments you make—bank and bond interest, mutual fund and stock appreciation, etc. Passive income is so-called because you don't earn it through your work. Instead, the money you save and invest works for you earning interest, going up in value, and so forth.

Active income pays your business and personal expenses. What's left over is your savings. By saving and investing a portion of your active income, you begin generating passive income. As these savings appreciate over time, the passive income augments your active income earned through daily business activities. Eventually, you can even grow your nest egg big enough to *replace* your active income. When you no longer have to work to support your lifestyle, and can live off the proceeds generated by your investments, you become financially independent. Whether you reach financial independence before retirement age depends upon how diligently you earn, save, and invest your music-success fortune.

Regular investing is the primary way to grow your savings. If you are currently 25 years old, start with no savings, deposit $200 a month over the next forty years, earn 10 percent compounded monthly, you will have $1,264,816 at age 65. If you are 35 years old, start with no savings, deposit $200 a month over the next thirty years, earn 10 percent compounded monthly, you will have $452,098 at age 65. If you wait until you are 45 years old, start with no savings, deposit $200 a month over the next twenty years, earn 10 percent compounded monthly, you will have a paltry $151,874. What this shows is that you can grow your savings with a minimum of fuss (just two bills a month). Also, the sooner you begin, the better off you will be. The ten-year increments show substantial differences in the ability of the money to compound and grow significantly. So, get your moneymaking music machine up and running right away!

Royalties. Now, there may be some active income that appears to be passive at first glance. The most obvious example of this is royalties. Your CD sells and the record company sends you regular royalty checks. Your publisher sends you royalty checks for mechanical license fees. And if your music plays on the radio, ASCAP or BMI send you regular performance royalty checks. This income requires little intervention on your part.

An argument might be made that royalties are passive income because they function as an investment of sorts. Some people even believe that royalties from music generated products and services would *be* a retirement plan. I disagree. Unfortunately, royalties are rather unpredictable and they rarely grow like other investments. In fact, they usually diminish gradually and you make less and less as each year goes by. Therefore, consider royalties as the ongoing payment for your hard work. You can only sell so much time, but royalties let you earn money from the repeated use of a product or service without devoting more time to it. Royalties are nothing more than a deferred, time-payment plan where the money arrives over time rather than all at once.

Instead, take this approach. Take your royalty money—if you

don't need it to eat—and invest it to make those same royalties grow over time as your investments appreciate. Plus, as you discovered in the previous chapter, sending your advances and royalties to a qualified retirement plan can save you money on your taxes, too. Personally, I deposit the money earned from my books directly into my retirement account. I'm counting on my writing to go a long way toward supporting my future. If the books stay in print, they continue to pay me. However, by saving all the money they already produce through continued sales, I develop my retirement fund as well.

INVESTMENT INCOME

Your investment or passive income falls into three categories: taxable, tax-free, and tax-deferred. Taxable passive income would be those savings and investments that generate income on which you must pay taxes in the year the investment income was earned. For example, you stash a grand in a Certificate of Deposit and the bank pays you interest on the money. You then report this interest as income on your taxes. Tax-free passive income would be investments you make where the income generated is not subject to incomes taxes. Municipal bonds and the Roth IRA are examples of this. Tax-deferred passive income is active income you earn and shelter from taxes. You then pay taxes as you withdraw the funds. The traditional IRA, SEP, and 401(k) plans are examples of this.

INVESTMENT STEPS

As the oft-quoted advice says: pay yourself first. After you've met your business obligations, but before you pay your personal expenses, set aside a certain amount or percentage and save it, 10-15 percent is a good start. Pay your personal bills with what is left. And if you still have some money remaining, send that to savings, too!

Your first goal should be to set aside enough funds for emergencies. Scrimp and save until you build a safety net with at least enough money equal to three months of your typical expenses. Put this money in a safe, interest-bearing account that you can get to quickly. A money market account is the perfect place for parking your emergency cash.

Invest in your debt. Make sure your total long-term debt (mortgage, vehicles, and credit cards) doesn't exceed 40 percent of your monthly gross income. Pay off any high-interest credit cards. The interest rates are staggering if you carry a balance. Paying the minimum will extend your debt for years. Start sending in the maximum amount you can afford until the balance gets to zero. Promise yourself to never carry a balance again. Use your card for convenience and to help your cash flow, but don't use it to finance your life. Paying off the CC debt is a way to earn 17-22 percent on your money (the equivalent savings by not paying the high interest rates). Pay off your car loan and/or shop hard for better rates, too. It's hard to earn 10-15 percent on your money without a lot of risk. Paying off a 15 percent car loan is much easier, with little to no risk.

Pay down your mortgage by adding a few extras dollars to your check every month. You will shave years off the loan and big dollars off the total payments. Here's an example. How much would you have to pay today to save *just one* mortgage payment in the future? Let say you took out a loan for $100,000 at 8 percent for 30 years. Your monthly payment would be $733.76, principal and interest. If you include an additional $74.42 to your first mortgage payment check, you would save $733.80 in interest charges over the life of the loan. And that means you'd pay off your home one month sooner. That's right. A *single* payment of slightly more than 10 percent of your monthly mortgage payment saves you one entire mortgage payment in the future. Paying just slightly more each month can add up to huge savings down the road. On that same $100,000 30 year loan at 8 percent, paying just $50 more each month saves you $34,211 in interest and you pay off the loan five years sooner!

Invest for retirement. Put as much money as you legally can into tax-free and/or tax-deferred retirement accounts. Invest these funds long-term for maximum growth.

Invest for income. Once you reach the maximum contribution limits for the qualified retirement plan you choose (and you still have money left over to invest), turn your attention toward taxable investing. Use these other investments to supplement your music income, and ultimately replace, some or all of it. This strategy lessens your need for making more money from your music career directly or allows you to earn that much more when you add passive investment income on top of your active income. Of course, you can choose to grow these investments larger and tap the funds in the future instead of using the income to support your lifestyle now.

PAY ZERO TAXES ON YOUR TAXABLE INVESTMENTS

It is possible to have your taxable account appear to be tax-deferred. If you own shares in a mutual fund or stock, and the value goes up, you do not pay taxes on the value increase until you cash in the shares. If you hold the shares for a long time, and slowly cash them in the future, you can carefully control how they affect your tax burden. Savings bonds work this way, too. They accrue interest, but unless you cash them in, you pay no taxes on that interest. Savings bonds interest is not subject to state and local taxes either.

STEPS TO FINANCIAL INDEPENDENCE

Doesn't it feel good knowing that you can pave the road to your financial independence with your music? Answer these questions to get the information you need to hit the pavement running ... and arrive sooner.

How much money do you need? Return to the exercise earlier in this book that helped you determine how much money you need to earn each month to meet your bills. For this example, let's use $3,000, or $36,000 a year.

How much do you have? This is a two-step process. One, determine your net worth by adding up all your assets (bank and investment accounts, fair market value of your house, wholesale value of your car, insured value of your personal property, etc.) and subtracting your liabilities (mortgage and other loans including CC debt). The resulting figure is your net worth, the value of your estate. Two, look up your current investment capital (savings). For this example, let's say you have $5000 set aside. Save these two figures; you'll need them in a minute.

How much money must you save? Figure out how much in savings, and at what investment return, you need to have to match your monthly income. For example, you'd need $360,000 in investments that grows 10 percent each year to make $36,000. The $360,000 in savings has the ability to earn $36,000 through passive growth (interest, dividends, stock value appreciation, etc.).

SAVINGS = INCOME

Money you save can pay you income. The more you save and invest, the more money you can potentially make. For example, let's say you have $10,000 and you invest it in a Treasury bond that pays 6.5 percent interest. You will get $650 a year in your pocket for the term of the bond. That's $54.16 a month. But that amount is not going to make you rich. Look at it another way. What can you buy with that fifty-four bucks and change? Does it pay your phone bill? A couple of tanks of gas? In other words, your savings generate income that can be used to pay a portion of your living expenses. Now let's say you save $100,000 at 6.5 percent. That's $6,500 each year. Save a cool million, earn 6.5 percent on that, and you pocket $65,000 a year without touching the original million-dollar principal. That's how financial independence works!

Feel there's no way you can save that kind of money? Determine how much money you've earned in your lifetime. Consult your annual Social Security statement. You may be pleasantly surprised by your earning potential. Now return to your net worth figure. That's what you've been able to accumulate from those earnings. I hope you see that you already have the ability to both earn and save the money you need to support your current and future lifestyle needs. You just need to keep doing it diligently (and perhaps contribute a little more in the right investments).

How much do you need to save each month at the same interest rate and for how long to reach your goal? If you start with $5,000 today, put aside $236.50 each month and earn 10 percent compounded interest, you will save $360,000 in 25 years. If you are bringing in $3,500 a month, you need set aside a mere 6.8 percent of your income to reach your goal, in this example. Plug in your numbers to see how this strategy works for you.

What about inflation? Now this exercise was done basing future income against today's expenses. Though prices do go up, I'm not convinced that a steady 3 percent each year, compounding, is entirely rational. Don't be paralyzed by inflationary fears. Everything does not go up in cost every year. Some things go down. Some things go up in price, but have more value. Some of your high bills will be paid in full. There's a good chance in 25 years you'll pay off your mortgage. That could be upwards of 30 percent of your expenses. When you pay off the loan, you immediately increase your income (or reduce your expenses depending on your viewpoint) by a whopping 30 percent+ instantly. That single windfall can make up for some of the shortfall in your savings whittled away by inflation.

Don't lose hope. The very act of doing this work can overwhelm you. Sometimes the figure you need to save may seem totally outlandish. Don't be discouraged. It takes small, regular, diligent steps to reach these goals. You must think long-term. Make some necessary sacrifices today to save more money now, and you will make your future bigger, better, and brighter.

SS STATEMENTS

The Social Security Administration sends a free earnings statement a few months before your birthday each year. Unless your are close to retirement, you can ignore the estimated payment you would receive (though they are good for a laugh). However, you must pay attention to your earnings records. It shows the money you reported as earning each year for your entire work history. You really need to check it for accuracy. One of my years showed earnings of only $50. I still had my tax return for that year clearly showing a different figure. It only took a phone call to the SSA to correct the dollar amount.

Live within your means. Spend less than what you earn. You must sacrifice and learn ways to live the life you want at your current income level. Use the Time/Money diary example mentioned earlier in this book to find spending waste. Budgets are especially hard, even for persnickety people like me. Waiting until you have sufficient cash before spending it is a sure-fire tactic. Also, setting limits for bigger purchases is a worthwhile.

Cut down on utility costs by shaving a few degrees off the thermostat. Add a clothing layer in the cold months and fans and cool drinks in the hot months. Replace incandescent bulbs with more expensive, but cheaper to run (and longer life) fluorescent units. Get a flat screen computer monitor which uses considerably less energy than a standard CRT.

Save at the grocery store by clipping coupons, buying in bulk when on sale, and so forth. It does not take that much extra time to shave big bucks at the store. Behind mortgage interest and taxes, my third biggest expense is food and related household items (TP, cleaners, soap, etc.). It pays to save here.

If you think looking for bargains is not worth the time, you're not trying hard enough. Every Wednesday, free flyers arrive in my mailbox for the major grocery stores in my area. It takes about five minutes to scan the flyer and see what's on sale. It helps to know your prices a little, particularly on regularly bought items (use a notebook and jot down prices). Often one store's sale price is still more than another store's regular price. On sale does not equal best price. You may also think it's not worth it to drive all over to save a few pennies on dishwashing detergent. I would agree. Fortunately for my family, two of the grocery stores are literally across the street from each other. One averages an overall better buy on most items; we make a quick trip to the other store to get real savings on certain items. Time invested, about an hour a week between menu planning, shopping lists, flyer scanning, and shopping. Savings? Huge! We average about 12 percent off of regular prices and once cut 31 percent from a grocery bill.

Also, shop around for deals on rent or mortgage rates, music gear, insurance, telephone service, Internet fees, office supplies and services, travel expenses, and more. When it is *your* money on the line, it pays to save a little here and there. Check out these Web sites for more money-saving advice: ***www.lowermybills.com***, ***www.tightwad.com***, and ***www.mmintl.org***.

CREDIT REPORT

Get a copy of your credit report from Experian ***(www.experian.com/consumer/)*** *every few years and check for erroneous information (and get them fixed, if that applies). The cost is under ten bucks. You will need to provide them with:*

- *Your full name*
- *Current address (If you've lived at this address less than five years, list your previous addresses for a five-year period).*
- *Spouse's first name*
- *Social Security number*
- *Year of birth*
- *Your signature*

Having your full name, address, Social Security number and year of birth helps prevent your credit information from being mixed with the credit information belonging to another consumer with the same or similar name. Having your spouse's name provides extra assurance that your joint accounts are included on your credit report. Your previous addresses help them link the credit you may have established in another region, or at another address in the same region, to your current credit information.

Focus on the long term. It is oh-so-easy to live in the present, but you need a better view. Growing investments takes time. At first, you see very little progress. That is not the time to stop. Work through these steps to know for sure how your savings will grow. Then, resolve to make it happen. Most of all, start doing this today for the maximum reward.

CHAPTER 18

Investment Options

"There's a mighty big difference between good, sound reasons, and reasons that sound good." — Burton Hillis

How are you going to invest your retirement or other savings? For some people, the investment world is shrouded in mystery, nevertheless it is important to your music career. This section aims to keep it simple. Bruce Eaton, in his *Conquering Your Financial Stress* book said it best: "You can either loan or own."

• You loan your money when you take your profits and put them in a savings account, money market account, certificate of deposit, treasury, municipal, or corporate bond. You loan the money and the institution that borrowed the cash pledges to pay you back in full with interest. Loans are less risky than owning something, but come with a lower return.

• You own something when you buy something tangible such as ownership in a company through stocks and stock mutual funds, real estate, and other collectibles such as gold. The value of what you own goes up or down based on several factors. Owning all or a piece of something comes with greater risk and usually higher returns.

Savings, money markets, and CDs. These are no-brainer investments. You put your money in the bank and they pay you an interest rate. Money market accounts yield a better interest rate if you meet the minimum deposit requirements. They are ideal for parking cash for the short- to medium-term. Certificates of Deposit are issued by banks at specific interest rates and terms. You get all your money back, plus interest, when the CD matures. There are substantial penalties for cashing in the CD before it matures, though.

Bonds. U.S. Savings bonds ***(www.publicdebt.treas.gov/sav/sav.htm)***

are often unjustly maligned. They come in two varieties: Series EE and I. You can convert them to cash instantly after the first 6 months (paying a three-month interest penalty if not held for more than five years). You don't pay taxes on the growth until you redeem them. They have little risk as these bonds are backed by the full faith and credit of the United States. EE bonds pay a decent rate (90 percent of the six-month average of the five-year Treasury note yield) and can be bought for half their face value in convenient denominations ($25, $50, $100, etc.). I bonds pay a fixed-rate (typically 3 percent) plus a semi-annual inflation rate based on the Consumer Price Index (CPI) and are bought at face value. If you have little to invest, US Savings Bonds might be just right for you. Later you can redeem them and invest in other, higher growth vehicles when your earnings and savings have appreciated significantly.

The U.S. Treasury issues securities to fund government activities. They are backed by the full faith and credit of the United States government and that makes them the safest investment in the world. Treasuries are actually three varieties: bills, notes, and bonds. T-bills are short-term bills that mature in one year or less. You buy them at less than their face value and get the full amount upon maturity. For example, a $10,000 treasury bill might cost $9,750, paying the full amount at maturity. The $250 difference is the interest.

Treasury notes and bonds pay interest every six months until maturity. At maturity, they return the full principal amount. Notes mature in more than a year and less than 10 years. Bonds mature in more than 10 years. You buy them at face value and can choose either fixed-interest or inflation-indexed varieties. The fixed pays interest twice yearly at the rate set at auction. Inflation-indexed notes and bonds pays interest twice yearly with the rate adjusted to reflect inflation as measured by the CPI. Treasury securities can also be traded on the market (see below). The interest they pay is also exempt from state and local income taxes.

You can buy Treasury bills, notes, or bonds at auction through Federal Reserve Banks, other banks, and most brokers or dealers. The minimum amount to purchase is $1,000 and larger amounts must be in $1,000 increments. The auction announcements are published regularly and you typically submit a non-competitive bid. You can even buy them through the Treasury Direct program *(www.publicdebt.treas.gov/td/tdstorefront.htm)*.

There are two ways to invest in bonds. One, you buy them and hold them to maturity, earning interest along the way. Two, you buy them and trade them based on moves in interest rates. When interest rates fall, treasury bonds increase in value. For example, you buy a five-year $10,000 note paying 6.5 percent interest. You get $650 each year for five years (half that amount every six months). If interest rates fall, the bond's value could go up to $10,500. If you sell it, before maturity, you would get the original principal plus the premium. The theory is that you can invest the higher amount at the new lower interest rate and still realize the same total return. Where this theory falls apart is you *can't* reinvest $10,500 because bonds are sold in $1,000 increments. Unless you have $100,000 for bonds, don't bother actively trading them. You are better off buying bonds and earning the interest and ignoring swings in interest rates. Let the interest you earn feed other investments, such as stocks, mutual funds, paying down debts, and so forth and forget about bond trading.

Municipal and corporate bonds. Municipal bonds are issued by state and local governments and function similarly to Treasuries. Their interest is also exempt from federal, state, and local taxes which can make them attractive for people in higher tax brackets. Corporate bonds are issued by companies. They usually yield higher returns, but at increased risk (the company can go bankrupt).

Stocks. When you buy a stock, you purchase ownership in the company. As an owner, your shares represent a stake in the company's future. You hope the company's earnings allow it to appreciate in value so that, at some point in the future, you sell your shares at a higher price and make a healthy profit. Some stocks also pay a dividend, which is a share of the profits realized by the company distributed to its shareholders at regular intervals. Stock prices fluctuate with changes in the market. This volatility is what causes some people to avoid the stock market altogether. It can be difficult and time-consuming to pick the right stocks, and survive their roller-coaster ride, too.

Mutual funds. Rather than invest in single stocks, you can purchase multiple stocks all at once through a mutual fund. As its name implies, mutual funds pool the money provided by the investors to purchase stocks, bonds, and other investments. Each mutual fund follows a specific philosophy professed by the mutual fund company and its managers. For example, it might invest only in the technology sector, or only international stocks, and so forth. You purchase shares of a mutual fund at its Net Asset Value (NAV) which represents the total value of the fund at the end of each trading day divided by the number of shares outstanding. Much like stock, the prices of mutual funds fluctuate with changing market conditions.

There is a particular class of mutual funds that all investors should know and understand. They are called Index funds because they attempt to mimic the returns of a given market index. The Dow Jones Industrial average and the S&P 500 are two such indexes that investors use to measure their investment performance. The S&P 500 index is comprised of the 500 largest publicly traded companies. An index fund tied to the S&P 500 tries to match the return of that index (and the stocks that comprise it). There are even index mutual funds that try to mimic the *entire* stock market!

Index funds make for particularly attractive long-term investments. First, they require very little research to choose up front. Just choose an index fund that matches the index you want and make sure your choice has low fees. Second, when you pick a broad-based fund (such as an Index fund that matches the S&P 500) you get all the market has to offer in terms of gains (and losses) with a minimum of fuss. You don't have to worry about stock picking, buying, or selling. If the market goes up, your portfolio goes up; if it's down, you're down, too. The S&P 500 in recent years has had phenomenal returns, but over the last 70 years or so it has returned around 10 percent average a year. That implies that your portfolio will average 10 percent gains a year. While there is no guarantee that will happen, it is the historical average and useful percentage when doing your financial planning. Once you've been investing for a little while, you can start plugging in your actual returns as you review your financial goals.

INVESTING FEES

When you buy a stock or shares of mutual funds you sometimes pay a commission or fee. You can trade stocks for under $10 at some on-line brokerage firms. Sometimes you pay a fee to purchase mutual fund shares, too. However, most mutual funds, especially index funds, are usually free to buy and sell (within certain parameters). These mutual funds do have *other fees to cover administrative costs, trading commissions, and promotional expenses. These fees range from .3 to several percentage points depending on the fund. Index funds do very little trading and therefore often have the lowest expenses of all mutual funds. If a fund has a .5 percent fee, that means that they keep 50 cents of every $100 you make. It is this fee that keeps an index fund from matching the actual performance of the index it represents. Because of these fees, your shares will always return less than the actual index. You want to minimize these fees by choosing only those funds with the lowest expense ratios.*

Real estate. You can invest in real estate in several ways. You can own your own home, you can buy land, you can buy homes and/or commercial property and rent them to other people, and you can buy homes and/or commercial property, fix them up, and sell them for profit. For most music professionals, owning your home is the only real estate investment you need to make. The mortgage interest you pay on your own home can decrease the amount you'd otherwise pay in income taxes. And should your home appreciate in value substantially, you may take away a healthy profit when you sell. Plus, there is something comfortable and, well, American, about owning your home. It feels and looks successful. If you want to become a landlord or pursue other moneymaking real estate ventures, investigate the possibilities carefully.

Tangibles. Owning stocks and bonds sometimes seem unreal as their is nothing tangible that goes with them (you can get stock certificates and physical bonds, but typically these are "paper-less" transactions). Having some gold or collecting antiques or art grounds your investing in reality. It makes fiscal sense to include some of these investments with your overall portfolio, too.

Caveat emptor. Always, stay away from any investment you don't understand. Stick to the tried and true.

ASSET ALLOCATION AND RISK TOLERANCE

You need to know how to divide up your investment portfolio by spreading your money among the aforementioned investment options. You also need to know your tolerance for risk by knowing what's at stake when you invest. The percentages of savings that you allocate among investments reflect both risk and reward. If you can take on more risk, and have a longer time frame to invest, you can allocate more of your funds toward the owning side. That way you have the potential for larger gains, in the long run. If you lose sleep over slight losses in your investments, and/or have a shorter time frame to invest, you can allocate your funds toward the loaning side. Investing in Treasury bonds is relatively safe, but their returns are somewhat meager. Stocks are thought to be more risky, but the rewards are often greater still. You need to determine your asset allocation in a way that makes you comfortable.

You can't avoid risk. You must reduce its impact. Diversification—spreading your money around several different investments—is the tried-and-true way to lessen your risk. Savings bonds and US Treasury securities are good, solid conservative investments. Use a money market fund to park short-term and emergency cash. Buy a home. Grab some gold or art or other antiques. Stocks are the only way to go for maximum growth.

Also, ask yourself the purpose of your investing. Where is the money going? Are you investing for your retirement? Or are you saving for some other purpose (to buy a house, for instance)? Your answer to this question gives you a time frame for your investing. The longer you plan to not need the money, the more you should be invested in owning (stocks). If the sum total of all your investments is through your retirement fund, probably close to 100 percent of it should be in the stock market. You'll have a wild ride over the couple of decades, but overall you should come out way ahead of any other investments if history's past performance continues. If your investment needs are shorter term, you should probably avoid stocks for the most part as their volatility can adversely affect your financial goals. Stick with loaning in this case. The stock market could be way down (such as when I'm writing this) when you need the money and there would be little you can do about it.

Once you know where your money is going, you can start to divide up your capital into a portfolio that matches your needs. A balanced portfolio would put 60 percent in owns, 35 percent in loans, and 5 percent in cash (money market account). An aggressive portfolio would be 95 percent in stocks and 5 percent in cash. A conservative investor would be 75 percent in bonds, 20 percent in stocks, and the rest in cash.

PUT YOUR INVESTMENTS ON AUTOMATIC

You do not need to devote untold hours managing your investments. Once you determine your portfolio's asset allocation, you can select a few index funds, buy some bonds, and keep making your deposits. Monitor your statements monthly and re-balance your portfolio allocations occasionally, too.

Start saving today. Get into the habit of putting aside an amount of money you feel is possible; 10-15 percent of every dollar you make is ideal. Even just $20 is something ($1,040 a year). It's no good to tuck your savings into a mattress (or a passbook savings account either). You need to invest that money for growth.

Choose solid investments. Index mutual funds and Treasury securities are the simplest methods of letting your money grow. Invest in stocks through a discount broker, buy your bonds direct from the U.S. Treasury, and park your emergency money and other cash in a local bank money market account.

Select your broker. When you invest in the stock market, you need to go through a broker. A large, well-known discount broker is the best bet. You can have your accounts there and choose from a variety of investments with no additional fees. Here's how to make your selection.

- Choose a few discount brokers
- Read about their accounts
- Get their prospectus on their mutual funds and read them carefully
- Choose the right fit for your situation.
- Fill out the forms and deposit your money
- Set up an automatic investment plan
- Keep contributing additional funds and buying more shares
- Monitor your transactions carefully

Compare your return to well-known indexes and make appropriate portfolio changes as necessary.

Build a core, then explore. To make investing easy, follow the "core and explore" approach popularized by Charles Schwab. For the money you earmark for the stock market, consider the index funds first. You want your piece of the large company pie. Along with those big companies you are going to want a slice of the little up and coming companies, too. These Small Cap stocks—stocks of companies with smaller market capitalization—are fast growing sectors of the market. You want to have some money there. Last, the International market is another place for some of your investments. You want to be invested in some of the biggest International companies at a percentage that makes sense.

Put about 70 percent of your stock market investments in the U.S. funds (50 percent large company and 20 percent small caps) and 30 percent in the International funds. With this strategy, you'll take most of what the stock market has to offer with little intervention on your part. It will fluctuate wildly from day to day, but at the end of a year, your portfolio will reflect what the market does. If it's up, you'll be up. The reverse is also true.

If you've chosen bonds as part of your investment portfolio, purchase your U.S. securities direct from Treasury Direct and pay no commissions. Have the semi-annual interest payments directly deposited into your personal account, too.

After you've invested your core amount in long-term, buy and hold investments, you may want to turn your attention to exploring other options. With your core portfolio, you are trying to match the return of the stock market. With the explore portion, you are trying to beat the stock market with explosive double-digit growth. Don't devote more than 10 percent of your portfolio to this exercise. This means you probably need in excess of $10,000 in your core portfolio before you can try other options. Why? Most mutual funds carry a $1,000 minimum. And buying shares of a stock with less than $1,000 is not worth the trouble. The trading costs in the form of commissions (up to 60 bucks) means your $1,000 stock investment must return over 6 percent to break even. Ouch!

Start an automatic investment plan. After choosing your broker, have a set amount automatically deducted directly from your checking each month and invested in the stocks and/or mutual fund(s) of your choice. This automatic investment program keeps a constant flow of money into your investment account. Consider increasing the amount of the monthly deduction until it starts to put a squeeze on your finances. That's the right amount. Investing regularly in the same mutual fund also lets you take advantage of dollar cost averaging. Another tactic is to have your loans feed your owns. In other words, let the interest you earn from your loans buy more owns (stock and/or mutual fund shares).

Dollar cost averaging. Dollar cost averaging is investing the same dollar amount regularly in the same stock and/or fund. For example, you buy $200 worth of shares monthly. This minimizes your risk during wild swings in the market. In essence, you buy more shares when the price is low and less when the price is higher. When you average out the costs, you usually come out ahead slightly.

If you have a lump sum to invest, consider buying shares over time. Park the whole balance in a money market fund and buy shares regularly in your key investments over time. I didn't do this and once took a fast, hard hit. It took nearly a year to get back to 0 and was down 32 percent in one fund at one time. I made sure to buy extra shares at the lower price, too. This meant that once the original shares returned to their purchased level, I'd still have some growth from the shares bought at bargain basement prices.

Forget about market timing. Can you pick stocks or mutual funds that are low and sell them when they go up? Timing the market is virtually impossible, as the market is hard to predict. Since you are usually guessing as to what is going to happen, it might as well be gambling. However, buying stocks and mutual funds during a general market decline *is* a good tactic. During these so-called "corrections" many stocks take a hit and drop in value/price. Buying shares of these stocks and mutual funds at this time can boost your overall return. These hit stocks and/or funds often jump right back to their former level quickly and continue their usual growth. This is especially true of larger, more stable companies, less so for smaller ventures.

Know when to sell. When you buy an investment, also take the time to set an exit strategy. What has to happen for you to sell. If you've taken a huge downturn, do you sell and then lock in your losses? What if you've doubled your money in three months, can you make even more? You can never lose money selling too soon after a substantial gain.

When a particular investment of mine unexpectedly skyrocketed, I was reminded of a story. A man was crossing a desert when an elder told him to pick up as many rocks as he could carry along his journey. The elder told the man he would be both happy and sad at the journey's end. The man did as he was told. When he completed his trek, he found that all the rocks he had collected had turned to gold. He was very happy with his newly found wealth. And, as the elder foretold, he was sad, too. Why? Because he wished that he had picked up more rocks. This is how I felt, too. I doubled my money on the investment and was very happy. However, if I had held on a little longer (three days!) I could have quadrupled my investment. And that made me sad. Success is often like that. You should always be content and satisfied with such profound returns. Regrettably, some successes still leave a nagging feeling of "if only I ..." This paradox is one of the hardest psychological hurdles to overcome. However, dealing with this positively will always help you better sustain your investment success.

Plan your estate. When you follow the tips in this resource, you substantially increase your ability to earn good money from your musical endeavors. Your income will grow and your overall net worth should increase exponentially, too. Make sure you take some time to plan your estate and how you will distribute your wealth to your heirs. Depending on your financial resources, there are several tactics you can take to avoid estate taxes. You should investigate your options and put a plan into effect accordingly.

• *One of the best places for financial advice on the Web is Kiplinger's* ***(www.kiplingers.com)***

WHAT DOES IT MEAN TO BE WEALTHY?

Does wealth mean just the salary you earn? Or is it something else? The books, *The Millionaire Next Door* and *The Millionaire Mind*, offer a clever definition of monetary wealth. According to the authors, earning a large income, and spending it all, is not being wealthy. They say building wealth means saving and investing in such a way that you accumulate assets. In other words, what do you have to show for your hard work? They offer a formula for computing your expected net worth based on age, income, and savings. If you are at or above this figure, you are a wealth accumulator; below the number and you are an earn and spend person.

Expected Net Worth = Age x .112 x Income

Using your age, annual income (from your last 1040), and net worth, see how you measure up. Compute your actual net worth and compare this figure to the expected net worth figure. To find your actual net worth, total up all your assets and subtract your liabilities from that number. Here's an example: 39 x .112 x 52,000 = $174,720. In this example, this fictional person's net worth should be *at least* $175,000 preferably more. According to the authors, truly wealthy people have an actual net worth that is 2 to 10 times their expected net worth. How did your arithmetic come out?

CHAPTER 19

Build a Core, Then Go Explore

"The secret to happiness is not in doing what one likes, but in liking what one has to do." —James M. Barrie

I borrowed this concept from Charles Schwab after finding the approach worked not only for investing, but for all moneymaking business pursuits. First, establish a base income doing what you do the best. This base income should come from a diversified core of moneymaking music activities. The core should include your own music products and services along with those produced by others that complement, augment, support, and parallel what you offer. Second, dabble a little in other areas to test the waters and potentially expand your earning opportunities. Limit the downside of these explorations to no more than 5-10 percent of your resources (time and money). This approach can yield some surprises and bring about new ways to earn more music money. Alternately, it can expose some bad ideas that you can then avoid without losing your shirt.

Where does your core come from and in what areas should you explore? Carefully examine the skills you bring to the table. What do you want to be your core income producing activities? Where would you like to explore? The earlier chapters provided an overview of some possible directions. Pick and choose from these guidelines to arrive at your optimum music products and services business mix.

Here's another tip. It's worth doing *any and all* work you can land. Even the tiniest gig can grow to something bigger. Small fish often get to swim in bigger ponds. In many cases, they take their friends with them. Stay in touch and build relationships with people who, at first, may seem inconsequential. You may be surprised when the time and effort you put into these relationships comes with due rewards down the line. The small fish who hired you for pennies last year is now a big fish with an even bigger budget—and she wants to hire you again!

CORE/EXPLORE IN ACTION

For example, a band's core might include:

- *Making a little money playing live*
- *Making a little money from their CD sales (at gigs, on Web, through brick and mortar distribution, etc.)*
- *Making a little money on their swag (ditto)*
- *Making a little money working a part-time day job.*

The band could explore opportunities such as:

- *Making a little money selling CDs and swag from other artists*
- *Making a little money playing on, writing, and/or recording other people's tracks*
- *Making a little money teaching lessons*
- *Making a little money __________ (fill in the blank)*

MONEYMAKING MUSIC ACTION STEPS

You've devoured a great deal of information up to now. At this point you might wonder how to bring everything together into a cohesive action plan. This details several example scenarios that you can use to model your successful career.

Everybody do this first. No matter how you decide to pursue your music career, make sure you complete these fundamentals. Follow Andrew Jackson's credo: "Take time to deliberate; but when the time for action arrives, stop thinking and go in."

• Research. Find the people who buy what you sell and uncover specifically what these buyers want. Then, adapt what you sell to what these people want to buy.

• Plan. Take the time to formulate a detailed road map for your moneymaking music career. Where are you now, where do you wish to go, and how are you going to get there?

• Acquire resources. Determine what you need (content, people, equipment, money, etc.) and begin to put everything in place.

• Establish an image. This image must appeal to people who buy what you sell. Create promotional material that conveys your image and to show buyers you have what they want. Remember: Image + Credentials = Reputation. People buy your reputation because they trust you'll deliver what they want, need, and desire.

• Start your business. Take all the steps necessary to begin legally conducting business.

• Follow the ruthless self-promotion tactics from this book to get your name out and make sales.

• Manage all the financial aspects of your business—bookkeeping, taxes, and investments.

Songwriter. These action steps are for the non-performing songwriter.

• Create your songs. Either record demos or draft sheet music (a lead sheet with chord changes, a melody line, and the lyrics).

• Register your copyright to the song. Copyright protection is automatic, but if you plan to publish and shop your songs, you should take the extra step of registering your claim of ownership with the U.S. Copyright Office.

• Start your own publishing company or work to get picked up by an existing publisher.

• Join either ASCAP or BMI to earn performance royalties for your songs. You should sign up as an individual songwriter and your publishing company should join separately, as well.

• If you start your own publishing division, have your company join with the Harry Fox Agency. This will enable you to both collect mechanical royalties and synchronization rights for your music.

• Put together your promotion kit, including your song demos, and start promoting your songs to labels and artists.

Musical act. These action steps apply to performing songwriters, solo artists, duos, and bands.

• Find other members and form the band. Create a formal agreement that details the duties, responsibilities, pay, and rights of each of the band members.

• Choose your content. Will you be a cover band? Or play only originals? Even if you decide the latter, consider sprinkling in a few covers that people recognize when these songs show your musical roots. Either pick the songs you plan to cover or write your own songs. If you do use your own material, follow the action steps for the songwriter above, too.

• Rehearse your act. Your live act can't be cobbled together. You must take the time to not only learn your material, but refine your presentation. Videotape and/or record your rehearsals and learn from what you see and hear.

• Put together a demo CD and/or video of your best music performances. You will use this music to get booked to play. Find possible venues. Promote to land some local gigs. Make sales calls to get booked. Use each gig's success to get more club dates.

• Develop promotional material to pitch your act to your market. Put together a Web site that appeals to fans and include specific information for the media and for venues that book your live act.

• When you get hired to play, make sure you have a contract with all who hire you.

• Soon after playing your first gigs, start your own record label. Produce your act's independent recording under the auspices of your own record label. Find some other swag to sell, too. Sell your products at gigs and through your Web site. Create new CDs and augment your other products regularly.

• Put together your own CD. Create a budget. You need to know what it will cost you to record, mix, master, duplicate, package, distribute, and promote your music CD. Choose songs. Find a studio and finish the recording. Develop promotional material and start promoting and selling (including finding distribution).

• Keep promoting both your live act and your CD(s). Get reviews and articles written by and about you published. Get your CD into retail stores (on- and off-line) and catalogs. Get Internet and over-the-air radio airplay of your CD. Place other promotions, too.

• After building your reputation locally, expand regionally, and even nationally if that fits with your plans. When you establish a firm fan base and stable CD sales, consider approaching a distributor to get your CDs into more stores and a record label for better distribution and tour support.

Individual band members. The band as a whole is only one opportunity for a talented musician. You can also pursue a parallel career while in the band.

• Pursue other songwriting opportunities (follow the steps for the songwriter above) including composing soundtracks and jingles (see below).

• Take on solo gigs or work part-time in another band (playing different music).

• Put together a promotional kit and demo of your playing and land session work playing on other's CDs, even jingle and soundtrack gigs.

• Create other products such as a sample CD or instructional video. Sell lessons or project studio production services.

• Promote these other aspects of your career to increase your earning opportunities.

Soundtrack and jingle composer. Similar to a songwriter, the difference being most composers both create and produce the music they sell.

• Follow the steps for songwriters from above (music, copyright, publishing, Harry Fox, etc.).

• Put together a promotional kit and demo CD and/or video of your work. Pitch your services to companies that buy original music.

• Use contracts when hired and make sure you understand the licensing issues related to this industry.

• Create other products, such as a music library, and offer other production services besides music to diversify your business.

Project Studio. You can use your personal project studio as a supplement to your other music activities or you may decide to make it your primary moneymaker.

• Put together a viable studio.

• Decide on the services you will offer (music recording, sound production, etc.).

• Develop a demo of your services along with other promotional material. Pitch your services to people who need what you sell.

• Work with clients on their projects and your own.

• Diversify into related ventures (as mentioned in the text).

MAKE $3000 A MONTH

Let's say you decide that you need to earn $3,000 a month to support your chosen lifestyle. How can you do that? Here are a few suggestions.

Band member or solo artist. If you can land three gigs that pay $500 each, sell some CDs and other merchandise both at gigs and through your Web store, collect some royalties on songs, and teach lessons to four students once each week, you can get to your goal:

Gigs 3 x 500	= 1,500
Gig CD sales 40 x 15	= 600
Web sales (CDs, swag, etc.)	= 150
Royalties	= 350
Lessons 25 x 4 x 4	= 400
TOTAL	**= 3,000**

Soundtrack and jingle composer. If you can land just two scores or jingles each month that pay a low-end average of $1,250 each, do some other production work (voice-over session, for example) and sell some music library CDs, you can reach your goal.

Two gigs at $1250	= 2,500
Other productions	= 300
Library CD sales	= 200
TOTAL	**= 3,000**

Project studio. You don't have to fill the room 24-7 to reach the goal.

32 hours at $75/hr	= 2,400
Supplies sold	= 200
CDs, merchandise	= 150
Duplication commission	= 250
TOTAL	**= 3,000**

Fisher Creative Group. Here's a typical month's earnings at my company. I don't include this to impress you; I share it to give you an idea of what's possible. I have had much better months than this and recently took in $11,764.52 in just 30 days. Contrast that to my first month in business when I brought in a meager $225.

On-hold gigs	= 398
Audio production	= 665
Multimedia production	= 1,520
Music fees	= 998
Music library	= 99
Web sales	= 358
Royalties	= 855
Writing, promotion consulting	= 760
TOTAL	**= 5,653**

What each of these examples shows is that by offering several different music products and services, it is much easier to reach your goals. It also clearly shows that by working a little harder to bring in more business (land one extra gig, sell another jingle, book some more recording time), you can substantially increase your income and exceed your goals. While some months may be bonanzas, others may be somewhat thin. Set these goals and work hard to meet them. If you come up short one month, you must make it up the next.

AND IN THE END ...

"'Why not' is a slogan for an interesting life."—Mason Cooley

What are the real secrets to success?

First, know yourself. Find out what it is you truly want to do and accomplish. Then, arrange your life accordingly to make it happen. Become who you want to be and recognize what you need to satisfy your desires. Along the way, collect the knowledge and experience you need to realize your life vision in your own way. Don't let anything interfere with your vision. Work to overcome any obstacles placed in your way. Don't put your trip off either. Get started today in some small way. Most of all, embrace your destination when you reach it, and enjoy your journey, too. Have you found what you're looking for? Are you even searching?

Second, follow the techniques explained in this resource. Concentrate on a specific audience. Discover what these people want to gain and/or what pain they want to eliminate. Adjust your music products and services to meet their needs. Establish your image. Acquire credentials. Build a reputation and ruthlessly self-promote it. Nurture relationships with people and help yourself by helping others. Develop and use your promotional material. Publish your news. Update your Web site. Capture names through your promotions and contact your hard-won leads with new offers regularly. Work hard to get gigs and sales. Treat your buyers exceptionally well, build strong relationships, and keep in touch. Get repeat business from existing clients. Always look for new business, too. Watch for opportunities and adapt. Create new music products and/or services and let your audience know about them.

Third, turn on your moneymaking music machine. Make the most money possible from your musical pursuits. Simultaneously, keep more of that money you do make by controlling both your personal and business expenses. Manage your finances carefully by tracking every business dollar earned and spent. Use every legal means available to reduce your personal and business taxes. Protect your assets through copyright and insurance. Save a significant amount of your profits and invest them for growth and future income.

Fourth, keep going.

Jeffrey P. Fisher
December 2002

Moneymaking Music Success Resources

Here are my candid and honest reviews of other books that can make your music career better.

Of course, first check out the books and videos offered by **ArtistPro Publishing** ***(www.artistpro.com)*** to further expand your education and make your musical endeavors more successful.

Moneymaking Music Ideas

Start Your Own Band, Marty Jourard. Sensible advice for putting together a band, writing and recording songs, and taking your act on the road.

The Musician's Guide to Making and Selling your Own CDs and Cassettes, Jana Stanfield. Planning an indie release? Grab this book and devour its practical advice about recording your act and selling your music through touring, newsletters, and online.

Profiting From Your Music and Sound Project Studio, Jeffrey P. Fisher. Discover how to set up, manage, promote, and sell your personal project studio. Great for musicians, composers, producers, engineers, sound designers, voice-over actors, and other audio professionals.

This Business of Artist Management, Xavier M. Frascogna, Jr. and H. Lee Hetherington. Here is the initial information you need to manage musical acts.

How to Make Money Scoring Soundtracks and Jingles, Jeffrey P. Fisher. Do your friends say your music sounds like movie music? Do you find yourself hearing radio and TV commercials and saying to yourself: "I could write a better song than that"? If you answered yes to either of those questions, perhaps you have a future in the commercial music industry scoring soundtracks and jingles. This is THE definitive book on the subject.

VO: Tales and Techniques of a Voice-Over Actor, Harlan Hogan. If you have "one of those voices" you should be letting it earn some money on its own. Reading ad copy, on-hold messages, commercial and corporate narration, and more can bring in some big bucks. Harlan's one of the best voice-over talents around, and he shares the secret to success in this book.

Music Promotion

Ruthless Self-Promotion in the Music Industry, Jeffrey P. Fisher. Join thousands of your music peers who already successfully use the techniques in this book to sell more of their music products and services today. It is the companion volume to this book.

The Neatest Little Guide to Making Money Online, Jason Kelly. There are lots of books on the Internet; this one is really worth reading. It's a basic guide to getting connected, designing your Web site, and making money selling your own and other people's products and services.

Music Business

All You Need to Know About the Music Business, Donald Passman. By far, the best book I've seen about music business issues: concise, thorough, and easy to understand.

Music, Money, and Success, Jeffrey and Todd Brabec. An exhaustive account of the business of music—royalties, contracts, and so forth. A little too legalese for some, but solid information anyway.

A Cure for Gravity: A Musical Pilgrimage, Joe Jackson. This autobiography thankfully avoids the mundane my-life-as-a -rock-star syndrome. Instead he shares his early life and all the people, places, and events that lead up to the release of his phenomenal *Look Sharp* album. It's a real, witty believable, and poignant musical journey that is entertaining, enlightening, and inspiring.

Music Production

Musician's Guide to Home Recording, Peter McIan and Larry Wichman. Provides a solid primer for the novice packed with basic recording information.

How to Run a Recording Session, Jayce De Santis. Before you pay a dime to record your music, follow the tips in this helpful guide.

Behind the Glass: Top Record Producers Tell How They Craft the Hits, Howard Massey. Interviews with the people who made and continue to make the best records today. Learn from George Martin, Glen Ballard, Arif Mardin, Phil Ramone, Geoff Emerick, Jack Douglas, Chuck Ainlay, and more. The book discusses working with artists, recording tricks and techniques, and various ways these people approach the challenges of recording and producing.

Inside Tracks: A First-Hand History of Popular Music from the World's Greatest Record Producers and Engineers, Richard Buskin. Interviews dozens of the people behind the scenes of the Beatles, Stones, Doors, Dylan, Hendrix, Nirvana, and more. It's a terrific read especially when you go back to the recordings mentioned and listen with fresh ears.

Money

Keep Your Hard-Earned Money: Tax Saving Solutions for the Self-employed, Henry Fellman. Clearly explains all the tax saving benefits of running your own company including how to convert everyday living expenses into legitimate, deductible business expenses.

Charles Schwab's Guide to Financial Independence, Charles Schwab. This straightforward overview of the investment world is ideal for the novice who needs basic information to get started.

Eight Steps to Seven Figures, Charles B. Carlson. Learn the secret investing strategies of millionaires. Contains solid, understandable, and easy-to-put-into-action advice.

Conquering your Financial Stress, Bruce Eaton. If financial stress is ruing your life (and your ability to make music), rustle up some scratch and buy or just visit your library and read this book. It will open your eyes and help you manage your money better.

The Money Mentor: A Tale of Finding Financial Freedom, Tad Crawford. Are your seriously in debt? Unlike a typical how-to, this resource uses a fictional approach to spin its advice. You follow the fascinating story as one woman learns to overcome her debt.

Inspirational

Zen and the Art of Making a Living, Laurence G. Boldt. I highly recommend Laurence Boldt's intense, innovative and unconventional book. It forces you to uncover the work you really want to do. And then it helps you take the steps necessary to create the kind of work and life that you want.

The Rebel Rules, Chip Conley. The book explores the new rules for business success and profiles the four primary traits of today's real business leaders: vision, passion, instinct, and agility. Also, Conley exhaustively includes exercises and action plans for implementing his rebel rules.

Success @ Life: A Zentrepreneur's Guide, Ron Rubin and Stuart Avery Gold. This is a more imaginative approach to starting and succeeding with your own creative business drenched in Eastern philosophy.

Creating a Life Worth Living, Carol Lloyd. This inspiring resource helps you design a creative career. Part career counsel, part inspiration, you will better map out your journey through the advice and exercises in this book.